TRY DYING

JAMES SCOTT BELL

TRY DYING

A NOVEL

CENTER
STREET

NEW YORK BOSTON NASHVILLE

Center Street
Hachette Book Group USA
237 Park Avenue
New York, NY 10017

Visit our Web site at www.centerstreet.com

The Center Street name and logo is a registered trademark of the Hachette Book Group USA, Inc.
Printed in the United States of America
First Edition: October 2007
10 9 8 7 6 5 4 3 2 1

Library of Congress Cataloging-in-Publication Data
Bell, James Scott.
Try dying: a novel / James Scott Bell.—1st ed.
p. cm.
Summary: "A fast-paced legal thriller in which lawyer Ty Buchanan will enter a world of unbelievable evil to discover the cause of his fiancée's death, prepared to kill for the truth"—Provided by the publisher
ISBN-13: 978-1-59995-684-8
ISBN-10: 1-59995-684-5
1. Lawyers—Fiction. 2. Los Angeles (Calif.)—Fiction. I. Title.

PS3552.E5158T79 2007
813'.54—dc22
2007005918

FOR CMB

TRY DYING

1

ON A WET Tuesday morning in December, Ernesto Bonilla, twenty-eight, shot his twenty-three-year-old wife, Alejandra, in the backyard of their West Forty-fifth Street home in South Los Angeles. As Alejandra lay bleeding to death, Ernesto proceeded to drive their Ford Explorer to the westbound Century Freeway connector, where it crossed over the Harbor Freeway, and pulled to a stop on the shoulder.

Bonilla stepped around the back of the SUV, ignoring the rain and the afternoon drivers on their way to LAX and the west side, placed the barrel of his .38 caliber pistol into his mouth, and fired.

His body fell over the shoulder and plunged one hundred feet, hitting the roof of a Toyota Camry heading northbound on the Harbor Freeway. The impact crushed the roof of the Camry. The driver, Jacqueline Dwyer, twenty-seven, an elementary schoolteacher from Reseda, died at the scene.

This would have been simply another dark and strange coincidence, the sort of thing that shows up for a two-minute report on the local news—with live remote from the scene—and maybe gets a follow-up the next day. Eventually the story would go away, fading from the city's collective memory.

But this story did not go away. Not for me. Because Jacqueline Dwyer was the woman I was going to marry.

2

AS ERNESTO BONILLA'S lifeless body was falling through the air, I was in the conference room of Gunther, McDonough & Longyear, high above Westwood Boulevard. An African mahogany conference table the approximate value of the GDP of Ukraine separated me from one Claudia Blumberg, plaintiff. She was, at first glance, impossible to think ill of, which was a big consideration here. If this case ever went to trial, and she testified, she could make a great impression on a jury.

It was my job to see that never happened. I had to tear into her so subtly and expertly that she and her attorney would not dare take this all the way. Do a *Sopranos* on her with sharp-tongued skill. Which I had in spades.

The walking ego and boogie-woogie bluster sitting next to her was one Barton Walbert, a Buddha-like figure if you're going by belly size. But his tactics were anything but divine. He was just waiting to throw legal grenades at me during the deposition.

And he could do it. Walbert was one of the most successful plaintiffs' attorneys in the country. He had won twenty multimillion-dollar verdicts, including one for close to a billion against one of the biggest corporations in the world.

I was a pup compared to Walbert. He was fifty-three and in his prime. At thirty-four, I was just hitting my stride. But the arrogance of youth is a good thing for trial lawyers. Like the young gun who comes to town looking for the aging outlaw, wanting to test the best, I was loaded and ready.

"Ms. Blumberg," I said, "your attorney has explained to you why we're here today, has he not?"

"Yes." She was cute, with short, auburn hair and intelligent brown eyes. There was a fragility about her that made her seem like porcelain. A jury would warm to her. I was Iceman.

"You understand that you are under oath and that your answers must be truthful, just as if you were in court?"

"Yes."

"Did you confer with your attorney before coming here today?"

She hesitated a moment and glanced at her lawyer. "I'm okay," she said.

"I noticed that you looked at Mr. Walbert just then," I said. "Is that because you're not sure what your answers should be?"

"Objection," Walbert said. "What you notice is not relevant, Mr. Buchanan. Just ask questions."

"That's what I'm trying to do, Mr. Walbert."

"Relevant questions."

It was all just jockeying for position here. A couple of sumos stamping their feet, circling. Standard stuff. I liked to get the other attorney riled if I could. That might lead to a little game of *quién es más macho?* I always wanted the other attorney to lose a little cool in depositions, because it would be captured in transcript and maybe come out at trial. Of course, I'd never faced a Barton Walbert before. This could get interesting.

Modern American litigation makes no pretense of the old collegiality. Back in the days when Melvin Belli was hoisting a skull and crossbones over his San Francisco office, trial lawyers could fight all day in court, then go out for dinner and drinks and tell tall tales of enrapturing juries by the sound of their voices. At least, that's what my law professors used to say. But now, in keeping with the general tenor of the times, incivility is more the order of the day, and gloves are off. You used to take ten paces, turn, and fire. Now your opponent is as likely to turn on eight and shoot you in the back.

"You need any water, Miss Blumberg?" I gestured at the silver pitcher on a tray on the table. Little drops of sweat on the outside of the pitcher mirrored what was going on in my pits. Which told me I was ready to go.

"I'm fine," Claudia Blumberg said. She was nervous, naturally. This was not her domain. And besides, being deposed ranks with root canals on the scale of things people most like to do.

She was twenty-three years old and suing our client, Dr. Lea Edwards, for ten million dollars for libel, invasion of privacy, and harassment.

3

CLAUDIA'S STORY, AS laid out in the immortal prose of Barton Walbert's complaint, was this. At seven years of age she was molested by her father. Shortly after that, her parents filed for divorce. The abuse became a central issue in the divorce proceedings, as her mother fought for custody. And won. She won largely because of the expert testimony of a psychiatrist, Dr. Kendra Mackee.

Mackee was considered an expert in repressed memory therapy. Not everybody believes this to be legitimate science, including our client, Dr. Edwards.

After the divorce, Claudia continued to see Dr. Mackee. But Claudia, as her story went, could not remember her father's abuse. Her father, of course, denied the accusation and publicly called Dr. Mackee a quack and a menace. That Mackee did not sue for defamation was seen as a great career move. It got her a lot of publicity and tons more work with victims.

When Claudia Blumberg was seventeen something startling happened, something that turned Dr. Mackee into a media darling. Under hypnosis, Ms. Blumberg suddenly recalled her father's sexual trespasses in gross detail.

And it was all caught on videotape in Mackee's office.

Mackee got a whole hour on *Larry King* as a result, smacking softball after softball into the seats. And stoking the ire of the noted memory skeptic, Dr. Lea Edwards.

Edwards was so disgusted she wrote an article questioning Mackee's methods and suggesting that Claudia was either lying or being manipulated. Edwards backed it up with information gathered, it was alleged, through means that invaded Claudia's privacy.

Which is why Claudia Blumberg went to Barton Walbert and why we were all dancing that day in the conference room of Gunther, McDonough & Longyear.

"Ms. Blumberg, you first went to see Dr. Mackee when you were how old?"

"Seven."

"Do you remember that, or have you been told this?"

"I remember Dr. Mackee's office."

"What do you remember about it?"

"I remember that it had plants and a nice lady sitting in the front."

"What nice lady?"

"The receptionist."

"Do you remember what she looked like?"

Before she could answer, Walbert said, "I'll object as to relevance, and instruct my client not to answer."

Walbert knew exactly what I was trying to do. If I could show that Claudia Blumberg's memory of her experience as a seven-year-old was actually pretty sharp, that would undercut her claims of having lapsed into repressed memory. That, in turn, would strengthen my client's position, as expressed in that article debunking the repressed memory claim in this case.

The article that had prompted the lawsuit.

"For the record," I said, "you are instructing your client not to answer a question about her memory, correct?"

"Relevance, Mr. Buchanan, that's all."

"Your client's memory is central to this case, sir."

"Your client is being sued for invasion of privacy and defamation, sir," Walbert shot back.

"And truth is a complete defense to the latter, sir."

All these *sirs* were like little gloves to the face. We were a couple of sword fighters insulting each other.

"Ask your questions, Mr. Buchanan, and I'll decide if they're relevant, and if you disagree you can go ask a judge."

That was another ploy guys like Walbert used to great effect. If you had to keep going to court to get a judge to rule that a question had to be answered, the game could get pretty expensive.

I went on. "So you recall certain things about Dr. Mackee's office when you were seven, only those things your attorney has allowed you to share with us today."

Walbert's cheeks pinkened like a Christmas ham. He touched Claudia's arm and shook his head. *Don't dignify that with an answer,* he was saying.

I let it pass. "Did you continue to see Dr. Mackee after that first visit?"

"Yes."

"Have you continued to see her up to the present time?"

"Yes."

"That would be about sixteen, seventeen years, right?"

"Yes."

"And would it be fair to say that over the years Dr. Mackee and you discussed on numerous occasions the alleged abuse by your father?"

"Objection," Walbert said. "Doctor–patient privilege."

"I'm not asking about any content," I said. "Just if such discussions happened."

"Same objection. I'm instructing my client not to answer."

I looked at Claudia Blumberg. "You can ignore your counsel's advice and make life much easier."

Walbert stood up. "You will not address my client, Mr. Buchanan, unless it's with a relevant question. Do it again and I'll walk her out of here and seek sanctions against you."

Quién es más macho?

I stood up, too, because Barton Walbert was about five-ten and I am six-two and wanted him to be reminded of that at every opportunity. "No need to blow, Mr. Walbert. The truth is what we're after."

"You're wasting everyone's time. And if that's what you want to do we'll just end it right here."

"If you would allow me to ask a question, Mr. Walbert, we won't have to waste Ms. Blumberg's time by dragging her in here again."

"Relevant questions, Mr. Buchanan." Walbert sat down again, as did I.

"Ms. Blumberg, since Mr. Walbert is giving such sterling advice, perhaps he has discussed with you the concept of free speech, which is quite relevant to a suit for defamation. Has he?"

"Objection. Attorney–client privilege."

"A whole lot of privilege going on," I said. "I'll ask you, Ms. Blumberg, if you gave Dr. Mackee permission to videotape your sessions."

This detail was key, and I knew Walbert could not in good faith object. Our contention was that by giving Dr. Mackee permission to shoot video, Claudia Blumberg had waived any claim to privacy, which was part of her lawsuit.

"Yes."

"And did Dr. Mackee tell you the reason she wanted to videotape your sessions?"

"Yes."

"Tell me what she said."

Walbert said, "I'm going to direct my client not to answer, on grounds of privilege."

I was ready for him. "Then I'll ask my question this way, Ms. Blumberg. And I remind you again that you are under oath here, just like you would be in a court of law. Dr. Mackee told you she wanted to video the sessions because she thought you were on the verge of a breakthrough, and that this breakthrough could be very informative and helpful to all sorts of victims suffering from repressed memories of abuse, and that she would call you Margaret and that would protect your identity, and here was your chance to do a great service to humanity. Have I got that pretty much right, Ms. Blumberg?"

Claudia Blumberg's eyes got as wide as truck tires and I knew I'd nailed it.

Walbert knew it, too. His face twitched. In the world of Barton Walbert versus everybody, that was a taste of victory for me.

What they didn't know was that I had prepared this question based on a mere hunch. Having read everything there was on Dr. Mackee, I had gotten sufficiently into her head to know she was a supreme self-promoter. She had made a lot of speeches and presentations to both psychological and legal audiences, and made the video of Ms. Blumberg a big part of the show. She had to have suggested something like I'd imagined.

"Isn't that right, Ms. Blumberg?" I repeated.

Walbert knew better than to object at this point. It would look too much like he was covering up the truth, and this section would be brought out and read to the jury at the appropriate time.

"Not in those words," Claudia Blumberg said.

"But that was the substance of what she said, right?"

She nodded.

"I need a verbal response for the stenographer," I said.

"Yes," she said.

So there it was. Maybe the most important piece of evidence in the whole case. Because if we could show that Claudia Blumberg knew she was going to be used in public, her claims of invasion of privacy would evaporate and would make defamation that much harder to prove.

I had to work hard not to dance on the table in front of them both. That wouldn't exactly have been in keeping with the decorum demanded by the firm of Gunther, McDonough & Longyear, where I was about to be deemed a superstar.

I thought of Jacqueline then, how proud she'd be of me. I'd tell her all about it at dinner. We were going to discuss wedding plans over oysters in a restaurant by the sea in Malibu. And then we'd watch the moon rise over L.A., huddled together on the beach.

It was going to be the perfect night.

4

HOW DOES A hot young lawyer on the rise, a guy with a future draped with Brioni, go from the twentieth floor to the county jail? How does a guy become something he's never been, more animal than man, able to and wanting to hurt people? Kill people? How does he go from light to darkness as fast as you can flip a switch in a mortuary basement?

It begins with a phone call.

"Oh God, Ty."

"Fran?"

Fran was Jacqueline's mother.

"Oh God, oh God."

I was in my office, about to leave in the glow of deposition victory, when the call came. I knew from Fran's voice it was about Jacqueline. Accident maybe. Slip and fall. In the hospital.

"Fran, what is it?"

"She's dead, Ty. Oh God . . ."

Her voice was spectral now. I could hear her crying.

"Can you talk to me?" I managed to say.

"An accident," she said. "On the freeway."

Jacqueline.

"Where is she? Where'd they take her?"

"I don't know."

"Who told you?"

"Someone . . . I don't know . . ." She was lost to tears and I knew she couldn't say any more.

"I'll be right over," I said and hung up. I was vaguely aware that light was fading outside my office windows. The phone may have rung a couple of times, but I didn't pick up.

I heard some part of myself suggest I was sitting on a movie set, and they'd remove the walls any second now and the director would yell *Cut* and the lights would switch off and we'd all go home with cheerful good-byes.

Nobody yelled *Cut.*

What was I supposed to do now? Go identify the body? Look at Jacqueline on one of those beds they slide out of the metal drawer?

The world receded like a stinking tide.

All that was left was memory. That's where I wanted to hide.

5

WE HAD MET a year before at a Mexican place on Pico. Usually three or four of us from the office would head there, order up the "grande sampler," and start ragging on the Dodgers.

On this particular night there were three of us —Danny, the geek genius who was head of the firm's IT; Al, another associate; and me. Al was into his third maggie (Al always started quoting Charles Bukowski on his third margarita —"*Love is a dog from hell*" —but we allowed him to stay anyway) when a vision of unbelievable loveliness walked in with a second vision almost as beautiful. But only almost.

My eyes must have bugged because Al grabbed my arm. "Listen!" he said. "These are the dead, the lepers. Seagulls are better. Seaweed is better."

"Will you shut up?" I said. Al was married to money and always joked about the *graveyard* of marriage. His Bukowski obsession was based on the poet's misogyny, no doubt.

Danny laughed.

"You're missing the point," Al said.

I shook my head. "The point is the hottest woman in the world just walked in here and you, my friend, do not appreciate it."

Al said, "If you do this, you are the dead."

His words stick with me, even now.

But I was not dead then, anything but. I was in love (I usually fell in love during the second pitcher, but somehow knew this was going to be different—*real*). I called the waiter over and told him to send two margaritas to the two women who had just come in.

"Fool," Al said.

I could see her face a few tables away. She had dark hair, long. Made me think of walking on the beach at night when the moon is full. Her eyes were feline, which made my heart kick even faster. When she smiled, she seemed to add another light to the building.

Al kept quoting poetry. Danny tried to start a conversation about the Dodgers' starting lineup. I only half listened as I watched the waiter deliver the drinks.

The waiter pointed at me.

The vision looked my way. I smiled at her, trying not to let her see my chest heaving as my pulse raced toward stroke level.

She looked back at the waiter, shook her head, said something to him.

The waiter looked confused for a moment, then sheepishly came back to me with the margaritas still on his tray.

"They say thanks," the waiter said. "But they don't drink."

"Good," said Al, reaching for the maggies. "More for me."

Don't drink? I looked toward her again, feeling exposed, like one of those dupes on reality TV who allows cameras into his bathroom.

The vision smiled at me and mouthed, "Thank you."

"Tyler!" Al wailed. "Don't go there. Disaster awaits!"

And *those* words haunt me. And probably always will.

I did go over and attempted to put on my best George Clooney. "Ladies," I said, "I hope that I did not offend by my offer, but I . . ." Suddenly, my tongue felt like a tree sloth. I just stood there, staring dumbly, a target for hunters.

The other vision said, "But you just wanted to meet Jacqueline, right?"

Jacqueline. Classic. (I never called her Jackie. Not once.)

I noticed the other vision had a wedding ring on her finger. Was I too obvious when I looked at Jacqueline's left hand? And saw no ring? And said to myself, *There is a God*?

"Was I that transparent?" I said.

"Like Glad Wrap," the other vision said, but I wasn't offended. Because I was still standing there. Jacqueline had not indicated I should take a flying leap.

"As a matter of fact," I said, "I did want to meet you. Ty Buchanan." I extended my hand to Jacqueline. She took it firmly and said, "Nice to meet you, Ty Buchanan. This is Rachel."

I shook hands with the other vision.

"I've got to tell you," I said, "I don't do this. I mean, I guess I do because, here I am, right?" *Idiot. Make a point!* "I mean I'm not usually this forward."

"I find that hard to believe," Rachel said. She had curly blond hair and an impish smile.

There was a silence, during which someone shouted an epithet in Spanish from the kitchen. The three of us laughed.

"Would you like to sit down?" Jacqueline said.

Al was glaring at me from our table, pointing at the pitcher of margaritas, only half empty. *Be here now,* he seemed to be saying, *you dead, you leper.*

I sat. "You sure this isn't an intrusion?"

Rachel spoke first, which was to be the pattern. "Frankly," she said, "you're an interesting experiment."

The experiment, it turned out, was something Rachel had cooked up and Jacqueline was embarrassed to have revealed. It boiled down to the fact that Jacqueline had broken up with a boyfriend of three years —*There is a God*—and had not dated anyone for over five months. Rachel had decided it was time, but Jacqueline was not so sure.

"I think she's ready," Rachel said. "What do you think Ty?"

Jacqueline's face was turning red, and I was more deeply in love than at any time in my entire life. "I think," I said, "that I would like to take Jacqueline to lunch and get to know her better."

6

I HELD FRAN all through the funeral. Her poor body shook the entire time. Fran Dwyer was a good woman who had endured more pain than anyone ever should. Twenty years of an abusive marriage. And now this, the death of her only child.

For Fran's sake, and maybe for my own, I wished with all my being that I could switch places with Jacqueline. If one of us had to be dead, let it be me. At least Jacqueline would have Fran, and they could go on together.

Now life had no meaning. No, that's too generic, too Philosophy 101. It was that life had no flavor, no color; no texture or taste. With Jacqueline I'd been on a bridge, walking across a gorge, she leading me, holding my hand, helping me to pass from one state of being to another. Through Jacqueline I was walking away from the blithe selfishness that had been my mental landscape toward an unfamiliar place I could barely see. I could only perceive that the light was better over there, that the colors were richer, the smells sweeter. And while it was going to mean setting up in unfamiliar territory, she would be with me and we would be there together forever and that was all that mattered.

Now that was gone, the bridge had fallen down the gorge, I was back on my side again, and it wasn't home anymore. It was lifeless, colorless.

I stared at Jacqueline's coffin, up in front, covered with flowers, and a big framed portrait of her for all to see.

The portrait was beautiful but still could not do justice to the woman I loved.

The firm—I always spoke of it as an entity, with its own personality and ego and vindictiveness—had given me a week off, but I didn't know how I was going to be able to work again.

They say time heals all wounds.

They're full of it.

I kept thinking of that first lunch. It was the day after I met her. A seafood place in Santa Monica. Lunch dates are a good invention. Low pressure, and you have a chance to see if things should go further.

There was no doubt in my mind that I wanted to go further with Jacqueline. And not in a sexual way. That was the weird part, for me at least.

Usually sex was the first thing I thought about, but when I saw Jacqueline walk in for lunch my knee-jerk reactions melted away like butter sauce. I was feeling something deeper.

And if lunches were opera singers, this one was Placido Domingo. The term *click* seemed invented for Jacqueline and me.

We talked about a whole range of things. She wanted to know all about me and what she called my *ruling passions*. I told her about my days as a rock drummer in high school and college, about my love for the Dodgers. She seemed most interested in the drumming part and begged to hear me play.

I found out why she didn't drink.

Her father had been a raging alcoholic. Raging in every sense of the term. Jacqueline and her mother, who still lived in the Reseda home Jacqueline grew up in, had never left. Once Jacqueline had run away, but she willingly came back because she couldn't bear to have her mother living with him alone.

Her father died when she was in high school. And unlike most of her friends, she had never had the desire to drink.

We didn't just talk about that, of course. We spent three and a half hours at that lunch. Jacqueline was on summer break from teaching, so the time didn't matter to her.

I was expected back at the office for a two o'clock meeting, which didn't matter to me. I skipped it.

When we parted, she let me kiss her and then she said, "Keep warm."

Those were always her parting words, for some reason. No matter what the weather was. I liked it. It fit her.

Keep warm.

Two weeks after our lunch she was at my house and I got out my old practice pad and sticks, and gave her my imitation of Neil Peart.

She ate it up, and that's when I asked her to marry me. She said No. Six weeks later I tried again, and she said Wait.

Eventually she said Yes.

And now she was dead.

She had so many friends, and they all came it seemed. Many of them had a few words to say before they lowered the coffin. The cemetery—Eternal Valley, it was called, which messed with my mind—was just off the 14

Freeway, overlooking Santa Clarita. The day was sunny and clear, the kind Jacqueline loved.

When it was my turn I tried to say something. Everyone looked at me with complete understanding and support.

"I just want to say, first off, how much I appreciate all of you being"—a knot in my throat. I looked down, breathed deep—"for being here. So many of you are lucky. You knew Jacqueline longer than I did. Her whole life some of you. I really envy you that."

The faces in the chapel pews started to go fuzzy. I wiped my eyes with the back of my hand.

"I mean, everything Jacqueline was, as a person, you can see just by looking around. Seeing her family and friends. And that means I was the lucky one after all. That she chose me to spend her life—" The knot came back. The tears kept coming. I knew I wasn't going to be able to finish.

"I just want to say, I hope she can hear us now. Because I want her to know I loved her more than anything."

That was all.

7

RACHEL CAME TO me after and held me close. "Ty, she loved you so much. She told me how much."

I just closed my eyes and felt the last of my tears fall into her hair.

"Want me to drive you?" she said. Rachel was having the reception at her house.

"I can make it."

"You sure?"

"Yeah. Take Fran, will you?"

"Of course. See you there."

I waited until everyone left and sat in the chapel alone for a while. Looked at the stained-glass window. Jesus, with a halo, hand held out to comfort the bereaved.

It wasn't working for me. But I didn't blame Jesus or God or the glass or the chapel. I blamed myself.

For not telling Jacqueline more how I felt about her. For not telling her from the deepest part what she meant to me. I've never been accused of wearing my emotions on my sleeve. Iceman, like in *Top Gun*. I wish I'd killed that guy off when I met Jacqueline.

Now it was too late.

When I finally left the chapel, I saw the guy in the dirty clothes again. I say again because I'd noticed him at the beginning of the ceremony, standing outside the chapel, across the drive. I figured him for a maintenance guy at the cemetery. But here he was again, at the grave site, watching from afar as I made my way back toward the parking lot.

There are people who frequent cemeteries. They get vicarious pleasure from watching the mourners. Hey, whatever works to take away pain. I can understand *that* desire.

So I didn't pay the guy much mind at first, until I saw him following me.

He didn't get too close. Not right away. I'd take a few steps, stop to talk to one of Jacqueline's friends, and notice he was a few steps closer, too.

Looking at me.

That's when I started to burn. What right did he have to intrude? I was this close to turning around and smashing him one in the mouth.

Now, stepping out of the chapel, seeing him again just looking at me, I knew I was still close.

"Hey, what's your problem?" I said.

He was Latino, maybe forty, maybe homeless. He had that look, though it was just an assumption on my part. His flannel shirt was splotched with black stains, like deep fried grease. The front of his jeans almost glistened with oily residue of some kind.

And his eyes. They were haunted, like he'd seen things a person should never have to see. His eyes froze me.

"Please," he said.

There was something in his voice that was either insane or a call that I absolutely needed to hear. Maybe some of both.

"Please what?" I said.

"You are him?"

"Who?"

"The man of the woman?"

Somehow this made sense. "Yes, yes. What about it?"

"She die in the car."

How did he know this? "Who are you?"

"I see it."

"See *what*?"

"See her die."

Unreal. If he was telling the truth and not just making a play for inclusion in my misery, he was a witness to the defining moment of the rest of my life.

"You saw the accident?"

"*Sí.*"

"So?"

He shook his head hard.

"*What!*" I spat.

"She no die like they say."

My hand squeezed the car keys, causing pain.

"They kill her," he said.

8

MY INSTINCT WAS to grab the guy by the shirt and shake him until his neck cracked. But his shirt was filthy. I kept thinking *rat* as heat ripped through my chest.

He must have seen something in my eyes. What I felt was a blinding whiteness. Not anger as much as anguish, mixed with grief. A mourning cocktail. He took a step back, put his hands up.

"Who are you?" I matched his step with one of my own.

"Look—"

"How did you get here? What do you mean *kill*?"

My hands were clenching and unclenching.

"I want to tell you, man."

"Then come on." A thousand things were flashing through my mind at once. This guy was nuts. This guy knew something. Jacqueline was killed by somebody *on purpose*. It couldn't be, a sick guy's body fell on her car—

"Hey, man, I came for you," the guy said, pleading now.

"All right," I said. We were the only ones left in the parking lot now. "Start with, Who are you?"

He put his hands in his pockets and looked down.

"What about Jacqueline getting killed. How do you know anything?"

"Look, man, you help me little?"

"Help you out?"

"You know." He pulled out one of his grungy pockets.

"Money?" My fists were now clenched big-time. "You came here to try and get money from me?"

"I saw, you want to know or no?"

"You tell me, right now, how you found me. Or you get nothing."

He shrugged. "The paper." He motioned at the ground, like he was a real estate agent showing the place to a buyer. "You need to know, man."

I made the decision. I took out my wallet, snatched a crisp twenty. "I give you this, you tell me something I think I need to know."

His eyes narrowed in rodent-like displeasure. "You got to trust me."

"I don't got to trust you or anybody."

"You need to hear."

"So tell me."

"Forty."

I've negotiated with Koreans, New Yorkers, and the California Highway Patrol. But never with a guy whose only bargaining chip was my insane misery.

"Fine," I said.

At just that moment a cloud rolled between sun and earth. I swear it was like a Halloween moment. The cemetery fell under heavy shadow. I half expected somebody to rise from one of the graves.

"Let's see." Ratso, bolder now, moved closer.

I opened my wallet and took out another twenty. That left me with about four more.

"Talk," I said.

"Under . . . freeway," he said, making a motion. I assumed he meant the overpass. "I seen the body. *Boom*." He clapped his hands.

My heart jumped. And I was there, at the scene, in my mind.

"Dude's body, on the car. Car stop, man, sounds *eeeeee*."

I imagined tires squealing. Jacqueline inside the car.

"Nobody do nothing. Other cars getting around. No stop. People no want to get out. Guys honking. Seen her in car. Trapped in there, cause of dude's body."

"Alive?"

"Moving."

I couldn't say a word.

"Then I seen somebody off the hill. Coming right down. Hill under the pass. I'm up in the corner, watching."

I was trying to get all this to make sense. It was weird, something out of a David Lynch movie. Dark, like my insides.

"He goes to the car and he attacks the dude."

"What? Attacks?"

"I don't know, it looks like. He grabs something, I don't know. It's loco, man. Then he goes to the door and opens it. He has to pull it hard."

"What about Jacqueline?"

"She turns her head."

Alive.

"The dude he . . ." Ratso stopped.

"You better tell me fast what—"

Ratso shook his head hard. "Man, it's no good!"

Now I didn't care about the guy's shirt. I didn't care about anything but having him finish this bizarre story. I dropped my wallet and the twenties and grabbed his shirt with both hands.

"Tell me!" I shook him.

He pushed away and almost snarled. "This worth more, man. You got to come up with more."

"Money? You're asking for more—" I grabbed my head. It was going to burst. The picture I'd formed of beautiful Jacqueline being killed—

"You sick. . . . Get out of here, now! Or I call the cops."

At least I remembered to bend down and get my wallet and money.

Stupid. What I think was the guy's foot slammed into the side of my head.

9

IT WAS DARK and cold when I came to.

My face felt two sizes bigger. I couldn't breathe through my nose.

"Don't worry, son," a gentle voice said. "Ambulance on the way."

In the distance I heard a siren. Things started coming back to me. I felt my pocket. "Wallet," I said.

"Just lie here," the voice said. I blinked a couple of times and saw the outline of a man. He was kneeling beside me.

"But the—"

"Shh. You took a nasty fall."

"No—"

"Ambulance coming."

The siren got louder, and I took the guy's advice. I just lay there. The world was spinning, and I didn't have anything inside me to stop it.

I spent half the night in emergency at Northridge Hospital. They contacted Fran Dwyer for me, and she showed up to get me out of there.

"You're coming home with me," she said.

And I did.

Fran lived in the same little stucco job where Jacqueline had grown up. On Hemmingway Street (two m's) in Reseda. Not more than a thousand square feet, it was built in the fifties when the San Fernando Valley was exploding into the biggest suburb in the world.

She set me up in Jacqueline's old bedroom, making sure I was as comfortable as possible. Which, under the circumstances, was not very. She sat on the side of the bed.

"Who would do such a thing?" she said.

I decided not to give her the whole story. She'd been through the grinder. I wasn't going to give her some whacked out account when I didn't know what to think about it myself.

"Some guy wanting money," I said. "Can you believe it? At a cemetery?"

"You should call the police."

"I've got to run around and get all my stuff together—license, credit cards, all that. Can you help me?"

"You need to rest."

"I'll be all right," I said. "My legs are fine."

"I don't just mean your face. It was a hard day for all of us."

"I bet I ruined the reception when I didn't show. Would you do me a favor?"

"Of course."

"Call Rachel and tell her I'm fine, and have her call people. Explain. I'm just not up to it."

"I will."

She patted my hand. "Ty?"

"Yes?"

"I have a box of Jacqueline's things, from school. I wonder if you'd like to have it."

She left the room for a moment, returned with a simple brown box that might have held anything—old clothes, oranges, records of the dead. It had a thin veneer of dust on the flaps.

"I think she'd want you to have this," Fran said. "Promise you'll take care of it." She put it on the floor next to the bed.

I looked at the box, afraid to open it. Afraid it would gnaw the wound of loss. But, at the same time, needing to see what it held.

"I'll take good care of it, Fran, I promise."

She left me there again. A box of Jacqueline's things. What would I find in there? What did I want to find? Jacqueline alive, her voice in my ear.

But her voice was silent. Instead, I heard something else. Another voice. Over and over.

They kill her, it said.

10

NEXT MORNING, FRAN drove me to the Department of Motor Vehicles so I could get a temporary license, then back to the cemetery to get my car. I gave her a hug and told her I'd call her later.

She looked worried about me.

She should have been.

I did not go home. Instead I found myself driving, heading for the Harbor Freeway. I was going back to the scene of Jacqueline's death.

Did I expect to see him? Sitting in a corner under the overpass? The rational part of me said no. But something beyond, or below reason, argued. It wasn't the money or the credit cards or anything else I wanted. I wanted to know if the story was *true.*

As I got closer to the place where Jacqueline died —down the 110 Freeway past the Sports Arena and Exposition Park and just after Imperial Highway —my nerves started to hum. All of a sudden it was like I was taken over by some alien light beam controlling my body.

I almost rear-ended a semi carrying office furniture.

Closer now. I could see it, could see the connector freeway where Ernesto Bonilla had stood, gun in his mouth.

Traffic was light, but I was only going 40. Cars were honking behind me. I didn't care. I had something to see.

Almost there. I started looking under the concrete bridge. For him.

Nothing. It was shadowy, but clearly no one was on either side. Ratso was not at home.

What I did see was the hillside. The place Ratso said the guy had scurried, down to where he would break Jacqueline's neck. It was mostly dirt, with a couple of oleander bushes struggling to be fertile.

And I swore I saw, in the middle of one of the bushes, a trampling down.

I got off at the next ramp and doubled back on Figueroa to Imperial. I parked my car and walked to the freeway overpass. On the chain-link fence hung a sign that said *Complete Funeral Service—$2,170.50. Direct Cremation—$695.* It gave a phone number. I wondered why they picked this particular spot to post a bill. Maybe they knew things.

From the fence I could see where a guy like Ratso could sit himself in the shade. And I could see quite clearly, in the shadow of the connector freeway, the stretch of Harbor Freeway where Jacqueline died.

Murdered?

Could it possibly be true? The whole bizarre story?

I had to tell somebody.

11

I DROVE DOWNTOWN, parked in one of those lots that require a second mortgage, and walked across Los Angeles Street to Parker Center, headquarters of the LAPD. It's a big, aged white block of a building with windows and three skinny, tired-looking palm trees in front. The new headquarters was being built then, making the old place seem all the more weary. Still, it was the nerve center of the whole department, and I figured why not start at the top.

I walked into the cavernous lobby. A big tile mosaic depicting images of the city dominated the left-hand side. At the reception desk sat two uniformed police officers, a man and a woman. The woman gave me a skeptical eye as I approached. Maybe it was the marks on my face that did it. The nameplate on her uniform read *Stevens*.

"Is this where I report something?"

"What is it you want to report," Stevens said.

"A possible murder."

The other officer gave me a look.

Stevens said nothing. Skeptical face, waiting for me to continue.

"There was a guy last week," I explained. "Shot his wife, then shot himself on the overpass, where the Century goes over the Harbor."

"I read about that," the other officer said. "Fell on a car, right? Killed somebody?"

"The woman who died was my fiancée," I said.

The officers now looked at least a little interested. I said, "There was a witness, and he said he saw somebody go down to the car and kill her."

"He saw this?" Stevens said.

"That's what he said."

"He needs Southeast," the other officer said.

"Isn't Robbery-Homicide down here?" I said.

"That's a separate unit," Stevens said. "This is administration. Jurisdiction starts with division, and that would be Southeast." She took a yellow Post-It note from a pad and wrote an address on it. "It's on One Hundredth and Eighth. Need directions?"

"I've got GPS. She'll tell me where to go."

Stevens smiled. "I been told where to go lots of times."

Southeast Division was in a two-story brick building just east of the Harbor Freeway. I parked in front. Inside, windowless, it gave off the sterile feel of the local government's idea of renovation.

The front desk had three computer monitors and a couple of uniforms standing behind. To the right, a woman was fiddling with a QuickDraw ATM machine. Getting bail money no doubt. To the left, on a bench, sat a fat guy in shorts holding a wadded-up T-shirt to a bloody face.

"Help you?" one of the uniforms asked. At least the LAPD had that phrase down. The officer was slim, mid-twenties. The other, stockier and a little older, kept his eyes on his computer monitor.

"I want to report a homicide," I said.

The slim uniform squinted. "Homicide?"

"There was a shooting last week, a guy named Bonilla shot his wife, then himself, on the Century Freeway."

Stocky, without looking up, said, "Yeah. Murder-suicide."

Slim said, "Already in the pipe."

"No," I said. "I'm talking about the woman who was in the car he fell on. Remember that?"

"Terrible," Stocky said.

"She was murdered," I said. "Maybe."

That got Stocky's attention. He looked at me. "That's not murder. Guy shot himself—"

"She was murdered after that, after the body fell on her car."

Stocky and Slim looked at each other.

The fat guy on the bench moaned and shouted, "Where is she?"

"She's coming," Stocky told him. "Just hold on."

"I been holding for an hour! This place is a freakin' prison!"

Stocky turned his attention to the fat guy. Slim said to me, "If you'll leave your name, I'll pass it along to the detective in charge—"

"Is he here?" I said.

"Just give me your—"

"Can I talk to him, please? He'll want to hear what I have to say."

"Sir—"

"Five minutes."

Slim must have seen something in my discolored face. He picked up a phone and punched an extension and mumbled something. I couldn't hear what he said because the fat guy was screaming now, and Stocky was shouting *Sir! Sir! Sir!* at him.

Slim put down the phone and pointed at a pea green door behind me. "Through there," he said, and went to assist his partner.

I walked past the screaming guy and through the green door. That took me to another reception area with pale yellow walls with nothing on them, except a clock. A bald black man with an earpiece sat at a desk. He wasn't a uniform; he was dressed in civilian clothes. He said, "Just wait there."

A minute later a guy who looked like a Golden Gloves contender came out, gave me a handshake, introduced himself as Detective Ramón Fernández, and had me follow him past a large copy machine and a few filing cabinets into a room of waist-high cubicles.

He led me around a corner and motioned for me to enter an interview room. Spare white walls. A table and two chairs.

"Get you some coffee?" Fernández said. He was maybe thirty-four, thirty-five. Short black hair and photogenic face, marred only by the little white scar under his left eye. He wore a tan shirt with a plain brown tie.

"I'm good," I said.

"Okay, take a chair, I'll be right with you."

I sat and listened to the sounds of the detective room through the open door. It was a low-level hum of voices and keyboards and shoes on floor. For a second I thought of myself as the suspect. Jacqueline was dead. I had to be guilty of something.

Fernández came back in with a yellow pad and file folder. He closed the door, plopped the pad and file on the table. "Okay," he said, taking a chair, "why don't you tell me what this is about?"

I made like Greg Louganis and dove right in. "My fiancée was the one who died in that Bonilla incident."

"Shot his wife, then himself. Fell off the overpass and killed a woman. She was your fiancée?"

"Yeah."

Fernández leaned forward. "I'm very sorry. That was a freak thing to happen."

"Maybe it wasn't an accident."

"Not an accident?"

"Something else happened, I didn't find out until the funeral." As I spoke I could tell I was moving into odd territory, stuff that wasn't going to sound too plausible. But I had to make it known.

"A guy came up to me in the parking lot, told me he'd come looking for me. Said he witnessed the accident. Someone had gone down to the car and Jacqueline was still alive . . ." The words stopped cold in my throat.

"Go ahead," Fernández said. He removed a pen from his shirt pocket.

I took a deep breath, "He said they killed her."

"They?"

"Yeah."

"This guy, says he saw this?"

"That's what he said."

"How far away was he?"

"I don't know. I didn't ask."

"This guy was in a position to see?"

"Yeah."

"You have the man's name?"

I knew where this train was headed. "I'll tell you, I really thought the guy was telling me the truth, but then I ticked him off and he attacked me."

Fernández's eyebrows went up in the universal sign of skepticism. He didn't write anything. He tapped his pen on the pad. "You're going to have to explain that one."

"I gave him a couple of twenties for his information. I got mad and dropped my wallet and bent over to get it and next thing I know I'm out. I wake up on the ground, and my head feels like it's been kicked."

"I can see that."

We fell into an uncomfortable silence.

"Anything else you want to add?" Detective Fernández said.

"What else you need?"

"Any witnesses to this guy beating you up?"

"I don't think so."

"This guy who attacked you, what did he look like?"

I gave him the best description I could.

"Well, I have to tell you off the bat that the chances of finding this guy are pretty slim. I can have a patrol take a look. But even if we do, to prove the attack from your word alone isn't going to—"

"I don't care about the attack."

"Excuse me?"

"I'm here because of the murder."

Fernández opened the file folder and looked over some papers. "Mr. Buchanan, Ernesto Bonilla popped his wife and then got on the freeway, stopped on the overpass, and ate a bullet. His body fell onto the Harbor Freeway. That's about a hundred foot drop. So how does a guy get to the car and find your fiancée and kill her? More to the point, why?"

"I've been trying to think. Somebody follows Bonilla for some reason? Maybe it's Bonilla he's after."

"Then he has to stop on the freeway and get down to the Harbor. I mean, I think it could be done, but it would be a real stuntman thing to do. Problem is, we got three witness statements from the scene. It was pretty confusing down there. A lot of rain. But nothing about anybody doing anything to the occupant of the car. Did this guy give you a description?"

I shook my head.

"Same problem. We'd have to find this guy to talk to him. Unless we do . . ." Fernández shook his head.

"You don't believe me, do you?"

"Do you believe it?"

My hands curled around the arms of the chair.

"Easy," he said.

"Maybe I have to believe it," I said.

He cocked his head. "Come again?"

I didn't say anything. Didn't feel like telling him my dad was a cop in Miami who got murdered when I was ten. That he'd been working on a major drug case, went out one night on his own, and they found him the next morning behind a motel with two holes in the back of his head. That the cops turned the town upside down for a month and no one was ever arrested.

The detective took a cardholder from his pocket, fished out a card, handed it to me. "Look, you find anything else, and I mean anything, feel free to call. You have a number I can reach you?"

I gave it to him. But it seemed strictly *pro forma* that he wrote it down.

After leaving the station I took the Santa Monica Freeway all the way to the beach and drove to Venice to watch the moon come out.

She loved the moon.

She loved it most when it was big and round and looming over the ocean, throwing silver streaks on the water. And the way it cast light over L.A., the cool softness of it, an illumination to mute the hard edges of night and the city.

Once she said it reminded her of the night-light she had in her room as a child. It was round and glowy and plugged into the wall, and when she woke up from a bad dream she'd stare at it until she felt right again, safe. Then she'd go back to sleep, knowing her light would be there in the morning, waiting for her.

She thought that's what you needed in the city—a big night-light in the sky, because there's so much unseen, streets of bad shadows, and you need something to stare at until you feel right again. Safe.

She even said I made her feel safe.

Alone in the night and the city, I heard myself whispering her name, over and over and over.

12

TWO DAYS LATER I worked up the guts to return to the office. It was the Friday before Christmas, so it would be light work, and everybody would be in a good mood. Good enough, I hoped, that I wouldn't have to talk to anybody about *it*, the incident, the loss. I didn't want a lot of well-meaning, tight-lipped, understanding nods.

So I came in through the back way, seeing only Nelson Richards, one of the partners who outworked everybody else in the firm. He gave me a well-meaning, tight-lipped, understanding nod. I gave him half a wave and shot down to my office. It felt foreign, something to be preserved in a museum.

Future gawkers could walk by and see the authentic abode of a once alive person who practiced law.

I tried to get back in the saddle, as they say. Churning through piled up e-mails, I found out that work doesn't make you forget, not this soon.

A little before ten, Al bounded in after a quick knock on the door. "Welcome back, dude," he said, arms akimbo like a televangelist on speed.

"I'm not all here yet," I said.

"Your face, man."

"Shut it, will you?"

"It'll come back to ugly in no time." He sat in a chair, loping one leg over the arm. "What was it Bukowski said? '*It all begins and ends here, in the moment*.'"

"Bukowski was a beer-soaked yutz."

"Not a bad idea. Let's grab a pitcher and get hammered."

"I don't think so."

"Best thing for you. Bring you back to a resemblance of normal."

"Al, you don't have to work so hard on me. I'll come around."

I was not at all confident this was true.

"Dude, I know it hurts. The fact that you're here now is, like, inhuman."

"What?"

"Not like mutants from Planet X inhuman. Wait. Superhuman, how's that? Whatever. Just thought getting back to a couple of drinks after work would be nice. The old routine."

"Another time."

"Your call." He flicked something off his pants. "So I had a phone conversation with Lea Edwards, covering your cute little keister."

"Yeah? What about it?"

"Just doing you a favor. You remember she's coming in today?"

Truth be told, I hadn't been thinking about the case at all. Jacqueline's death was all over my mind.

I quickly checked my calendar. There it was. Giving me about an hour to prepare.

"You're a saint, Al. I don't care what your mother says."

"Kiss my—"

"Good-bye, Al."

13

DR. LEA EDWARDS was beautiful in that classy Lauren Bacall sort of way. Also formidable intellectually. Bachelor's, master's, and PhD from Harvard. Danforth Award winner as one of Harvard's top teaching fellows.

Author of ten books, highly sought after expert witness, and reputedly a killer gourmet chef.

She was blonde, tall, and divorced from a professor of psychology who now taught at Berkeley. For the last fifteen years she'd been teaching at UCLA, on her way to becoming one of the country's leading experts on the memory and the tricks it can pull.

But at the moment she was holding my hand warmly in my office. "I heard all about your fiancée," she said. "I'm so very sorry."

She wore a nightshade blue suit, the coat unbuttoned in deference to a white, lacy blouse. Around her neck was a large silk scarf that complemented the color scheme. Her perfume was just the right balance of subtlety and come-hither.

"Are you sure you'd like to do this now?" she asked.

"Professional duties don't go away just because of personal trouble."

"Well said. My father would have liked you. He was the publisher of a small-town newspaper, but he took it every bit as seriously as if it were the *New York Times.*"

"Old-fashioned work ethic."

She nodded. "When my mom was in a bad way and I was over in Japan speaking, he still had to get out the paper. He was proud he never missed a deadline. That's why I say he would have liked you, Ty. You even look a little like him."

"Yeah?"

"He was about six-three, sandy blond hair, blue eyes. A real athlete in his day. Football."

"I'm more of a hoopster."

"I bet you look good in a uniform."

Whoa. I quickly opened a drawer, pulled out the case file, and plopped it on my desk. "The Blumberg depo went pretty well, I think. I want to go over some of her answers and get your feedback. We've got to be prepared to cross-examine if it ever comes to that."

"Certainly." She gracefully slipped into a client chair. "What did you think of her?"

"Overall, she makes a good impression. Things like demeanor, directness, vulnerability."

"All of which have alternative explanations."

"Why don't you expand on that a little."

She assumed a pose in the chair that exuded power, the kind that comes from knowing more than anybody else about what you're going to say. "Psychology, properly practiced, is the art of digging beneath surfaces. What you saw were the surfaces of Claudia Blumberg. That's the part Kendra Mackee presents in her seminars. Only Mackee gives it her spin. What's got them so mad is that I found out the truth."

"You think it's a, what did you call it, neuro-something or other?"

"Neuro rationalization. She has embedded a hatred of her father into her nervous system, so to speak. It's much the same phenomenon as the false memories that were implanted in her by Dr. Mackee."

"Pretend I'm a juror. Can you give this to me in terms that are understandable to a layperson?"

"Of course. The whole debate comes down to whether memories are fixed, like concrete, or malleable like warm clay. Is that easy enough?"

"Fine."

"But it's not just a scientific debate. We've raised up a generation of victims. One might even call it a victim industry, with people like Mackee making big bucks. The victims themselves see the financial rewards court judgments can bring. And they get to be on the *Today* show or *Good Morning, America*. Do you know I've never been asked to be on either?"

"I'm not surprised."

"There is an incentive now to make things up, you see?"

"You don't believe repressed memory ever happens?"

"It's so rare as to be statistically insignificant."

"But others disagree."

"Others are wrong."

At that moment Dr. Lea Edwards looked like someone who could chew through steel to bite her critics. We'd have to soften that up a little before trial. If it ever came to that.

"So Claudia Blumberg was acting?"

"Not necessarily. She probably really believes what she's saying. But that's because those memories have been implanted in her."

"How?"

She got up and walked around the chair, her scarf trailing behind her like a comet's tail. "Years ago a very bright advertising man figured out that in order to sell deodorant, you first had to convince as many people as possible that they stank. He came up with a television campaign that showed nice-looking young men in social settings making life stinky for the people around them. You follow?"

"I'm all over it."

"It was a brilliant bit of group brainwashing. The product sold itself. It took off. That never would have happened without the soil being prepared."

She was at the window now and turned around. The light caught her eyes. Violet.

"A doctor can easily do this to a child, the most vulnerable among us. He can prepare the soil in a child's mind, then through questions actually plant the toxic weeds that will come out in falsity."

I had the impression for a moment that she was trying to implant something in me. And succeeding.

"Ty, are you getting this?"

"Oh, yeah. Of course."

"I lost you there for a second."

"No, I'm fine."

She took her chair again. "Assure me then."

"Assure you?"

"That you're going to be all right. That your, how did you put it?, *professional duties* won't be compromised."

"You've got nothing to worry about, Dr. Edwards."

"Then I'd like one more thing," she said.

"Yes?"

"For you to call me Lea."

And that look came at me again. Thankfully it was broken by the tweeting of her cell phone. She picked up and from what I could gather was talking to someone about a possible newspaper interview.

When she signed off, she looked at me and said, "Is that not a good idea?"

"You can do interviews," I said. "Just don't mention the Blumberg litigation, okay?"

"I promise, Ty. I'm in your hands." She smiled at me, and it was one dazzling look.

14

LESS DAZZLING WAS the day in L.A. A thick haze had settled over the city just in time for the lunch rush. Made Hollywood look even dirtier than it was as I drove to the Channel 5 studios on Sunset. Their offices were located in the former Warner Bros. building. They filmed *The Jazz Singer* there in 1927. It still had a white, Greek revival façade and a huge broadcasting tower on the corner with the call letters. You could see the Hollywood sign up in the hills.

"You can't go in," the gate guard said. He was SUV wide, dressed in a black security uniform. His black baseball hat had *KTLA 5* in yellow across it.

"I just want to talk to Ms. Westerbrook," I said.

"What, you think you can just drive in and talk to her?"

"Sure I can. I step on this gas pedal and use this wheel to steer. See?"

"Sir, nobody can just—"

"Would you please tell her I'm here?"

I needed to talk to Westerbrook. She was the first reporter on the scene where Jacqueline died. I guess it wasn't much of a story to her because she never bothered to try to get in touch with me. No one did.

It was all an accident, you see. Held up traffic on the Harbor Freeway for a while, and the fatalities made it somewhat significant. But then it was on to the next story.

"You need to turn around," the guard told me, "and call up and talk to the desk, and they'll see what they can do."

"But I'm here now. If you were to make the call and use my name, they might make you sergeant."

The humor was lost on him, as well it should have been. My delivery that day was not Letterman quality.

"Can't let you in," the humorless guard said. "I'll write down the number for you to call."

He wrote it on a big yellow sticky note and handed it to me. "Now back out," he said with gusto. He must have practiced that phrase at security guard school.

I drove down Van Ness, the walled-off studio to my right, and pulled over in the *No Stopping Any Time* zone. I'd left my cell phone in the car. Fortunately, it still had some juice.

I punched the number the guard had given me. A recording walked me through to the directory. I entered the first three letters of Westerbrook's last name and got her voicemail.

I said, "If you want a lead on another murder in connection with the Ernesto Bonilla freeway death, call me." And I left my cell number.

Then I drove to a Noodle Express on Hollywood Boulevard near Gower and got some noodles and orange chicken. The place smelled like hot oil. There was no place to sit inside so I sat on a hard, curved bench at an outside table that had some graffiti on it. The orange chicken tasted like glorified McNuggets.

My phone chimed *Flight of the Valkeries*, and I saw the call was from Al. I toyed with not answering, but finally did.

"What're you doing, dude?" Al said, concern in his voice.

"Killing baby seals."

"Great! You coming back?"

"Of course. Why?"

A short pause. "The old man was asking about the Blumberg summary."

I'd forgotten all about it. I was supposed to prepare a pretrial summary of the key issues in the Claudia Blumberg litigation for the senior partner who'd try the case, Pierce McDonough. It was on my to-do list and everything.

"What'd he say?" I asked.

"He wanted to know where you were."

"What did you tell him?"

"I covered for you, man. I told him I thought you were bustin' your hump at home."

"Thanks."

"Anything else I can do for you? You need some help on the summary?"

"No, I'll get to it. Thanks for the heads-up."

I finished the last of the noodles, cold now and sticking in my mouth, then walked out to the street. The Hollywood Walk of Fame stretched out here, and I found I was standing on the five-pointed star commemorating the career of Veronica Lake. All I knew about her was that she had that famous peek-a-boo hairstyle that drove men wild in the forties.

The *Valkeries* struck again.

A woman's voice. "This the guy with the murder story?"

"Channing Westerbrook?"

"So what about a murder?"

"Can we talk?"

"What have you got?"

"Let's meet and talk about it."

"I don't do that," she said. "If you have something that can be substantiated, that I can check out, then maybe we can set something up, but I'm—"

"Look, this is real. I promise you. You remember the name of the girl who died?"

"Dwyer," she said. "I have the summary in front of me."

"Jacqueline Dwyer."

"That's right. Did you know her?"

"Oh yes," I said.

15

THE GUY WITH the muscles did not smile at me. He wore a Gold's Gym sweatshirt with the arms cut off so his own could be seen in all their ripped glory.

He was Westerbrook's cameraman. She had told me to meet her at the corner of Normandie and Santa Monica where she was doing a remote about a bomb scare.

"I've got five minutes," Channing Westerbrook said. She had short chest-nut hair and looked a little younger than she did on TV. I figured her for around thirty. She was made up for the camera. She wore a designer jacket, light pink with a pearl brooch of some kind. Below the waist it was blue jeans and sandals. Then I thought about the times I'd seen her on the tube. They always shot from the waist up.

Muscles was setting up his camera on an industrial tripod, casting glances our way as he did. Behind us was the strip mall where the bomb had been reported. Half a dozen black-and-whites were in the parking lot. Cops were milling around.

"Thanks for seeing me," I said.

"So you were her fiancé?"

"Yes."

"Can you prove it?" Her expression was no-nonsense. She had high en-ergy, and it seemed that she couldn't speak fast enough.

I reached for my wallet, which had Jacqueline's picture in it. Then I real-ized I didn't have my wallet. Ratso had taken it. I only had my temporary license and some cards in a billfold.

"Why would I make this up?"

"We get calls like this all the time. Gummies. We call them gummies. Peo-ple who want to stick themselves on a story. Wackos who say they were the ones who saw the real killer of Bonnie Lee Bakley or Nicole Brown Simpson. Or did it themselves."

"Do I look wacko to you?"

"Boy-next-door looks, Ted Bundy had 'em."

"That's right. I'm a serial killer. What a scoop for you, huh?"

She took out a package of Marlboro Lights from her jacket pocket and lit one. She shot the smoke out of one side of her mouth. "Let's say for the mo-ment you are who you say you are. What's this about a murder?"

"When did you get to the scene?"

"What's that got to do with it?"

"I want to know what you heard or saw. Did you speak to anybody?"

Channing Westerbrook took another deep drag on her cigarette. "I'm not here to be questioned by you."

"Did you question anybody at the scene? Did you follow up on Bonilla?"

"Hey." She put her hands in the air. "You said you had something for me. Tell me what it is now or this conversation is over."

"Somebody may have killed Jacqueline," I said.

Channing Westerbrook squinted within a plume of smoke. "Bonilla's body fell on her car," she said. "Freak accident."

"What if the body didn't kill her?"

Muscles stood up straight. My voice had grown a little louder than normal. Channing Westerbrook did not flinch. "I did some quick background on Bonilla. Nothing remarkable. Ex-gang member, I guess, but he was working now. Your fiancée —if you're telling me the truth —was a schoolteacher."

"Elementary. Fifth grade. And I am telling you the truth."

She looked at me as if I were a witness and she the cross-examining attorney. "What else could it have been?"

I gave her the story up to the point where Ratso took me down.

"That's it?" Westerbrook said.

"Yeah."

"That sounds like a shakedown to me."

"But what if there's something to it?"

"Too bizarre," Westerbrook said.

Channing Westerbrook looked behind her, saw that Muscles had the camera in place. He was now standing there like a eunuch in a harem, watching everything that was going on between me and the princess of television.

"I'd like to help you out," she said to me, "but you've got to understand this business. This is an oddball story you've got here. Possible murder? Unless you have some kind of evidence or eyewitness or something like that, what do I have to go on? If you ever get something like that, you can—"

"I can't get something if I can't find the guy again. I thought maybe you could help by giving me what you've got. You said you had a file."

"I don't give out my files," she said, laughing a little, like I'd said the dumbest thing.

"Maybe you can make an exception," I said.

Her face got granite solid. "Sorry."

"I'm not going away."

"This conversation is now over," she said.

"No," I said. "It's not."

Before I could say another word Muscles stepped over. He had the macho look, the WWF stare. Maybe I could have landed a good kick in his classified abs, but like I said, my fighting days were behind me.

Or so I thought then.

16

FRAN COLLAPSED ON Christmas Day.

I'd spent the night at her house, sleeping once more in Jacqueline's childhood bed. I didn't want Fran to be alone. I'd even bought her a little tree and set it up in the corner of the tiny living room. It made the place smell nice, but Fran hadn't put up any decorations.

In the morning, before she got up, I slipped a present under the tree. It was a portable CD player and a CD collection of Dean Martin. Jacqueline told me once how much her mom loved Dean Martin and had a bunch of his albums on vinyl.

Then I did my imitation of a cook and made up a pancake breakfast for her. I had the TV on to some morning Christmas show, and everybody was happy.

Fran ate half a pancake before dissolving into tears. I sat there, wordless, not knowing what to say. Everything seemed inadequate.

Then she fell off the dining room chair. I thought she'd had a heart attack. But the cause was just the unbearable sadness of it all, and I got her on the sofa and let her rest her head on my shoulder as she cried some more.

"We're in this together," I whispered. "We'll hold each other up."

A chirpy woman on TV said, "Happy Holidays to you and yours from all your friends at KTLA Channel 5."

17

JONATHAN BLAKE BLUMBERG was known around town as B-2, and not just because of the initials in his name. Like the bomber, Blumberg flew over the world of digital products, seeking competitors to wipe out. He took no prisoners.

I went to see him the Thursday after Christmas, in his building—yes, that Blumberg Building, the one that overlooks the 405 Freeway. I wanted to get his side of the story. The man deserved a hearing because for the last seventeen years he'd been painted as an evil child molester by a vicious ex-wife and a scheming daughter. Or so I was paid to believe.

His office seemed to be all glass, and not just the kind you look out of. The kind that keeps out weather and bullets. He had a very politically incorrect moose head mounted on one wall. He saw me looking at it and said, "I wanted to put Bill Gates there, but I haven't had a clear shot."

I tried to smile.

"You sit," Blumberg said. "I'll stand. I need to walk around."

The man was like a lion in a cage. His frame under a knit golf shirt was trim. He had full black hair, only slightly speckled with gray. No sign of thinning, either. I got the idea that if his hair tried to fall out, Blumberg would beat it back into submission.

I fired up my Mac. "I take better notes this way."

"No need to tell me. Soon enough we'll be able to talk and voice recognition software will distinguish our voices and take it all down."

"You think so?"

"Look at this." He held up his wrist and showed me his watch. A substantial silver thing. He whipped it off and tossed it to me. "Fifty years ago people thought only Dick Tracy in the comics could have something like this. You remember?"

"Dick Tracy?"

"Oh yeah. You're just a kid."

"I did see the *Dick Tracy* movie with Warren Beatty."

"Stinko! Don't ever let Madonna near a movie. Point is, we got TV, video, satellite coming in on a phone now. Here's a prototype of a watch that'll do the same thing. That's what JatDome is all about. We define the next generation, and when it arrives, we do the next."

And that's how Jonathan Blake Blumberg became a billionaire.

"Cool," I said. "Am I being watched, so to speak?"

"You're a funny guy." He took the watch from me, clicked it back on his arm. "But funny doesn't win cases."

"I can be unfunny, too."

"Good. I don't look to the past, Ty. That's old news. But the past keeps trying to bite my head off. I haven't been able to shake it in seventeen years."

"I know. In a way, it's good to have your daughter bring this lawsuit. With Dr. Edwards we can show the whole thing to be a fabrication."

"A little late in the day for me. I never got to watch my daughter grow up." He was looking out the window when he said this, toward the airport. It was a clear day, and I could see the air traffic to and from LAX.

"Would you mind going over it again, from the beginning?" I said. "I know it's painful, but if—"

"Pain doesn't do it for me. A long time ago I learned that pain avoidance is always an excuse for inaction. You ever see *Lawrence of Arabia*?"

"Sure."

"Great movie. At the beginning, Lawrence puts out a match with his fingers. Doesn't flinch. Another soldier sees this and tries it, burns his fingers and says, 'Hey, that hurts. What's the trick?' And Lawrence says, 'The trick is not minding that it hurts.'"

"That was in *All the President's Men*, too."

"Point is, you're a litigator, Ty, that's good advice for you, too."

I didn't tell him about Jacqueline. I didn't tell him that it still hurt and that I couldn't make the pain stop.

"So there was a divorce when Claudia was about seven," I said.

"Right. I'd had an affair. Ironically, with a lawyer. Sheila Katz, you may have heard of her."

I shook my head.

"She's quite a success up in San Francisco. Partner with a big firm up there. Anyway, it was only a fling, but when Dyan found out about it, she went nuts. Filed for divorce."

"And won custody of Claudia."

"Worse, she convinced Claudia to lie. Put it in her head that I abused her sexually. You know how many men are accused of that each year by angry ex-wives? It's the nuclear option. And quacks like Mackee come along and make it seem legit."

His voice caught a little then, in his throat. When he turned to me his eyes had the hint of glistening in them. "Ty, do this please. Beat this case back and rip the truth out. I've been waiting a long time."

I nodded, feeling I'd looked into the inner sanctum of the B-2, to a place few people ever got to see.

"Let's get down to it," he said, and for the next hour gave me his side of the tale.

He had married Dyan Collins of Providence, Rhode Island, after seeing her on the Miss America pageant. Decided he wanted her and that he'd get her. Pulled some strings. I got the impression this is what he did best, pull strings, though he didn't say whose strings they were. He arranged for her to fly out to L.A. He then took her on his private hydrofoil to Catalina Island for dinner. They stayed three days at the Hotel Metropole, overlooking Avalon Harbor.

They were married a month later. Daughter Claudia was born eight months after that. And Dyan Blumberg, twelve years younger than her husband, started looking for an acting career. Jonathan pulled a few strings again and landed Dyan a role in a Tony Scott action flick, a supporting role playing a nuclear technician for the CIA. The critics did not find this a convincing fit.

"That was the beginning of the end," Jonathan told me. "She started to go a little nuts after that. Couldn't take the rejection. As much as I tried to build her up, she seemed to go further down. She started drinking. To my discredit, I let her. I should have gotten her help right away. Maybe if I had, I could have stayed out of the ninth circle of Hell."

He stared out the window for about twenty seconds without moving.

18

"YOU KNOW," HE said at last, "the joker who said hell hath no fury like a woman scorned didn't know about a woman loaded who didn't believe anything her husband told her. She started to develop this paranoia. It was creepy. The only person she trusted was our daughter. She put her whole life into Claudia. Which left me out in the dark, which led to a whole lot of arguing."

What happened next was the all-too familiar tune played in the neighborhoods of the rich and powerful. Divorce featuring two overpriced lawyers and a custody battle that could have been staged by the Medicis.

The big bomb in many cases is the accusation of child abuse. Dyan found Dr. Kendra Mackee, and that was the beginning of the end.

"I could have continued to fight it," Jonathan said, "and maybe I should have. But I didn't want Claudia to be torn apart. I offered to settle for visitation. I thought the abuse accusations would dry up. Then about six years ago Dyan started keeping Claudia away from me, and Claudia decided she didn't want to see me anymore. That's when I went back to court, and found Mackee and Dyan waiting for me with this repressed memory business. Witches. Let's go back to Salem and burn 'em both."

I took copious notes, all the time assessing what sort of witness Blumberg might make. And I wondered, just slightly, if he was telling me the whole truth. How could I tell?

Well, it wasn't my job to guess. We had a case to win and B-2 might have to be a witness, unless we settled for some chump change.

Blumberg picked up on my thoughts, in an eerie sort of way. "You don't entirely believe me, do you?"

"Mr. Blumberg," I said, "I'm not a jury. I'm a lawyer. And whatever you say is good enough for me."

"Well, it's not good enough for me."

I had no idea what he meant.

"You want to make it as a lawyer?" he said.

"Excuse me?"

"Do you want success as a lawyer?"

"Of course."

"Then don't let anything be good enough but this—more information than your opponent. And right now I'm your opponent."

"You are?"

"That's right. Everybody is until you get the information. That's the only currency that matters, Mr. Buchanan. The reason I whip everybody else in negotiation is that I have more information than they do. I make sure I do. That's why I win."

Macho award to Jonathan Blake Blumberg. With a supporting nod for bluster. If he were ever to testify, he might just bluster his way out of favor with a jury.

"You'll appreciate what I've said the longer you live, kid." Blumberg stood up and signaled the end of the meeting with an iron handshake. He eyed me intensely, making me wonder if he wanted us to take off our shirts and bump chests. I got out of there before finding out.

As I was driving away from Blumberg's office, my cell bleeped.

"It's Channing Westerbrook. You busy?"

"Driving."

"Not a good time to talk?"

"About what?"

"Your story."

"I thought I didn't have a story."

"I'm sorry about last night," Westerbrook said, in that rapid-fire way she had. "We got off on the wrong foot."

Both feet. "What's different?"

"I've thought about it," she said. "Maybe there's something we can both work with."

Now I was being sold? There was something very strange about this. What could have possibly happened in the last twelve hours to change her attitude? But I learned long ago you always listen to the first offer.

"Go ahead," I said.

"I looked through my file again, and there was an interesting item I'd overlooked."

"I'm listening."

"Now before I tell you, let me give you the other part of this scenario."

"What are you talking about?"

"Ty, I am a reporter, okay? Reason is, I always had a nose for news, as my grandfather used to say. I know stories. You are a story."

"I am not a story," I said. "I came to you so I could —"

"Why don't we meet again? I'd rather do this in person."

The smirking face of Muscles flashed into my head. "Alone," I said. "I'll see you only if you are absolutely alone."

"Deal. Where?"

"I know a place."

19

WITHOUT POUNDS OF makeup for the camera, Channing Westerbrook was actually very attractive, in a girl-next-door kind of way. She
wore a dark red blouse and, once again, crisp blue jeans and sandals. Urban
casual.

"Why here?" she asked.

"Not likely to be interrupted," I said. "Unless you believe M. Night
Shyamalan."

"Pardon?"

"You know, seeing dead people. *Sixth Sense* and all that?"

"Ah," she said without a smile.

We were on the grounds of the Westwood Mortuary, not far from my
office. Having her come over to my turf was a little negotiating ploy, though
I still didn't know what would need to be negotiated. All I knew was that a
part of me didn't trust a news reporter seeking me out. It was quiet here,
with only a few other live people milling around. The place is tucked away
behind office buildings on Wilshire, keeping it semiprivate.

"How long've you been in L.A.?" I asked as we strolled onto the
grounds.

"I joined the station a year ago," she said.

"Where from?"

"Cincinnati."

"Want to visit Marilyn Monroe?"

I walked her to the crypt that's Marilyn's final resting place. "DiMaggio
used to have a rose in that brass holder at all times," I said. "Until near the
end of his own life."

"Cool," Channing Westerbrook said. "Where's Rudolph Valentino?"

"Not here. He's at the Hollywood Mortuary, across town. If you want to
visit Jack Lemmon or Natalie Wood or Dean Martin, you've come to the
right place."

"How do you know so much about all these dead people?"

I felt a twinge, let it pass. "Jacqueline loved old movies. We both did." I barely noticed the past tense applied to myself.

We found a bench in the back, looking at the grass plots and trees. Most of it was taken up by flat markers.

"I want to do your story," Westerbrook said.

"I told you I don't have a story."

"But you do," she said quickly. "A quest about lost love."

Oh brother.

She must have read my face. "No, listen," she said. "In just the brief time we've talked I can tell Jacqueline must have meant the world to you. In a way that's missing from so many relationships today."

I wondered if she was talking about herself. Certainly she wouldn't have had any shortage of interested males.

"Then this murder story gets you beaten up," Westerbrook said, sounding like she was pitching a screenplay. "But you can't let the possibility go."

"You know squat about me."

"I know about Jacqueline."

I stiffened. "What do you mean?"

"I called her school, talked to the principal. She gave me all sorts of good stuff."

"Hold it," I said. "What are you doing digging into her life? Why don't you tell me what this is really all about?"

She stayed cool. "I'm trying to, Ty. Really. You came to me with a story that was very hard to believe. The more I thought about it, the more I admired your determination. So I did some digging around. On Jacqueline. And on Ernesto Bonilla."

An older couple came shuffling by, smiling and nodding at us. As if we were some young couple in love. I waited until they were out of earshot.

"Tell me," I said.

"The Bonillas had a neighbor across the street, a Lupe Salazar. She gave a short statement to the police."

"How do you know this?"

"I have a copy of the police report."

Her eyes were starting to sparkle.

"Go on," I said.

"I went out to see Mrs. Salazar."

That was out of the ordinary. Westerbrook was not an investigative reporter. She was basically paid to show up and talk on camera, with a token interview thrown in. That she did all this showed something more than a passing interest.

"Okay," I said. "You went to see this neighbor. Did she have anything to say?"

"Oh yeah," Westerbrook said with a half smile. "Only not in words."

"What does that mean?"

"She was scared out of her mind."

A screech of tires wailed on Westwood Boulevard. It was midday traffic out there, always a study in madness and mayhem.

"What was she scared of?"

"Gangs."

"That doesn't make her unique."

"But it was in connection with Bonilla. And Bonilla was supposed to be an ex-gang member. Reformed. Working."

"Right."

"Got rehabbed at that honor ranch in Lancaster."

I'd read about that place. Out in the desert, on hell's stove. It was a private ranch that used tough discipline on gangbangers and whipped them back into productive citizens. Or so their PR said.

"So if he was a new man," I said, "why was this woman scared?"

"She wouldn't tell me at first." Westerbrook fished in her purse for a cigarette. "Mind if I?"

"I don't think they want you to smoke out here."

"The dead? Let them tell me." She lit up. "I managed to get her to talk a little. That's what I'm good at."

I was beginning to believe she was very good at that.

"Mrs. Salazar thought the Bonillas were into selling a little marijuana."

"Why?"

"She'd see cars coming around at all hours. People getting out, running up to the door, running back. Typical profile."

"Was Bonilla ever busted for it?"

"No, that's the thing. The cops came out once, Mrs. Salazar said, but nothing was found. She thinks the cops gave Bonilla a pass."

"That doesn't make any sense. And neither does this Mrs. Salazar."

"Hold on," Westerbrook said. "She said she started watching the house because of all this. And one day she's walking on the sidewalk and sees a guy watching Bonilla's house. Right in front of *her* house."

"What kind of guy?"

"Gangbanger. He's wearing a wife beater, and Mrs. Salazar can see, clear as day, the three dots on his arm."

"The three *what*?"

"Dots. A Latino gang tattoo."

I shook my head. "I don't get it."

Channing Westerbrook took a drag on her smoke. "I called a source we have on gang activity. I asked him about it. The dots stand for a phrase."

"What phrase?"

"*Mi vida loca.*"

"My crazy life?"

"Now here's where it gets interesting," Westerbrook said. "I also got the autopsy report on Bonilla. You'll never guess what he had on the back of his neck."

"Three dots."

"You're getting good. Only these dots were *connected*. A triangle."

"Maybe he was into geometry."

"There was a cut across it, right through the triangle. A fresh cut."

"You must have thought about what this adds up to, or you wouldn't have called me. You mind telling me?"

The reporter stubbed out her cigarette on the bottom of one of her sandals. Her toenails were painted purple.

"Suppose," she said, "Bonilla really was into drug trafficking. And the guy with the dots was watching him because he was a rival of some kind, or working for a rival."

"All right."

"Now, Bonilla shoots his wife. When he takes off from the house, Three Dots follows him."

I nodded, feeling again like I was being pitched a crazy Hollywood story.

"Then Bonilla shoots himself, falls over. Three Dots has stopped, too, only back a way. Maybe there's two of them. Three Dots runs to where he can jump the rail and scampers down. Maybe he wants to make sure Bonilla is dead. Unfortunately, Jacqueline is still alive and sees him."

Westerbrook stopped. I'm sure she sensed my discomfort. It must have been all over my face. "Go on," I said.

She cleared her throat. "So he killed Jacqueline."

My chest felt empty all of a sudden, all the energy sucked out of it. "You know how crazy that sounds? How could you prove any of it?"

"I don't have to," Westerbrook said.

"What is that supposed to mean?"

"I mean this is your quest. Your search for answers. You don't have to find them, you just have to look. I know you want to. And I want to record it. I want your story, Ty. Exclusive. For a *New Yorker* article, or a book. Maybe both."

"Not interested," I said. "All I want to do is find the guy who might have killed Jacqueline."

"I can help you."

"I appreciate it."

"*If . . .*"

"Why? Why me?"

"Like I told you, I can smell a story. And I don't want to do remotes for local news forever."

I started to consider the possibilities. Someone like this on my side, with resources and contacts, could help a lot. I didn't want any publicity, but maybe that would be a small price to pay to find out what really happened.

"How about I think about it?" I said.

"Call me at this number." She handed me a card. "And don't wait too long. Oh, and one more thing. Keep this between us, huh? I don't want to get in bad with the station. Yet."

"How about quid pro quo?"

"What sort of quid did you have in mind?"

"Get me a copy of the police report."

She thought about it. "Will that seal the deal?"

"It'll sweeten the pot."

"Not good enough."

Now it was my turn to think it over. "All right, Ms. Westerbrook. You've got a deal."

With a gleaming smile, one that was going to make her a star someday, she put out her hand. "Pleasure doing business with you, Mr. Buchanan. Let's make it Channing and Ty, huh?"

20

THE GENIUSES WHO designed two holidays to follow one after the other were maybe thinking, Hey, let's get all happy and festive at the end of the year. Give people a good excuse to shut down work, like Scrooge complained about, the old Humbug. We'll do the Christmas thing, then the New Year's thing, and the bubbles will flow.

Only when you've just lost the one you love, it's a double hammer blow. The Christmas hole and the New Year's pit.

Which is why I didn't go to Al's for his annual New Year's party. Besides, I thought I'd better spend the night at Fran's again, at least one more time. I didn't want her to be alone.

We ended up eating popcorn and watching an old episode of *Everybody Loves Raymond.*

"Thanks for being here, Ty," she said. "I know you could be out with—"

"Hey, come on. I love *Everybody Loves Raymond.* I'd much rather watch that than stay up with a bunch of people getting sloppy."

"Not much point, is there?"

"I'll crash in Jacqueline's room again if you don't mind."

"You're always welcome."

I kissed her cheek.

Fran smiled for what seemed the first time in weeks. "You know, when Jacqueline was a little girl, one of her favorite things was to be alone in the backyard, just thinking. She used to take out a bowl of oyster crackers and grapes and be by herself."

"Why do you think that was?"

"That was just part of her. She had friends and liked playing with them, but she liked to be alone, too. One time she said she thought there was more to the world. And when I asked her what she meant she said, *Just more.*"

"I can hear her saying that."

"When she was nine or ten I sent her to Sunday school at the church on the corner. She came home one day talking about Jesus and her father had a fit. But Jacqueline told me her secret that she had Jesus now and for me not to worry. Can you imagine that? A little girl telling her mother not to worry."

"I can totally see her doing that."

"In high school she always kept searching. That's just the way she was. And then she found you, Ty. You were part of her *more.*" She teared up then, and we just sat in silence as the TV droned on.

Fran went to sleep around ten. I sat on the couch and watched the ball drop in Times Square.

21

NEXT MORNING FRAN and I watched the Rose Parade and some football, and I hung around the house most of the day. I pulled some weeds in Fran's garden and soaked up a little sun. Around four I got the bright idea I might take a drive. Since it was New Year's Day, I thought it would be quieter in a little section of town I knew I had to visit.

Quiet was definitely the wrong word.

South Central Los Angeles was, at one time, a pretty nice place to live. Simple wood frame homes lined cozy streets and trimmed lawns. Now the windows have iron bars. Patios are enclosed with industrial strength grating. Chain-link fences surround patchy grass.

Gang tags mark commercial buildings along Figueroa. Even the Higher Ground Baptist Tabernacle looks more like a boarded up warehouse than a place of worship. The graffiti has something to do with it, along with the windowless brick façade.

A few years ago they started calling it South Los Angeles, dropping the *Central* to try to take away some of the stigma. Nice try. That didn't keep my pulse from spiking as I drove down West Forty-fifth Street.

Like everyone else in L.A, I was aware that gang activities were up, as well as killings. The political and civilian overlords had put a choke hold on the LAPD, and a federal court had extended a consent decree that made life harder for the cop on the beat. With all that cracking down on the cops, the word had gone out on the streets—life was good again if you wanted to score some turf.

So I was sure some gangbanger with a semiautomatic was going to gun me down the moment he saw my Westside face in the open window of my car. It didn't help that the late afternoon sun was darkened behind some mean-looking nimbus clouds. Sitting in my silver Cabriolet I stuck out like a searchlight.

I drove on. Maybe there was a little bit of me that didn't care if I got it. Jacqueline was gone. Why should I make a big effort to keep going?

It was easy to find Mrs. Salazar's house. I'd memorized Bonilla's address from the account in the paper and approached the house directly across the street. It was faded yellow with flaky, white trim and Spanish tile roof. An old-fashioned television antenna was stuck on top. I wondered if it did anything but sit there.

The yard had no fencing around it, and the grass was clipped next to the cement walkway that led to cement steps. There was a spreading bougainvillea near the steps that made the yard almost inviting. But the black iron bars on the windows sang a different tune.

From the sidewalk, a little girl on a pink bike looked at me as I started up the walk. I probably seemed as much a part of the neighborhood as a Mormon missionary.

"Hi," I said.

She smiled. "I got a new bike."

"It's very cool. Is it fast?"

"Uh-huh. I like to go fast."

"Me, too," I said. "High five."

She slapped my hand and I said, "Later," and proceeded up the walkway to the front door. It had a heavy black screen on the outside. I knocked. After a moment a voice from behind the door asked who it was.

"Mrs. Salazar?"

"Who is?" she said.

"I'm a friend of Channing Westerbrook."

Pause. The door opened a crack.

"I talk already to her."

"If I could just have a moment of your time—"

"For why?"

"It's very important that I—"

"No. Go way now."

"But—"

"No."

The door started to close.

"Your neighbor killed my fiancée."

The door stayed open just a crack. "I can no help."

"Please," I said. "Just two minutes." I felt like a vacuum cleaner salesman, and in a way I was. I just had to get in to see her, and then I could close the deal, whatever that turned out to be.

She unlatched the chain and opened the door. As I went in, I saw the little girl on the bike, still looking my way. She waved. I nodded.

The house smelled of fried food and air freshener. It was modest and neat, like Mrs. Salazar herself. She seemed to be in her late sixties. Skin the color and look of almonds, and graying black hair cut short. On the wall above a blanket-covered sofa was a crucifix. I was staring at it when she said—

"Ernesto kill your woman?"

"You know the story?" I said. "How he shot himself?"

Mrs. Salazar sighed. "He shoot Alejandra. I no know why. She is so pretty and nice."

"You have no idea why he'd do that?"

"No." Tears brimmed in her eyes. "The baby."

"What?"

She looked at me. "Baby. Alejandra. She was going to have a baby."

That was a bit of news that had been left out of the newspaper stories.

"Did she tell you this?"

"*Sí.* We talk. So sad. She was woman of God."

"May I sit?"

"No, please. I no want to say more." Fear had replaced the tears in her eyes.

"Believe me, I won't say anything to anyone. All I want is to find a man."

"Man?"

"The one you saw, with the three dots."

"I tell the woman and the police. That is all I know."

"You haven't seen him around here since?"

She shook her head. "Only police."

"You've seen the police?"

"They are driving around. I think they watch the house."

"Bonilla's?"

"*Sí*."

Why would they be doing that? What good would it do to watch a house that had no occupants?

"Can you tell me more about Alejandra?" I asked. "How well did you know her?"

With a shrug, Mrs. Salazar said, "A little. She work at the market."

"How long had they been married?"

"Only a little, I think. They move in maybe a year."

"You said Alejandra was a woman of God?"

"*Sí*. She is talking of God a lot. She seem to be happy. Until . . ."

"Yes?"

"Last time I see her, she is seeming, I no know—" She balled her fists. "*Ansiosa*."

"Tense?"

Mrs. Salazar nodded.

"How long was that before she was killed?"

"A day. Two. Now, please to go. I no want no trouble."

I didn't move. I felt like Mrs. Salazar was the last thread I had. If I let go, I'd never find my way back. *Jacqueline*. I just kept thinking she didn't have to die.

Before I could say another word, an explosion from outside rattled the house.

Mrs. Salazar screamed.

I ran to her window. I could see, about five houses down, a huge flame. A car was on fire. Black smoke billowed into the air. People from all over were running out of their homes to look.

"What is?" Mrs. Salazar said.

"I don't know."

"Go, please."

"Yes, I'm sorry."

My body was vibrating like a hot wire. I drifted toward the street, not sure what I was going to do. It was dreamlike, all these people—black, brown, white, young, old—charging toward the scene.

I floated forward, not wanting to get too close. This was not my neighborhood. I was an outsider.

Then I saw two things that took my breath away.

First was a smaller crowd gathering across the street from the fire and screaming. As I stepped closer I saw why. The little girl who had smiled at me was lying on her back on the street.

And then I saw the other thing. A man, walking rapidly, in the opposite direction from the fire. In the confusion no one seemed to notice him. But I did.

In the shadows.

Ratso.

22

HE RAN AROUND to the back of Bonilla's house.

Heeding a small voice in my head, I rushed back to Mrs. Salazar's and told her to call 911 for the little girl.

Then I charged across the street.

There was a small strip of brown grass along the side of the Bonilla house. No sign of Ratso. I squatted as I passed a couple of windows on the side. If Ratso was inside I didn't want him to see me.

At the corner of the house I put my back against the wall, like an escaping prisoner. I peeked around the back. The backyard consisted of a cramped lawn area against a wooden fence, a slab of cracked concrete, and a slatted overhang.

And no sign of anyone. There was a doorway about ten feet away from me.

I slid along the back wall. The screen door was closed, but behind it I could see the inner door open.

I couldn't hear any interior noise. What I heard instead was the distant sound of sirens.

To the side was a pile of what might have been firewood kindling. Perfect. I selected a chunk the approximate size of a child's arm. And slipped off my shoes.

My pulse drummed.

I slipped around to the other side of the screen door and slowly opened it. The door made only the barest squeaking sound.

I was inside. An old washer and dryer set took up most of the space here. An inner door led to the front of the house.

I listened. A faint scratching sound came back at me. Like sandpaper.

Stepping to the door I tried to form some sort of strategy. Maybe I should just run in, screaming, and jump him. Or give him a good shot across the legs with my club to get him down.

Or I could continue on my quiet pace and try to see what he was doing first.

I chose to sneak. Even though I had the jump, this was not my world. I was a lawyer, not a thug.

But I didn't care about that fine distinction. I was being driven by adrenaline.

The scratching sound got louder. I pressed forward in the tiny hallway. There was another open door up ahead.

Ratso was in that room doing something.

The smell of stirred dust hit me as I got nearer the door.

My piece of wood scraped against the wall. I froze.

The scratching noise stopped.

I raised the club in case he decided to jump out into the hallway.

No jump. Silence from the room.

I had to see what was going on. It was possible he was on the other side of the door holding his own weapon. A tire iron. A gun.

Now what?

All that came to mind were the innumerable cop break-ins I'd seen on TV and at the movies—fast, furious, loud, and ready to inflict damage.

Club at the ready, I took a deep breath and made my move. With a swipe at the air in front of me, I let my weapon lead the way into the room.

Empty.

There was no furniture in the room, but the carpet had been torn up in the middle, leaving a gaping wound. I knew then I hadn't heard scratching. It was tearing.

Then I saw the other door. Leading out of the room. Open.

Next thing I knew I was flying forward and down. A body on my back. My nose hit the floor and white fire erupted in my head.

Hot breath hit me in the ear. And pain like I couldn't believe.

He was biting my shoulder.

I lashed out with an elbow, drawing nothing but air. I felt a hot, sticky pulse of blood.

He grabbed my hair and pounded my face into the floor again. Little white pinwheels spun behind my eyes.

With all my might I jerked. No go. He had me.

My head whipped back again and down into the floor.

Now I could smell blood and taste it. It poured from my nose. I saw red splotches on the carpet. They swam around in circles, then started to fade.

And that's the last thing I remember.

23

A RUSTY SAW was cutting my brain in half. I was groaning. And moving.

Or being moved.

From a faraway place somebody said *Okay?*

Darkness. I was on my back. In a car.

"Hey," I said.

"You okay, man?"

From the front seat. The driver.

"What's hap . . ."

"You got hit pretty bad, dude. Hang on."

I tried to sit up. Couldn't. "Where . . ."

"Tell me what you feel like."

The driver had a slight accent. Who was he? And what was I doing in this car?

More to the point, where was he taking me? Possibilities started to form like crystals on frozen glass, patterned but not making immediate sense. But I was sure it couldn't be good.

"Let me out," I said.

"Hey man, you're hurt. You gotta—"

"Drop me."

"Listen, you don't want to be dropped. Not out here."

I made myself sit up. It was like pushing a laundry bag with a stick. I gripped my head, trying to keep the halves in place. "Where's my car?"

"Easy, man. First, how you feeling?"

I saw him only as a shadow, a dark form behind the wheel. The car itself wasn't anything to brag about. It had the feel of a lot of miles and fast-food wrappers.

"Why am I talking to you?" I said.

"I'm the only one here."

Comedian. I looked out the window and saw the lights of some part of L.A. We were on a surface street. The signs were mostly in Spanish. "Who are you?"

"Your guardian angel, man."

"Really? You suck."

"I got you in the car. Got you out of there."

"I could have used you before that. Who the—"

"You needed help. I helped."

"Okay, you helped. Now take me back."

"Just relax, man, and—"

"Take me back *now*." I didn't like the idea of being a captive, even to a guardian angel. I wanted to get to my car and to my house and my own bed and to my medicine cabinet. I wanted to chew aspirin. Maybe I was permanently messed up. Having your head turned into a soccer ball can do that.

"All right, no gratitude," the pseudo angel said. "What this city's like, you know, do something good for somebody, they spit back in your face. You lose faith in humanity, know what I'm sayin'?"

"Lose faith in angels, too."

He started to pull over. The street was barely lit by old-style streetlights. We were in front of a closed up mini-mart. It had hand-lettered signs, TOSTADAS DE CEVICHE and DESAYUNOS. Next to it was a fenced off lot, with razor wire and three Dumpsters overflowing with trash.

Overlooking it all was a huge, suited Latino guy, movie star looks, glaring down with all seriousness. LOS ABOGADOS! it said.

The Lawyers. You can't get away from us anywhere.

"First we need to talk," the angel said.

"Take me back to my car.

"You ever think somebody might be waiting for you at your car?"

No, because I wasn't thinking much at all. Thinking made my head hurt even worse. "Just take me back and drop me and I'll jump in and drive away. I don't care."

"I do, man."

"Who asked you to?"

We were just sitting there at the curb.

He didn't answer. He opened his door, got out, opened the back driver's-side door and got in next to me.

My adrenal glands started pumping like mad. He looked a little older than me, wore a white T-shirt and jeans, and was ripped. A guy who could do damage with his hands if he wanted to.

"Need to talk," the angel said.

"Don't want to talk."

"What do you think you were doing out there, in that neighborhood, huh?"

"Look, thanks for getting me out of there. You did do a good thing. I'm grateful. I just want to go home now. No more talk."

He shook his head. "Ah, man, that's not gonna help me at all. No way."

How long was this going to last? I closed my eyes and tried to will the pain in my head to downgrade into something less than a horse kick.

When I opened my eyes, I saw that my guardian angel had pulled a righteous-looking knife and was holding it in front of my face.

24

"SEE THAT?" HE said.

"Hard to miss."

"Can do a lot of damage."

"What's your point?"

He laughed. "That's a good one. Point." He twirled the knife a little. I thought about trying to make a move to the door but knew I'd never make it.

"You scared?" he said.

"What do you want me to say?"

"That you're scared, man. That you're gonna wet your pants."

"If that makes you feel better."

"You're not listening. I want you to say it and I want you to believe it. 'Cause it's real. Ain't no game."

I was scared all right. But it was a reflex. There was something else going on. A not caring.

"Whatta you really want?" I said. "Money? You want my money?"

He shook his head. "Be scared."

"Fine. I'll be Homer Simpson if you want. Just get on with it."

He lowered the knife. "Man, that 'tude's gonna get you nailed."

I started to say something, but he jumped in ahead of me. "Just listen. You're lookin' around at stuff you're better off forgetting. Okay? I'm doing you a real favor here. Stay out of it. 'Cause the next guy who shows with a knife at your face ain't gonna be so reluctant to use it."

"Who are you?"

"Tell me you understand."

"I'm all over it, but—"

"Then we got nothin' more to say to each other. Put your seat belt on, man. It's the law."

He drove me back to the neighborhood, back to my car, and didn't say ten words the whole way.

As far as I could see there wasn't anybody out on the street, looking for me or anybody else. All the earlier excitement was over. Just as well for me.

I hoped the little girl was all right.

The last thing the guy said to me, as I got out, was, "Remember what I told you. Don't come back here. Go home and get on with your life."

"Tell me your name at least."

"Have a good night," he said before peeling away.

25

THE NEXT DAY at the office my head felt like an outtake from *The Texas Chain Saw Massacre*. I must have looked like it, too. My assistant, Kim—a paralegal with a Roller Derby body but sweet disposition—looked at me in horror and said, in her indirect twenty-something way, "What happened to you?"

"Please get me four aspirin. Bring them to my office."

She bounded from her desk as I made it to my office, almost blind from the pain. I probably should have checked into emergency. Or maybe donated my head to science and been done with it.

Kim came in with the aspirin and a bottle of water. I popped the four tabs in my mouth and washed them all down in a gulp. "And please bring me my messages."

While she was doing that, I called Southeast Division and asked to speak to Fernández but got put through to voicemail. I left a detailed message about what happened to me and asked him to please call as soon as possible.

Kim came back with a few pink sheets. Even though the firm prefers we use voicemail, I try to have Katie or whoever else is on duty screen calls. It saves time. I went through the messages one by one and decided not to call anyone back.

Except one. The message was from a Father Robert. All it said was he had something relevant to offer on Dr. Kendra Mackee. *Father.* A priest. I thought I recalled Mackee having a client a few years back who said he was molested as a boy by a priest.

I punched the number and put it on speaker. A woman answered. I asked for Father Robert.

"We have been expecting your call," the woman said. "The father asks if you would come this afternoon."

"Come where?"

"St. Monica's Retreat."

"Wait, can I talk to him? Maybe we can set some things up over the phone."

"Oh, Father Robert has no phone."

"Doesn't have a phone? What kind of outfit are you?"

"We are a monastery, Mr. Buchanan."

I rubbed my temples, trying to put a rope on the horses kicking at them from inside my head. "Why don't you find him and have him call me, will you? I really can't be going all over the place."

"Oh," the woman said, "we are very easy to find."

26

ST. MONICA'S WAS tucked up against the Santa Susana Mountains in the northwest corner of the San Fernando Valley. At one time the valley was dominated by the Catholic Church, acting as sort of a trustee for the Spanish, and later Mexican, governments. Mostly they were there to Christianize the Native American population. Which meant assimilation, sometimes the hard way.

Later, the land was carved up into great ranchos, but when the inevitable tide of the Anglos swept in, the dons found themselves on the run.

When the dust settled, though, the Catholic Church had managed to come out with some sweet parcels of land. St. Monica's was one of them.

The parcel was just north of the 118 Freeway, which I'd always thought was uninhabitable. Brush fires burned through there every year, it seemed.

But here was this little oasis with a killer view of the whole valley. The spread up here would be worth tens of millions to developers.

Which is why I hoped the Catholics would stay true to their vision and never sell out. The city was already overstuffed with shoulder-to-shoulder houses thrown up by quick-buck artists who'd build on graveyards if they could. More houses brought more cars for the same amount of road space, and that meant more delays and traffic and road rage.

Welcome, friends, to the mess that never ends.

I drove through the open gate and up a small drive to a squat, tan-colored building. Not much for design, these people. Practical. Like a nun's shoes.

The reception area in the building was as plain as the outside, only with a crucifix above the desk. Behind the desk, in a full habit, was a nun. But not like any nun I'd ever seen before. I'd always thought it was Vatican policy that nuns have dried apple faces and tight lips. Not this one.

She wore a simple silver cross around her neck. I kept my shades on to hide the multicolored glory of my face.

"You must be Mr. Buchanan," she said, rising. "I am Sister Mary Veritas."

"Veritas. Truth?"

"You know Latin?"

"I took some philosophy in college."

"Cool."

Cool? What manner of divine was this? She seemed about twenty years old, though it was hard to tell with the habit. What blazed out clear were her acetylene-blue eyes.

Catholics were a mystery to me anyway. There was a Catholic family down the street when I was growing up, the Sullivans, and they seemed to produce a new kid every year. Sullivans were popping out all over the place, two and three to a room. One of them, Danny, was about my age and knew all the dirty fighting tricks his big brothers had taught him. He taught me how to hold something in my fist, like a roll of quarters, to take the give out of the fingers and make a punch rock-hard. All the Sullivans went to something called mass, and I wondered if they learned more tricks there.

"I will show you to Father Robert," Sister Mary said.

"I never knew this convent was here," I said.

"Oh, we're not a convent, Mr. Buchanan. We're Benedictines. This is a monastery."

"I thought nuns lived in convents."

"The Benedictine order lives in community."

"But you're still nuns, right?"

She laughed, but not condescendingly. "Oh yes. But to our vows of chastity, poverty and obedience, we also add others from St. Benedict, including hospitality."

"So if I order a beer, you can get it for me?"

"Not exactly. But if you come to us seeking a place to stay, we cannot turn you away."

I almost said, *If word gets out about you, you're gonna have a ton of guys showing up trying to get you out of your vows, sister.*

27

SISTER MARY WALKED me across the nicely groomed grounds. Spreading shade trees had the feel of the old ranchos, knotty and lush. The smell in the air, though, was something else.

"What's cooking?" I asked.

"Fruitcake."

"Fruitcake?"

"Fruitcake.

"I never associated fruitcake with Catholicism."

"What do you associate it with?"

"Aunt Betty. Every Christmas, without fail, an inedible fruitcake in a tin came our way, courtesy of Aunt Betty."

She stopped and faced me. "Every order such as ours needs a way to raise funds for ministering to our community. We are actually well known for our fruitcake, Mr. Buchanan. It's really good. If you'd like to try—"

"Thanks very much, but maybe another time."

"Send one to Aunt Betty." She had a cherubic smile.

"Let's go see the padre."

Toward the back of the property the green grass got scrubby and brown, melding into the dirt and rocks of a sun-baked hillside. Parked under a gnarly oak tree was a white trailer, maybe a twenty footer. Another of the same type was parked on the other side of the tree. I was surprised when the nun walked up to the first trailer and rapped on the door.

The trailer shook a little, then the door creaked open. A black man poked his head out, looked at the nun, then at me.

He smiled. His face had the weathered appearance of fifty hard years. His hair was short and the color of New York snow—not pure white, but mixed with the dirt of heavily trafficked sidewalks. He was not what I expected in a priest. I always thought Bing Crosby when I thought priest.

"Mr. Buchanan, I presume," he said.

I nodded.

"I'll leave you now," the nun said, and hurried away.

"I'm Father Robert," the priest said. "You can call me Bob."

Bob? Calling a priest Bob was a little too weird, like calling your gym teacher in middle school Frank. I decided to defer what I would call him until I knew what he had to say.

His modest crib was plain like everything else at this place. The vow of poverty thing showed. We sat at a Formica table and he offered me a lemonade. It was hot that day and lemonade sounded good.

"I want to thank you for coming all the way out here," he said. "I haven't had a visitor in a while."

"I guess the nuns take all the good quarters, huh?"

"This was my choice. It's like a little hermitage. Since I'm precluded from pastoral work, I thought spending more time with God would be a good idea. Fortunately, the diocese also found it convenient."

"Convenient?"

"They had entertained and then accepted an accusation against me, of molestation. I'll tell you about that in a moment. But what to do with me? Well, the abbey here needed a priest to say mass and hear confession, you know, so that's what I was assigned. Besides, I was beginning to be the cause of a little too much discomfort, claiming innocence and all. Funny how a little thing like false accusations can set the powers that be all a twitter."

"You maintain your innocence, then?"

"Do I detect a little skepticism in your voice?"

"I wasn't—"

"It's all right," he said, with a wave of his hand. "The context of the times does not lay a lot of benefit of the doubt on the priestly side. I understand your reaction."

Embarrassed, but fully in agreement with his perception, I took that moment to have a sip of lemonade.

As I did, he smiled and did a-rat-a-tat on the table with his two index fingers. Fast.

"Not bad," I said.

"What?"

"That riff."

"Oh, that. A little habit of mine, actually relaxes me. I used to pretend I was Chick Webb when I was a kid."

"One of the greatest drummers of all time."

His eyes lit up like Christmas lights. "You know about Webb?"

"A little. I played drums once."

"Get outta town!"

"Not a bad idea at this point."

"No, really. Tell me."

I shrugged, not wanting to get into it. The way you don't want to talk about a pet that died. "In a band once."

"Rock?"

"Yeah."

"So who did you like? Keith Moon?"

Amazing. A priest who knew about rock drummers. "Moon was great, sure," I said. "Neil Peart, though, is something else. And John Bonham."

"Who was he?"

"Led Zeppelin. He did a fifteen-minute solo on a song called 'Moby Dick' on the live album they did at Madison Square Garden. The best."

"Son," he said, beaming. "There was Buddy Rich, then everybody else."

"Oh yeah, I saw him play on *The Muppet Show* once. And Carson. You may be right."

"Brings back some good memories."

He reached into an Arturo Fuente box and pulled out a cigar. "Can I offer you one?"

"No thanks."

"Mind if I?"

"Not at all." The idea of a cigar-smoking priest wasn't entirely off my beam, but it was still a bit of a paradigm jab.

I finally took off my shades.

"Ouch," Father Bob said.

"Disgruntled client," I said. "It's always about the bill."

He laughed and lit up. He blew a plume of smoke and said, "A pleasure of the flesh God doesn't frown upon, I'm certain."

"Isn't self-denial part of this whole thing?"

"Sure, and I obey, though I sometimes wonder."

"Wonder what?"

He took another puff and said, "You know the joke, don't you? About the Pope going to heaven and getting shown to the Catholic section?"

"Go ahead."

"He sees all these priests walking around with sour looks on their faces. And he grabs one and says, 'Hey, you're in heaven. It's beautiful here. Why does everybody look so upset?' And the priest grabs the Pope by the shoulders and says, 'The word was *celebrate*!'"

I couldn't help smiling. It felt good.

Father Bob said, "A few years ago, I was named in a lawsuit by a man who claimed I had molested him repeatedly when he was an altar boy. I knew the name. David Townsend. Davey back then, a kid I tried to help. He was a troubled boy. I guess maybe I tried too hard with him."

"Too hard?"

"He was white." The priest stopped for a moment and looked at me. "I guess I was trying to prove myself, to everybody, show 'em a black priest could be the savior of a white kid, and not always the other way around."

I nodded and thought maybe I understood. Back then, it was probably a different scene. Or maybe not so different.

"So when the lawsuit comes down, the diocese is extra gun-shy. The priest scandals were hitting, and last thing they needed was a racial element in all of this. I told them I was innocent, and they were very understanding and deferential, and would I mind talking to Dr. Kendra Mackee."

"Did you know who she was?"

"I'd heard the name. She had a lot of these cases a few years ago. She was helping a lot of adults remember the terrible things priests did to them as kids."

"You think it was all a witch hunt?"

He shook his head. "Sadly, it wasn't. But it was inevitable some of the good ones would get caught up."

"And you're one of the good ones?"

"You think I'm being less than candid with you?"

I shrugged. "I'm not a jury."

"Well, the archdiocese didn't want this thing anywhere near a jury. So they brought in Mackee, right down there in the cardinal's office, and they let her at me, with all her reports and sweet voice. She could be your little sister, with pigtails and cute little face, and a stiletto behind her back."

"Did you contest what she said?"

"I told them I was innocent."

"And they didn't buy it."

"They weren't even shopping."

"Why didn't you fight it?"

"Regardless of everything, I love the church. I thought that fighting it would just inflict more hurt on her. I thought it was the will of God."

"I don't think it's the will of anybody that the wrong guy gets it."

"Tell that to Jesus." He took a sip of lemonade, thinking. "Some time after that I talked to Davey again. I wasn't supposed to, but I had to look him in the eye. I had to ask him. You know what? He looked scared. I tried to get him to come clean. Not for me, but for him. For his soul. He said something then, a name, it sounded like Lorimar."

"Lorimar? Who is that?"

"He didn't tell me and I never followed it up, but I felt like that was his confession. That's all he said to me. He never changed his story."

"So your superiors, or whatever you call them, gave you the boot?"

"They agreed to a big payout to Davey, but that wasn't the stiletto."

"What was it then?"

"She had a condition attached. To keep this from going further, she insisted that I be removed from my parish. She said that looking into my eyes, knowing I was innocent. It was nothing but an act of unadulterated cruelty."

"Are you sure she wasn't just doing what she thought was best? Maybe she really believes you did it, believes what her patient told her." As I, without saying so, also believed.

The priest shook his head, which seemed weighted with care now. "You're talking about someone who manufactured a memory. And she's doing the same thing in your case. Which is why I called you. I called you to warn you. I'm not concerned about what happens to me now. But I can't let her harm others."

I nodded. "Thanks for your time. If I need to talk to you more, maybe take a statement, I'll let you know."

He smiled, but with resignation, as if he thought it a brush-off. "I hope you come back anyway. I don't often get a chance to share lemonade with folks."

Just before I got in my car I heard my name called. Sister Mary was coming my way, carrying something.

"I wanted to give you this," she said. She placed the item in my hands. It was an official St. Monica's fruitcake in a blue and gold tin. There was a rendition of a saintly woman on the front, with light emanations.

"I note she is not eating," I said.

"Pardon?"

"The lady on the tin."

"Saint Monica."

"Not eating. Doesn't she endorse your fruitcake?"

"The whole heavenly host does, Mr. Buchanan. And you'll never know why unless you try it. Have a pleasant drive."

The drive was only okay. The fruitcake was still fruitcake. I broke a little off and munched it as I headed back to the Westside. Yes, it was better than the bricks Aunt Betty used to send. But it was still fruitcake, and I suppose not even a saint of God can overcome that minor snag.

28

AT THE OFFICE I had a couriered package waiting for me. I thought it might be something from Walbert's office, but found instead that it came from Channing Westerbrook.

It was a copy of the police report on the Bonilla murder-suicide. Channing had placed a sticky note on top and written *Deal!* on it. She was nothing if not pushy. She was going to go far.

The report was not much at all. Some handwritten notes describing, in broad terms, the physical aspects of the scene. I couldn't bring myself to read it all in detail. But when it got to some of the follow-up, the report listed a name to contact, someone called Tomás Estrada. There was a phone number after the name, and the notation, *Acquaintance of Subject Bonilla.*

Nice work, Miss Westerbrook.

I called and left another message for Detective Fernández, asking if I could see him again. A few little things had happened since the last time.

Al poked his head in. "Dude."

"Don't you knock anymore?"

He came in, all smiles. "Where you been?"

"What're you so happy about?"

"I'm away from home. *Got the world on a string...*" He did that in his Sinatra voice, which wasn't bad.

"You want to get within twenty feet of me," I said, "wipe that smirk off your face."

"Love you, man. Really, what's going on? You been out."

"I went to see a priest."

"About your face?"

"Hilarious."

"To confess your sins? You could have just told me."

"You'd be a lousy priest."

"You're right," he said. "I'm not celibate. Which would surprise my wife."

I shook my head. "Why don't you get some counseling?"

"Hey, my wife and I were happy for twenty years."

"Oh yeah?"

"Yep. And then we met." He slapped his leg. "Thank you! I'll be here all week!"

"Get out."

He made a bouncing motion with his hand. "How about a little half court? We got some guys at the club—"

"I don't think so."

"Come on! We need six. It'll do you good. You need some good, my friend."

Sometimes in life we do stupid things, like play basketball with a puffy face. *Quién es más macho?*

"All right," I said. "But only if you don't cheat."

"Me?"

"It's been known to happen."

Al grinned.

"Listen," I said, "we need to find a guy named David Townsend, a client of Mackee's who made a claim against this priest."

I gave Al the whole account. Then he said, "You told McDonough about this guy?"

"Not yet. I want to talk to Townsend first and find something good. Maybe then McDonough will think I'm the fair-haired one again."

"You are, dude. But can you still make a jump shot under pressure?"

29

WE PLAYED THREE on three at Al's club. He'd rounded up a couple of other lawyers, one of whom I recognized from a firm we'd once teamed with on some asbestos litigation. Another was apparently a friend of Al's from the club. The fifth guy, the biggest one—six-five at least, and thick across the front—was in Info Management for Sun America. Bruce was his name. Bruise was his game.

There's a wide variety of roundball species. You have your ex-jocks trying to relive their days of glory. You have guys out for fun, and guys out for blood. The worst are the trial lawyers, who are competitive enough in court.

They see a pickup game as another federal case, one to be settled by superior physical prowess.

Then you have those who play with a certain detached humor. That was me. I played because it was a good way to keep in shape, but I never took these games seriously. I would talk a lot of good-natured smack, just to keep things loose.

Some are the opposite of this. They find no fun in the game—at least their faces don't show it—and when they hear a little trash talk they take it personally.

Such a one was Bruce the IM. And he was the one who ended up guarding me in the first three-on-three. And wanted to show me, from the very start, who the Big Dog was.

The first time I touched the ball, at the top of the key, Bruce tugged up his shorts and assumed the squat position of the serious defender; practically chest to chest with me. He was saying *You are not going to score once, girl.*

This annoyed me more than anything else. You don't get this intense in a half court game, unless there's some money on the line.

So, instead of passing, I decided to take it to the hole. I could tell I was quicker than the guy, and if he was going to play me this close I'd make him pay.

I gave him the rocker step, one of my best moves, had him back on his heels, and cut right. A lane opened in the key and I made for the hoop. Bruce recovered enough to dog me from the side, but he was a step behind. He wouldn't catch me. It'd be an easy layup.

Only when I went up a huge paw came down across my wrist and knocked the ball to the floor, where it bounced up and was nabbed by one of Bruce's teammates.

I waited for the call. The code of half court demands that you call a foul when you commit one.

Bruce said nothing. Instead, he hustled out to the free-throw line for the offensive set.

"Whoa!" I said. "Foul."

Everybody stopped moving. When the word "foul" is uttered, play ceases and the offended party—in this case, me—gets the ball back.

But Bruce put on a disgusted look and cried, "No way!"

"You got my arm, man."

"All ball! No way!"

"I'm calling a foul," I said. "Our ball."

"No way, man."

This was not cool. You don't make a big deal about a call on the first play of the game. And it was his fault. A deaf man could have heard the slap.

"I called a foul, now gimme the ball."

"No way."

Did this guy know any other words? He looked at me, daring me to come at him.

Of all the types of baller, Bruce represented the worst—the guy who's never wrong and won't back down. I was ready to knuckle his face, which was not a normal thing for me, not in a game of half court.

Al, who was on my team, stepped between us. "Dudes! This ain't Lakers–Heat! Let's just play." To Bruce he said, "Your ball."

That did not please me, but I let it go. I knew now the game was going to get physical, and any civility I had left fell to the floor like a glob of sweat. I didn't care.

The game moved along without incident for a few baskets. Then Al fired up a fifteen footer and I blocked out Bruce, ready to go for the rebound.

The ball hit the rim and bounced to the side. I went up and Bruce the Jerk went over my back, grabbed the ball, and sent me sprawling to the floor.

No call again.

I jumped up ready to spit in his face. "No way! I'm calling that."

"Oh jeez." Bruce threw his hands in the air.

"Over the back, man. Play ball, why don't you?"

"What I'm doin'. Can't take it?"

I laughed out loud. "You are a piece of work."

"Play the game."

"Our ball," I said. "I'm callin' it." I motioned to one of Bruce's slack-jawed teammates, who held the ball, and motioned for it.

He tossed it to me.

"Un-freaking-believable," Bruce muttered.

If I'd had a shotgun then, I would have taken his knees out. Instead, I was this close to just walking out. I didn't need this.

"Let's go, buddy," Al said lightly. Smilin' Al. He should run for office.

Bruce got that little boy pout face on him, only stretched across his grown man's puss. There's nothing more grotesque than that. And when it's directed at you, it's a challenge as obvious as a slap.

So the second I got the ball I drove to the board.

Bruce was all over me. But I was ready. I put my shoulder down and pushed up and out with all the force my legs could muster.

My left shoulder caught Bruce in the chest. Only he had decided that he was going to do everything he could to stop me. We collided in the air like 747s in the same airspace.

My teeth rattled as Bruce's arm whacked me in the face. I went sprawling to the floor.

My eyes crossed with pain. Blood seeped from my nose. Again.

I heard Al yelling at Bruce, really ripping him, as he ran under the basket. I covered my face with my hand. Al grabbed a towel from under the basket and threw it to me, then faced Bruce again, who was just standing there with his hands on his hips.

"That's it," Al said. "Game over."

Not quite. I got to my feet and, still holding the towel on my face, started for Bruce. As I did, I had one of those moments when you step outside yourself and watch yourself about to do something that shocks you.

Even with one hand, I wanted to smash his face in. This wasn't one of those anger reflexes everyone feels. It wasn't like being cut off on the freeway. What I wanted to do was inflict real and permanent damage.

I've played a lot of ball, and know that the most dangerous weapon on the court is the elbow. Once I got a tooth knocked out by a guy six-eight who didn't like the way I was guarding him. An elbow to the face can really foul you up.

I wanted to elbow Bruce's face and give his nose a concave shape. I wanted to foul him up good.

Luckily, Al and the others got between us. After a lot of shouting, Bruce left the gym.

"I guess we win by forfeit," Al joked.

"I'd rather win by ripping his pancreas out," I said.

"Think it's broken?"

"I don't know. It hurts is all I know."

"You were really ready to go after him."

"So?"

"That's not like you."

"It's not?"

"Usually it's your rapier-like wit you use."

"I guess I'm not finding much funny these days."

30

AFTER A SHOWER, having cleaned off blood and rage, I got dressed and met Al in the parking lot. We got to his Escalade and he leaned against it. "You hanging in there?"

"Hanging."

"Think about her?"

"Oh yeah."

"I was there when you met her, remember?"

"Of course."

"I wish I'd known her better."

"Me, too." Memories started flashing on the screen, full color. "You know, I have this theory that you can get to know a lot about a person by their favorite *Twilight Zone* episode."

"Yeah?"

"What's yours?"

"I really don't know."

"Yes you do," I said. "Everybody has a favorite *Zone.* Come on."

"Well, what's that one where the guy is walking in Europe and he comes to a monastery? There's all these guys with beards?"

"Yeah. That's 'The Howling Man.'" These hermits have Satan in a cell, and he can't get out because a special staff is barring the door. But the guy who comes in listens to him and gets convinced he's just a poor prisoner."

"Right. And lets him out. And then he turns into the devil right before his eyes."

"That's it. The poor guy tells the head hermit, Sorry, I didn't recognize him. And the hermit says, That's man's weakness and Satan's strength."

Laughing, Al said, "You really do know your *Zones*. So what was Jacqueline's?"

"The one she loved was about this good-hearted street peddler who sells ties and jewelry and knickknacks out of his valise. Everybody in the neighborhood loves him, especially this one little girl. Well, Mr. Death has these appointments he's got to keep, and one of them is for this pitchman. He convinces Mr. Death to let him make one more try at a sale. See, he's always felt he had one great pitch in him, one for the angels he calls it. That's the title, I think. 'One for the Angels.'"

"What happens?"

"Mr. Death says, 'OK, I won't take you until after your next pitch.' So the peddler pulls a fast one. He tells Death, 'I'm not going to do any more pitches. We made a deal. I get to live.' Death, seeing that he got hoodwinked, he tells the peddler he's going to take another life in his place, and arranges, through the power he has, to have the little girl hit by a car."

I could see Jacqueline's face as she told me how much she loved this episode. I could see the tears in her eyes.

"They take her up to a room," I went on, "and Mr. Death is going to go get her at midnight. The pitchman and Death are sitting outside the building, waiting, and the pitchman, very slowly, starts showing Mr. Death his wares. He lays a line on him, and the next thing you know, Mr. Death is buying a tie. And then some other things. In fact, the pitch is so good Death can't stop buying. And he keeps buying and buying until the stroke of midnight. When he hears the bell toll, Death knows he's missed his appointment. The little girl is going to live. Of course, the peddler has now made his pitch for the angels. And, as per the agreement, must go away with Mr. Death. He asks Death if he's going 'Up there.' Death says, 'Yes, you made it.' And off they walk."

Al nodded. "That tells me a lot about Jacqueline."

"Yeah it does," I said.

31

I DECIDED TO drive out to Reseda to check on Fran. It was getting toward dinnertime, and I had the feeling she might need to see me. I took Sepulveda through the pass, trying to avoid the freeway traffic.

Somewhere past the Getty Center, a car started hugging my rear. It had a tinted windshield, and the way the light was in the canyon I couldn't see a face.

A guy too anxious to get home. In a blue Lexus. He could afford to wait.

But he didn't want to and kept close.

After the game, after the nose thing, I wasn't into this. Road rage is a cliché, especially in L.A. The *Honk While I Reload* bumper sticker was born here.

Only I was feeling like I wanted a gun in my hand for real. This was starting to freak me a little.

I thought about slamming on my brakes, letting the guy rear-end me the way those scam artists do to get the insurance.

Paranoia is mental illness, unless everybody is after you. Sometimes you feel that way in the city, especially when your head's working overtime trying to get a handle on lies and murder.

The car was still behind me as I passed the Galleria. And then I got a call from Detective Fernández. He said he could see me in the morning.

"I'll be there," I said.

When I looked in my rearview mirror, the Lexus was gone.

32

"THANKS FOR COMING in." Fernández seemed the slightest bit more friendly to me. "Can I get you some coffee?"

"No, thanks."

"Not missing anything." His attempt at humor seemed more like a dodge, as if he didn't have good news coming my way.

"I got whacked on the head again," I said. "As you can see."

"How'd that happen?" He lowered himself into a chair and positioned himself to listen. We were back in the same interview room. It looked even more sterile, like they did the occasional autopsy here.

"The guy who did it the first time, I saw him again. And he did it to me one more time. Do you find that an amazing coincidence?"

"Same guy? The homeless guy?"

"That's right. I was talking to one of Bonilla's neighbors. Mrs. Salazar." Fernández shook his head.

"You don't know who that is?" I asked. "On a murder case?"

"Mr. Buchanan, we're not treating this as a murder."

"Can I ask why not?"

"Lack of evidence. That's all it is."

"Well, can't you look around and find some?"

He shifted in his chair. "We did get three witness statements from the scene, but none of them saw anything we can determine is criminal. It was raining, you'll recall. Incredibly, there wasn't any contact with other vehicles. Ms. Dwyer's vehicle came to rest straddling the two and three lanes. There was apparently a lot of confusion. One guy did have the presence of mind to call 911. None of the wits got out of their cars. They were on the freeway, after all and—"

"Who are these people? Can I talk to them?"

"Of course I can't give you the names—"

"Help me out here."

"Mr. Buchanan—"

"Please. There's more to this. You've got to press it."

"We have eight detectives, three trainees, and seven hundred unsolveds. We just don't have the manpower to—"

"What about me? I just gave you some new evidence here."

"Mr. Buchanan, what you're telling me has no relation to the death of Ms. Dwyer."

"I *am* the relation. I'm sitting here telling you what happened."

"I understand that. But—"

"Listen, I went to see a woman named Salazar. She lives across from the Bonillas. She was going to tell me about them. Now why should the guy who tracked me down at Jacqueline's funeral be there, too?"

"I still don't see a connection."

"What more has to happen to me before you do?"

"Last thing I want is to see you hurt. Don't go messing around as if you're trying to solve a murder. This isn't TV. There are very bad people out there that if you happen to ask the wrong question at the wrong time, well, we can't be there to help you."

"You haven't been much help so far."

Fernández's face hardened. I took my foot out of my mouth and said, "Look, I'm tired of getting hit. I'm tired of not knowing what's going on. There is something out there, and I want you to know about it. I don't know what else to do."

After a long moment, Fernández said, "If anything changes from my end, I will certainly let you know. But my advice is this, that you let go of the thought that this was anything more than a bizarre accident. I mean, a man commits suicide and falls off an overpass and hits your fiancée's car. That could not have been planned. And the word of some mysterious homeless guy just isn't going to change that."

The whole thing did sound outlandish, like a bad Oliver Stone movie. I couldn't blame the LAPD for not spending time and resources looking into it.

So I stood and thanked Detective Fernández and walked out of Southeast Division thinking there would be no resolution and maybe I'd better just forget it. Bury the dead and get on with living. Get rid of the headaches for good.

But when I got out on One Hundred and Eighth Street I kicked a wire trash can so hard I almost broke a toe. And I knew then there was no way on God's asphalted earth I could forget it.

33

WHEN I GOT back to the office, I was surprised by the news that Jonathan Blake Blumberg was in the conference room wanting to see me.

McDonough was in there with him. He didn't look happy. He was used to his associates being in the office sharp and early, unless they were in court.

"I wanted to talk to you," Blumberg said.

That much I gathered.

"Alone," he said. McDonough, without a word, left the room. I felt like I'd been called into the principal's office.

"Something wrong?" I said.

"What makes you think something's wrong?" His eyes were like blue laser beams. I could understand how he melted his opposition. But he was supposed to be on my side.

"I can only assume because you're here," I said. "Is there something I should know?"

"Is there something *I* should know?"

"I can't think of anything."

"Think again."

Feeling under the gun after my fruitless visit downtown wasn't doing much to chill my brain. I told myself to take it easy.

"Mr. Blumberg, I am open to anything you have to say, but—"

"You think I'm a liar."

"What?"

"Buchanan, there is something I do that I do better than anyone I know, and that's get inside heads, and when you were in my office that's what you were thinking."

"Would it make any difference if I told you I wasn't thinking that?"

"You're denying it?"

"I was trying to get your statement," I said. "Like a real lawyer."

"And do what with it?"

"I don't really follow you, Mr. Blumberg."

"When I checked with McDonough, he wasn't overly enthusiastic about your recent work."

"That's news to me."

"I don't care if it's news or not. I want to know if you can do the job."

"Excuse me, sir, but what exactly are you talking about?"

"I'm talking about my daughter's lawsuit against your client."

"Yes, I can do the job."

"I hear you saying that. But I don't see the hunger. You have to get mad. You have to hunt meat. That's what separates the calves from the bulls."

What era was this guy born in? He was like some Victorian patriarch set loose in Africa with an elephant gun and pith helmet. "Mr. Blumberg, I am a lawyer representing a client, and my interest is in doing everything I can to win the case. And I will—"

"Everything?"

"Well, within the ethical guidelines."

"Guidelines are drafted by the folks who finish second."

"What is it exactly you want me to do?"

"I want you to get mad. I want you to get mad at the right people, like Kendra Mackee and my ex-wife. Have you been to see her yet?"

"No, and I—"

"Go see her. That'll tell you a lot."

"I can't just go see her. I have to wait to depose—"

"Find a way, Buchanan. Have you done anything else?"

"It so happens—"

"Tell me."

"Give me a chance, will you please?"

He folded his arms. He had his sleeves rolled up, and the dark hairs on his forearms looked like they could scrape a ship's hull.

"It just so happens," I said, "that I interviewed a priest who had a run-in with Dr. Mackee. He was accused of molestation by a guy who got his memory unjogged, so he said, by Mackee. Only it never got to the trial stage 'cause the archdiocese settled the matter. But this priest insists it was all fabricated, and I think I believe him."

"Is any of that admissible? I mean, can you legally use it?"

"Not his statement alone, I'm afraid."

"But this accuser, maybe you could find him?"

"I can try."

"Don't say *try* Buchanan." He slapped the conference table. "Come on!"

I stood up. "With all due respect, sir, you can call me Mr. Buchanan. No, I take that back—you cannot call me at all. You are not a party to this lawsuit and you're getting in my way. If I need anything from you I will get in touch." Signing your own professional death warrant is perversely cathartic. My little speech had spewed out of my mouth like lava. Something kicked in, and I couldn't control it. Now all Blumberg had to do was walk down to

McDonough's office and tell him what I said and my future at Gunther, McDonough & Longyear would go up in a cloud of dust.

Instead Blumberg just sat there staring at me, letting me stew in my juice for a moment. Then he smiled and stood up. "That's what I'm talking about," he said. "Mad! Good. Now go get some meat."

34

MEAT.

I kept thinking about it. Whatever else B-2 was, he had this kind of primal scream personality that made me think of pounding drums.

Maybe Blumberg was right about me, I had to get a little down, a little dirtier. In a lot of ways.

There was a time when I was snowboarding in Mammoth with Al, and my good buddy challenged me to air one out like never before. He was laughing at me, too, he being the expert, me the novice. But the time had come. And as I headed for the booter to make the jump I got nervous, but in a split second chucked it away and told myself I had to do it.

I did, and wiped out big-time. It's a wonder I didn't break my neck. But between the time I jumped and the time I biffed, I was living in the zone and went back and did it again.

You have to get back up and try again, and now was the time. If I biffed now, maybe I'd end up with more than a broken neck, but I didn't care. I just wasn't into caring at the moment, thank you very much.

And so, at four-forty-five in the afternoon, I entered the Beverly Hills office of Dr. Kendra Mackee. From a legal standpoint this was a fool's errand. She was the chief witness for Claudia Blumberg in the litigation. Didn't matter to me. I wanted to look her in the eye just once before I deposed her. Once without a lawyer in the room. Except me.

Her receptionist was an expressionless twenty-something with a silver stud in her eyebrow. In all other respects she was a classic Beverly Hills presence. Perfect skin and makeup, clothes that probably came from one of the high-priced boutiques on Rodeo Drive.

"May I help you?" she said tonelessly.

"The name's Buchanan. I'd like to speak with Dr. Mackee for a moment if I may."

"You don't, like, have an appointment, do you?"

"No," I said. "I, like, don't. I'm here on semiofficial business. It involves the Claudia Blumberg matter."

That got her eyebrow to rise. It looked like an effort.

"Can you wait a moment?" she said.

"I got nothing but time," I said.

She left the reception area. I sat in a chair that would have been an unaffordable luxury in most homes. The overhead on this location had to be killer.

The maple door next to the reception window opened. Dr. Kendra Mackee, even though she was no taller than five-four, seemed to fill it.

"I don't appreciate your coming here." Mackee seemed almost the opposite of Lea Edwards—short, with dark hair, and deep brown eyes. She wore a black suit with a multicolored scarf around her neck. For a moment, it seemed to be the only color in the place. She was a coil of energy, too.

If Lea Edwards was a waltz, Kendra Mackee was a tango.

"My name is—"

"I know what your name is. Buchanan. You represent Lea."

"First-name basis?"

"I wouldn't dignify her name with *Doctor*."

"Is there a place we can talk?" I said.

"I have nothing to say to you."

"I thought maybe you could enlighten me on some things."

"Oh please."

"Like repressed memory, for instance."

Her eyes sparked. "You think I'm going to give you anything?"

"Relax, doctor. I'm just trying to find out the facts."

"The facts are that Lea Edwards is a liar and a slanderer, and when Claudia gets through with her I'll sue her myself. Now please leave."

Not moving, I said, "You wrote a book about repressed memory, didn't you? I can't recall."

"That's not funny."

"Didn't mean it to be. I read *The Memory Book* by those guys, you know . . ."

Kendra Mackee looked at the receptionist. "Call Vince," she said. "Tell him we have an unwelcome presence."

Vince, I took it, was security. To the receptionist I said, "No need to call Vince. I'm, like, gone."

"Get me Barton Walbert on the phone," Dr. Mackee said, then leveled a glare at me that was not one you'd want to mess around with. It also told me what I wanted to know.

Kendra Mackee was a little well-dressed bomb, and given the right prodding she'd blow. That would make for a very nice cross-examination.

35

THE WORKDAY WAS over after my little visit to Mackee's. And the hunting of meat, as B-2 had put it, had given me the taste for more.

I drove east, then south.

Mrs. Salazar was shocked to see me standing at her door. I didn't wonder, considering what happened at our last meeting.

"Go away, please," she said.

"Mrs. Salazar, please, only a minute."

"Why?"

"I need your help."

"No, no."

"But why?"

"I am afraid."

"I am afraid, too, Mrs. Salazar. I'm really afraid I'll never find out what happened. And I'm running out of places to turn."

Her forehead creased. "Come in."

I went inside the small, warm house. Noticed again the crucifix on the wall above the sofa. In front of the sofa was a small, round table with a sewing kit on it. Some fabric was next to the kit.

Mrs. Salazar might have been your friendly neighborhood seamstress.

"You must go," she said. "I no want no one to see."

"Who?"

"The men."

"What men?"

"With Ernesto."

I took the folded copy of the police report from my back pocket. "Is one of those men someone named Tomás Estrada?"

"*Cómo?*"

"Estrada. Tomás Estrada."

"No know."

"What men are you talking about, with Ernesto?"

"*Malo.* Bad."

"In what way?"

"The gangs."

"Ernesto was a gang member?"

"I think."

"Do you know the name of this gang?"

She shook her head. "Please to go."

I made no move toward the door, and a flicker of fear moved across Mrs. Salazar's face. The last thing I wanted to do was scare her any more than she already was. As I was thinking of my next words, I glimpsed the crucifix on the wall.

"Last time you said that Alejandra Bonilla was a woman of God."

"*Sí.*"

"As are you."

She said nothing.

"As was my fiancée."

Mrs. Salazar's features softened. "I pray for her."

"You can do more, for both of them."

"How?"

"Help me find this man, Tomás Estrada."

"I do not know this man."

"Be my interpreter then."

"Eh?"

"I don't speak Spanish. I'm going to call this number and say there is a legal document to be hand delivered to Tomás Estrada. It's from the Los

Angeles Police Department. I want to get an address. But I'll need you to interpret. Will you do that for me?"

Mrs. Salazar was silent for a minute. Outside, a car drove by blasting music that rattled the windows. She closed her eyes and waited for the din to stop.

"The gangs," she said. "I am too afraid."

She looked it, too. "Mrs. Salazar, no one will know about this. I won't come back again, I promise."

"Please to go now."

"Last time I was here, there was an explosion."

"*Sí.*"

"There was a little girl outside your house, she had a new bike, I talked to her. I saw her lying on the street after the explosion."

She nodded. "Mashara. Live two houses that way." She pointed.

"Is she okay?"

"I do not think so."

"I just want you to know, Mrs. Salazar, I know who did it, and I want to find him and keep him from doing it again. That's a promise to you."

I turned to go.

"Wait," she said. "This thing you can do?"

"I can try."

She looked into my eyes as if trying to read a distant sign. "Okay. I will do this thing. To help you speak."

"Help me make the call?"

She nodded.

"Thank you." I opened my phone and dialed the number for Estrada. After two rings a man's voice answered in Spanish.

"Tomás Estrada?"

"No."

"This is the Los Angeles Police Department."

"Eh?"

"*Momento,*" I said. I handed the phone to Mrs. Salazar. "Tell him it's the police."

She translated for me. Then lowered the phone. "He want to know your name."

"Lieutenant Walbert," I said. "Tell him we have a city check for him."

She conveyed the message. "He ask what for."

"For his time in giving a statement."

Mrs. Salazar spoke in Spanish, then back to me. "How much?"

I rolled my eyes. "Three hundred. To be delivered today. By hand."

She told him and listened. They went back and forth a bit. Then: "He say to go to El Tapado. It is in La Puente. Tomás go there at night, but not come home."

"Tell him Lieutenant Walbert thanks him."

She did. I took the phone and closed it. "Thank you, Mrs. Salazar."

"You must be very careful," she said.

"Don't I know it."

36

TWO HOUSES DOWN, I knocked on the door. A woman of about forty, looking tired and suspicious, opened the inner door.

"Excuse me," I said.

"What is it?" She spoke through the heavy screen of the outside door.

"Are you Mashara's mother?"

"Who are you?"

"No one. I was here when the explosion happened. I had spoken to your daughter just before."

"Granddaughter."

"I was wondering how she's doing."

The woman studied me for a long moment. "Why do you want to know?"

"I just was in the neighborhood and I—"

"How'd you get this address?"

"Ma'am, I was just asking. I hope she's all right."

The woman said, "You with the police?"

"No, ma'am."

"Who then?"

"Just a guy who was here. Sorry I disturbed—"

The woman said, "She's hurt bad, but she's going to be all right."

"That's good," I said. "I hope she recovers real soon."

"Why do people do things like that?" the woman asked. "Why?"

Good question. One I couldn't answer. One that kept after me all the way into the night, when I drove down to El Tapado.

37

THE PLACE WAS dark and wooden, with some backlit signs for Dos Equis and Corona and a mirror behind the bar. A small TV was perched on a cantilevered mount in the corner at the far end, with the volume cranked up. A soccer game was on, and a bunch of men watched it with macho intensity.

I bellied up to the bar at the opposite end, aware of the looks I was getting, and stayed there until the glum bartender headed my way. He was short and dark, with a thick black moustache. He didn't say anything, just flicked his head a little to indicate he was listening.

"I'm here to see Tomás Estrada," I said.

After a moment's hesitation, the bartender said, "See your badge."

"We don't need no stinking badges."

He glared, confused.

"I'm not a cop," I said.

"What you doin' here?"

Not the usual greeting one gets from the service industry. "Tomás Estrada."

"Look around you, man." His accent was heavy, but his pronunciation suggested he could converse in English. "Hear what I'm saying? You come around here, not a cop, you get into a little hot water, eh?"

"No trouble," I said. "I'm not here to mess with anybody. It's a personal thing."

He looked me up and down.

"You want to check me for anything?" I offered.

He shook his head. "You do anything in here, man, you don't get out."

"I'm good with that. Is he here?"

The bartender looked over my shoulder. I turned around and saw a guy sitting in a wooden booth under an Aguas Frescas Cañita sign.

I walked to the table. The man was looking into a glass of beer. A Carta Blanca bottle sat off to the side. He didn't look up when I got there. It was obvious to me he knew I was in the bar and he wasn't going to acknowledge it.

"Tomás?"

He took a sip of beer, staring straight ahead.

"You knew Ernesto Bonilla?"

Now he looked at me through narrow eyes that had a slight downward tilt. They gave him a sad look. His brown skin was marred by a gash on his right cheek that looked three or four days old. "Who are you?"

"Name's Buchanan."

"Don't know you."

"Can I sit down?"

"Don't want to know you."

"Buy you a beer?"

He shook his head. A cheer went up from the bar. Somebody had scored a goal for the home team. Tomás looked past me toward the TV screen. I slid into the booth.

"You follow *fútbol*?" I said.

"Hey man—"

"Ever see Serriano?"

"You know Serriano?"

"Doesn't everybody?" I knew Serriano only because our firm once represented his agent in a contract dispute with Nike. Serriano was apparently hot stuff down Mexico way. He had rock star charisma, and they wanted to bring him up to the States. But a couple of years after the Nike deal fell through he got drunk with a bunch of his friends and decided to go bullfighting on a farm outside Mexico. He got a little unplanned groin surgery. Career over.

Tomás softened a bit. "I ask who are you."

"I'm a lawyer. I need to find something out about Ernesto's death."

"Don't know nothin' about that."

"When was the last time you saw him?"

"Man, I don't got to answer."

"No, you don't. And I don't have to buy you another beer, but I'm going to."

"You think then I talk? Happy little wetback likes his *cerveza*?"

"You can do whatever you want. But I said I would, so I'm going to and you can drink it or not, we clear?"

He shrugged. I went to the bar and ordered another Carta Blanca and didn't get any hard looks from the patrons, who were concentrating on the game and apparently had accepted my presence.

Back at the table, Tomás accepted the beer and poured some in his glass, then asked, "How come you interested?"

"Because when Ernesto's body hit a car a woman died. That woman was my fiancée."

He shook his head. "No lie?"

"No lie, Tomás."

He scratched the back of his neck like a man considering which shirt to put on. "Man, look, what is happen to Ernesto is no good. What is happen to you, I am sorry for. Yeah, I am. But look, I no can say nothing."

"Why can't you?"

His eyes flicked to the left, then back at me. "Don't want to."

"You afraid of something?"

"Look, man—" He stopped. Three men were at the table, laughing and pointing at Tomás, and saying a bunch of things in Spanish. My Spanish skills dropped off greatly after twelfth grade with Señora Padilla. But it was apparently something really funny—or else the result of too many beers—that had the trio in stitches.

Nervously, Tomás laughed and returned some banter. One of the men, with an ample stomach doing damage to a tight flannel shirt, looked at me and stopped laughing. He said something to Tomás, and I recognized enough of the words to know it had to do with me.

Tomás appeared even more nervous as he answered. Whatever he said rolled off the backs of the other two, but El Estómago kept glaring at me. I looked at Tomás and waited.

A few more words and the three left, bobbing and weaving between tables back to the bar.

"You better get out now," Tomás said.

"Why?"

"Just do it. Do it now."

"You haven't told me—"

He leaned over. "Let it go, man. I'm saying to you, let it go. You keep on about Ernesto, man, the guys at Triunfo gonna hear about it."

"At what?"

"Triunfo, man. Where you at?"

"How do you spell—"

Slapping the table, Tomás said, "You don't go now you gonna get hurt."

"But—"

"Shut up!" He slid out of the booth, grabbed the beer I'd bought him, and walked to the crowd at the bar, joining his three friends. The big one was still looking at me.

I got out.

38

THE NIGHT AIR was clammy. Lights from the bar cast a dull, multi-colored patch on the sidewalk, like a kid's melted snow cone. Even the mess of light seemed dirty. I'd parked my car at the end of the lot, where the light barely reached. That's why I walked quickly. But not quickly enough.

The fat one stepped out from the shadows. He must have gone out a back way. His face was barely visible, but I saw enough of it to see he was smiling.

I stopped. He looked at my Cabriolet. "She's a nice car, man."

He'd obviously had his fill of beer and now had nothing good on his mind. I wasn't going to be getting in my car anytime soon.

"Can I have it?" he said.

"You want my car?"

"Yeah."

"Go to law school."

I thought about turning and running. The guy, big and sodden as he was, would not be able to keep up. Then I could call a cop and get safely out of there. Meanwhile, El Estómago could mess up my car all he wanted. No big deal. I had insurance.

But I didn't run. I was through running from people like this. I had no idea what I was going to do at that moment, except not run.

"Car like that," he said, "cost money. Big money, eh?"

"Why don't you go have another beer?"

"Got no money."

"Ask one of your friends."

"You," he said.

"You're on your own." I started to walk around the back of the car so I could come up the other side. But he stepped in front of me and that's when I saw the knife. I don't know if he drew it just then or if he'd had it in his hand all along. The weapon seemed to have a personality all its own, big and blustery like its owner.

Running was the right thing to do. Instead, I put my hands in the air and said, "Sure. Fine. You can have my wallet. I don't want any trouble." I reached in my pocket and pulled the wallet out and tossed it at his feet.

The moment he looked down, I kicked him between his legs as hard as I could. It was a stupid thing to do. One wave of his hand and he could have gutted me.

But everything aligned just right and he doubled over. As hard as I could, I kicked him in the face. He went down on his side.

That's when I lost it. I entered an acid fog that burned my senses and took away all human will. What I did next was pure animal.

I jumped up and stomped his head with my right foot. He groaned but was clearly out. That's where I should have left it. But I did the same thing again. The rage that had been building up, all of the reactions against being knocked over the head by lower forms of life like this fat slob bubbled up in my chest.

Only a vague thought that I might kill this guy with the next blow stopped me. I picked up my wallet and when I got in the car I was shaking so bad I could hardly grip the wheel. I kept looking around. Had anybody seen me? Was someone taking down my license number even now? Calling the police, prepped with a full description?

I pulled out to the road, still trembling. Slow, hard realizations started falling on me.

I'd told Tomás exactly who I was. There would be no way I'd get out of this without being ID'd. It wouldn't take much for the cops to find me, and my tale of self-defense would be my word against everybody else.

If Tomás went to the police. He and his friends might decide to take things into their own hands.

The lights got brighter near the 134. I hopped on the freeway, almost running myself into a semi in the process.

It was near midnight when I got home. By then the shakes were coming and going, like I'd just been pulled from the Atlantic and handed a blanket. Sort of like going in and out of consciousness. When I shook, that was all I could think of. When I calmed down I thought of myself. And what I'd just become.

When I was a kid I saw *Death Wish II* with Charles Bronson. I remember thinking, as he took down punk after punk, that he seemed to like his "work" a little too much. There was some sort of pleasure in the destruction of loathsome human beings that brought a half smile to his face.

What I'd just done was a Bronson thing, but this wasn't the movies. There would be no half smiles, no credits at the end after rough justice had been meted out. You had the feeling Bronson was always comfortable in that craggy skin. My own skin was vibrating with adrenaline and fear.

I turned out all the lights and lay down on the sofa and tried to get my breathing steady. Couldn't.

I needed a drink. That would calm me down. I hadn't thought about drinking since Jacqueline's death. She didn't want me to, and it was no big deal not to. But I had some Jim Beam in a cupboard, and right now I wanted the smoky heat in my throat and stomach and head. What I wanted was to drink, put on Gretchen Wilson, and pour another round, and another, until I passed out.

The JB was half full. I took down a shot glass and poured one. Lifting it to my mouth, I thought of Jacqueline. She invaded my thoughts, like if I took the drink I'd be shaming her memory.

But she was dead. Dead and over, and she wasn't coming back, so what was I doing trying to find out anything about how she died? Would that make it any better? Would it make one bit of difference in the whole big world of things? Would I reach some sort of beatific vision or get closure or anything else worth getting?

At that moment I thought I might hate Jacqueline now, or the memory of her, for bringing me nothing but grief. Maybe that's what Poe felt like when he wrote "The Raven," which we all read in middle school thinking the guy should get over that stupid chick Lenore already.

Jacqueline wasn't coming back and I could get drunk again. I wanted to fall into that amber glow and pass out like I used to in my good old college days.

The shot glass hit my lips.

I didn't drink. I still don't know why. Poured it down the drain, took the bottle and did the same. And noticed, as I did so, that I was crying.

39

ON MONDAY I felt like the entire cast of a George Romero zombie movie. The weekend was lost to me. I hadn't showered or shaved, nor had I left the house. I didn't answer the phone or return messages. I felt like I slept through Saturday and Sunday, and probably did sleep through a lot of it.

But I had to go into the office, had to pull myself back to the old life. Had to find Tyler Buchanan again, the respected lawyer, not some half-animal prowling bars and kicking people in the face.

I wasn't succeeding, not even when I got behind my desk and fired up the computer for the day's work.

I couldn't concentrate. My head started pounding at nine-twenty. At nine-thirty I called Al and asked him to come see me. He was in five minutes later.

"What's up?" he asked, tossing himself into one of the client chairs.

"You talk to McDonough today?"

"Only about your future, which is sinking like a stone."

"I'm not kidding around."

"Neither am I. There's a spot in the Xerox room that has your name written all over it."

"I'm really not kidding, Al. Cut it."

"Hey, you all right?"

"No, I'm not all right. My head feels like it's being pulled apart by tractors. I can't sleep, and I know my work on Edwards is floating in the toilet. I just want to know from you if you have any word about what the big man is saying or thinking, so I don't go down the toilet with it."

Al fiddled with his tie. A regular Oliver Hardy. "All seriousness aside, buddy, he did make a little mention."

"Wonderful. What did he say?"

"Hey, no big deal. He just asked me if I thought you were all right. He understands about Jacqueline. I think he just wants to know that you're going to bounce back and be right where you were before this all happened."

"I'm not going to be where I was. I don't know if I even want to be."

"You're just talking out of frustration, you can—"

"I got plenty to be frustrated about. While this Edwards thing is going on, there's some weird stuff about Jacqueline's death. Stuff I can't leave alone."

"What kind of stuff?"

"I can't even begin to tell you. All you have to know is I can't leave it alone, and it may impact some of the stuff I'm doing here at the office. It would be a great favor to me if you would consider covering for me every now and then."

"Sure, but what exactly are you saying? You're starting to worry me a little bit."

"I'm worrying myself."

"Can I help?"

"Just in the way I've described. Will you?"

"Of course I will."

"Thanks." I rubbed my temples, my middle fingers making small circles on the skin. "You ever hear of a gang called Triune Foe, or something like that?"

"What kind of a name is that?"

"It sounds almost like it has a religious connotation, doesn't it?"

"Maybe it's a Catholic gang, a bunch of priests carrying concealed beads."

I ignored his goofy grin, which was starting to bother me. "I went to see a guy, a Latino, about Jacqueline, and—"

"What does a Latino guy have to do with Jacqueline?"

"Will you shut up and listen? Just concentrate on what I'm telling you. When I talked about the guy who fell on Jacqueline's car, this guy's friend, he got all mysterious and mentioned this Triune Foe. He said it would be bad if they ever found out I was looking into it."

"What are you doing sticking your schnozz in police business?"

"So I guess your answer is No, you don't know anything. Fine. Thank you. Get out of my office."

"Dude, despite my usual obnoxiousness, I'm concerned about you."

"If you are, then just watch my back with McDonough. Got to get a lot done today."

"Consider your back watched," Al said, standing. "And such a lovely backside it is."

"Get out."

After Al left I brought up my activity page on the computer, looked under Edwards, and saw the tasks piled up like bricks at a construction site. I needed to get on this.

For the next hour I forced myself to work on a summary memo of the Claudia Blumberg depo. For a little while that did the trick. I managed to get my mind off Tomás and Ernesto Bonilla, but my headache got about ten times worse. Halfway through I had my assistant, Kim, bring me aspirin and a bottle of water, and I downed four of the pills.

It helped a little, and probably tore my stomach lining since I hadn't eaten. But I pushed on.

A few minutes after I'd put the last touch on the memo, Kim buzzed me and said Lori, Al's assistant, wanted to see me. Lori Ruiz was a sharp, competent presence in our office. She was taking paralegal classes at night at UCLA Extension. She did a lot of grunt work for Al, and sometimes me, and did a nice job of it every time.

"You wanted to see me about something?" I said. "I hope Al has committed major fraud. He owes me a dinner, and only jail time is going to wake him up."

She smiled and said, "Nothing like that. He said you were asking about Triunfo."

I straightened up in my chair. "Yeah."

"Said you thought it might be a gang."

"Is it?"

She shook her head. "It's a self-help group. Started by a man named Rudy Barocas. Ever hear of him?"

The name sounded vaguely familiar.

"You see him in the papers sometimes," Lori said. "He's pretty hot looking. The kind of guy who always has his hair perfect, slicked back like Antonio Banderas, and all the right clothes. Real successful guy."

"So what's this group of his do?"

"Triunfo means triumph. It started as a way to help gangbangers get out of the life. He has a ranch or honor farm out in Lancaster, I think it is, where the courts sometimes send these kids. He uses discipline and hard work to turn them into productive citizens and all that."

"Does it work?"

Lori shrugged. "I guess sometimes it does. They also have a place in Hollywood where they do counseling with people."

"Anybody?"

"I guess so."

"You know where it is?"

"I could find out if you want."

"Would you?"

"Sure."

I said, "Do you know any reason why people might be scared of this group?"

"Scared?"

"Yeah. Like they might come after you or something."

"Not really. I just know my sister gets some materials from them and says it helps her. Says she's going to be a success with it. She's in real estate. She still thinks you can get good real estate deals in Southern Cal."

"A dreamer."

"Yeah, I guess. But . . ." She looked at the floor.

"What?"

"I get a little nervous about it. She's really buying into it. I don't want her to end up throwing her money away."

"Self-help scams have been around since Satan told Eve to have a bite."

"You believe in that?"

"What?"

"Satan."

I shrugged. "I don't know. But a bunch of people are sure making a good case."

She laughed, but in a way that made me think she was a believer in God's great enemy. When she left my office, I wasn't sure what I believed anymore.

40

TRIUNFO WAS HEADQUARTERED in one of those renovated office buildings in Hollywood, this one on Vine. The Pantages was around the corner, one of the last reminders of old Hollywood. I could see the stack of flying saucers that made up the Capitol Records building. Outside of Musso & Frank, and the Egyptian and Chinese theaters, there wasn't much recognizable from the days when Garbo and Gable went out among 'em. The local city powers were trying to make Hollywood a respectable place again, and a lot of building was going on. They were trying to stir up a good nightlife.

But this was daytime, and I could see the dirt on the black and gold-flecked Walk of Fame, as clearly as muck on a stagnant pond. Poor Audrey Hepburn. Her star had a big wad of old gum stuck to it.

Outside the building, in an alcove, was a book rack that had one offering. Same cover, but some titles were in Spanish. The English version read *You Can Do It*, and in the middle of the cover was the smiling face of the author, whose name was emblazoned in bold letters across the top—Rudy Barocas.

He had thick brown hair swept back, clear brown eyes, and a perfect, V-shaped jaw. I wondered if he'd had any work done on his face. Chin implant maybe. Botox.

I picked up one of the English copies and turned to the back cover.

> Rudy Barocas never should have made it.
>
> Born into poverty in Miami. Gang life at an early age. Destined to end up in prison or on a slab.
>
> Then one night a rival gang came looking for him and shot up his house, nearly killing his thirteen-year-old sister.
>
> At age nineteen, it seemed Rudy had little time.
>
> Deciding that family came first, Rudy packed up his mother and sister and drove across the country to Los Angeles, where he found work in a garment sweatshop.
>
> And where he decided to test the American Dream.
>
> Today, Rudy Barocas is a living testimony to the reality of that dream. As one of the country's most successful Latino businessmen, Rudy now gives of his time and talents to spread his philosophy of self-respect to everyone from gang members to movie stars.
>
> This is Triunfo.
>
> This is Triumph.
>
> And it can give you the American Dream.

At the bottom were a couple of blurb endorsements. One from a Hollywood star, an actor who had a running part on a hit NBC drama.

The other blurb was surprising. It was from L.A. County Supervisor Leland Rich. Surprising because Leland Rich was a Bizarro World Barocas. Red hair, skin that seemed almost transparent. Some had called him a Huck Finn type. That was something no one would ever say about Barocas.

> Rudy Barocas is helping transform our City, and will do the same with the whole country someday.

The blurb was a little over the top, but then it started to make sense. Leland Rich was just another ambitious politician, and in L.A. that meant you had to get as much of the Latino vote as you could. That was the political reality and would be from now on.

"Would you like a self-test?"

I turned around and looked into the eyes of a beautiful Latina. She was dressed in a blue business suit, held a clipboard, and wore a sales smile.

"Excuse me?"

"We offer a test," she said. Her accent was mild, her voice a smooth hum. I could see why they would want her out front as the face of the organization. "The test will help you identify your areas of greatest potential."

"Oh yeah?" I craned my head to look at what was on the clipboard. She tipped it back.

"It takes about twenty minutes. Would you like to come inside?"

"Can you tell me a little bit more about your group?"

"What would you like to know?"

"This guy on the book, Barocas?"

"Mr. Rudy Barocas. You mean you haven't heard of him?"

"Should I have?"

"He's a great man."

"Does the great man have an office here?"

The smile began to melt. "Mr. Barocas has several offices. He is constantly on the go."

"You ever met him?"

"If you would like to come inside and take our self-test, we would be more able to help you."

"I don't need any help at the moment, except to set up an appointment with Mr. Barocas."

"I cannot help you. If you would like to call the main office—"

"Where is the main office?"

"You will find the number here." She handed me a slick, color brochure. Another picture of Barocas, this time leaning on a Mercedes, was on the front.

"Why don't I just go in and—"

"Inside is for anyone interested in—"

"Your self-test, yes. How much will it cost me?"

"The self-test is free."

"I mean after that."

"Sir, if you would like—"

"I would not like. I just want to —"

A voice behind the woman said, "Is there a problem?"

He was a little stubby, maybe thirty, with a shaved head and an ill-fitting green suit with a black knit shirt underneath. He and the suit did not look like they belonged together. It was like an old joke my dad used to tell, that sometimes he felt like life was a tuxedo and he was a pair of brown shoes. Maybe it was the dull blue of a web tattoo on his neck, sticking up above his collar. You don't usually associate gang tats with finer clothes.

"This gentleman wishes to make an appointment with Mr. Barocas," the woman explained.

The man said, "Are you a reporter?"

"No, just an interested bystander."

He paused, shook his head. "You will have to call the main office."

"If I do, will I get to see him?"

"I can't say."

"How long have you worked for this place?" I asked.

The two of them gave a sideward glance at each other. "Thank you for coming by," the man said. "Feel free to come back and take our test."

"How about I buy a book?" I said quickly.

"You can certainly do that," the woman said skeptically. "Nineteen-ninety-five, you can pay inside."

"Twenty bucks?" I hefted the anemic paperback.

"All profits go to help turn gang members around," the woman said.

I bought the book and drove home, wondering if I had what it took to realize any dream, let alone the American kind.

41

AT HOME I microwaved a burrito, popped a Coke, and sat out in the back, munching and drinking and trying to feel normal again. The last couple of weeks was like a kid's fingerpainting—awash with strong colors but formless. Messy.

Chasing after a phantom killer was stupid. It was getting me hurt, almost knifed, turning me into something unrecognizable.

Where was the high school kid voted Most Likely to Succeed? What had become of the editor of the *UCLA Law Review,* who had his picture taken with the governor of California during his visit to the campus? In the picture I'm shaking the governor's hand and smiling like Oprah's agent. Life was supposed to be one smooth ride after that.

So where was the kid now? Eating a lukewarm burrito outside a home that would never hold the only woman he'd ever really wanted.

I put the burrito down and walked back in through the French doors I'd had installed because Jacqueline liked them. There was something I had to see.

The box Fran had given me sat on the coffee table, next to a picture of Jacqueline and me in a gold frame. It was the time we went skiing in Big Bear with Al and his wife, Adrienne. Jacqueline has her arms around me from behind. She's wearing a blue wool cap. Her smile is pure happiness. My smile is cool. I am trying not to show the camera that I am crazy in love.

I hate myself in that picture. I wish I'd let my feelings show.

It was only six o'clock now, but I was thrashed.

I was tired of hurting.

I wanted Jacqueline.

And some part of her was in this box. Stuff from her school years, Fran had said.

But I was also afraid as I slit the brittle tape that Fran had used to secure the box. What would I find? Was this even a good idea?

I couldn't stop.

Three high school yearbooks were on top. Grover Cleveland High School. The Cavaliers. 1991, 1992, 1993. Neatly stacked.

I took the first one out. Opening it, I smelled dust, and ran my hands over the cool, slick pages.

Jacqueline was in here, waiting for me.

Turning to the page marked Sophomores, my hands were shaking and sweaty. I flipped to the D's, and was actually having a hard time breathing as I scanned the row of square photos, the young hopefuls of 1991.

And then I saw her. *Jacqueline Dwyer.*

She was beautiful even then, in a fifteen-year-old way. Her dark hair was long and silky, her eyes pure and clean. You could already see jadedness in some of the other kids. Not Jacqueline. She could have been a poster for

American youth in 1946, when the country was cocky and confident. But there was something in her eyes. A searching. Like she was ready to look for something but didn't quite know what.

I reached for the next annual. 1992.

She was there in the Juniors, looking more mature, more confident.

What was she like back then? What was she thinking? Who was she going out with? What did she want out of life?

What would it have been like if I'd met her then?

Then the last annual. Jacqueline as a senior. This time her picture was larger. She was smiling. I recognized the smile. It was like the one in the frame on the coffee table. Only difference was that the one in the frame was bigger and fuller, as if with me she'd found what she was looking for at last.

I set the yearbooks on the coffee table and looked in the box. There were some pictures of kids, snapshots Jacqueline must have taken at football games and dances. She was popular.

And smart. A couple of her high school report cards were there. Straight A's. Great comments from the teachers, like her eleventh-grade English teacher. "Real talent for writing. A pleasure to have in class!"

More items. An athletic letter for volleyball. A stack of papers, stapled, which looked like reports for history and other classes. A+ on most of them.

Some jewelry. A pair of earrings. A stuffed animal dog the size of my fist, filled with bean baggy stuff.

And a plain, black composition book. Nothing on the cover.

I opened it. The first page had the date of Jacqueline's sixteenth birthday.

Below, in neat but flowing handwriting, was this line:

There has got to be more to life than this.

More what?

JUST MORE.

My neck started to tingle. It was like hearing Jacqueline's voice. The heart of the woman I had loved, when she was a teenager. And now it was in my hands, talking to me.

Should I read this? Would it be a violation? Jacqueline had never mentioned this journal to me. Maybe she'd forgotten about it.

Or maybe she didn't want anyone but her to see it.

But she loved you. She'd want you to read it.

I knew I would.

But not then. I closed the journal and just held it. I didn't want to rush through it. I wanted to savor it, as if I had been given the ability to travel through time, to sit down with Jacqueline and just listen to her.

I carried the journal with me to the couch and lay down with it. I closed my eyes. At some point, I don't know how long it was, I fell asleep.

42

NEXT MORNING, FEELING a little more human, I left a message for Channing Westerbrook and drove to the office. I actually got some good work done, prepping for the depo of Dyan Trudeau, Claudia Blumberg's mother and Jonathan's ex. Al dropped by to check up on me and seemed pleased I was looking pretty good.

Channing called saying it was about time we met, and she gave me the name of an eatery in Hollywood.

The restaurant was located a block off Ivar. It was in a renovated house, the old Craftsman-style that was big in the twenties and thirties. Now it was upscale and, according to Channing, the perfect place for rising stars to chow together.

She ordered a glass of Chardonnay and I asked for a Pellegrino. Taking out a pad and pen, she asked, "How are you feeling these days?"

"Like Paris Hilton thinking."

"What?"

"My head hurts."

"Got it."

"Been a strange few days."

"Uh-huh."

"I wanted to ask you a question."

She frowned. "Wait a second, you owe me a little material here."

"I'll get to that."

"Why don't we start with it and go from there?"

I realized then how little I liked this arrangement. I almost asked to call the whole thing off, but knew she could be the source of valuable information. "All right. Last night was hard. I was thinking of Jacqueline, looking at pictures of her when she was in high school. It was strange."

"How?"

"You know, odd."

She sighed and took a sip of wine. "Ty, you're going to have to try to cast off that male reticence and lay it out a little more fully for me. I want to know how you *feel*. I want to get that in the book."

"I'm not sure I want that to be in the book."

"That's the only thing that'll set it apart. You *are* the book. Come on, try, will you?"

The young waiter, some embryonic soap actor, chose that moment to take our order. Channing selected the chicken piccata. I went for the overpriced cheeseburger.

The waiter poked everything into a handheld, smiled with perfect teeth, and walked away like James Dean.

"So," Channing said, "you were saying?"

"I feel mostly a sense of loss," I said. "A real deep sense, the kind where you know nothing will ever make up for it."

Channing was writing. "That's right."

"You ever felt that way?"

She looked up. "Is it my turn?"

I nodded.

"I was married once, right out of college. To a guy who went on to do sports at a local channel in Cincinnati."

"What happened?"

"I was more successful than he was, and that he couldn't stand. Anyway, I had a serious boyfriend for a while, but nothing . . . and why am I telling you all this?"

"Because you want to. You're building up trust."

"Let me ask you something, off the record. You ever think of—" she paused. "Doing yourself in?"

"Doesn't everybody at one time or another?"

"No, I mean because of this. Don't answer if it's too uncomfortable."

"I hardly know you."

"I'm a reporter and I told you this would be off the record."

"Then the answer is yes. One time. It was the day before the funeral. That's when it really hit me in the gut. I only thought about it for about five seconds. It was almost like . . . I was tempting myself, daring myself to do it. Does that seem strange?"

"It is what it is."

And then she put her hand on mine. For one of those pregnant beats you see in Drew Barrymore movies, she looked me in the eyes.

I slipped my hand away and said, "I have a question for you now."

"All right."

"You know anything about a group called Triunfo?"

"A little. I mean, I've heard about it. A couple of the techs at the station are into it."

"What do you know about it?"

"Some sort of self-help, I think. One of the techs told me he was going to use it to become a TV news anchor someday."

"Maybe he will."

"I doubt it. I mean, positive thinking is one thing. Having a face made for radio is another."

"You're not saying it's all looks, are you?"

She stiffened a little. "You have to be good, too. Very good."

"I'm just saying, you don't see many three-hundred-pound reporters."

"They couldn't exactly run after a story, could they? Speaking of which, you owe me some stuff."

"Fine. I'll give it to you. But I need to know about this Triunfo and the guy who runs it, Rudy Barocas."

"Why?"

"Because there may be some connection with Bonilla and Jacqueline's death. Maybe nothing at all, but at this point I'm not willing to look away from anything."

"That's good."

"What is?"

"Obsession."

"Isn't that a perfume?"

"That smells like a bestseller."

"Makes you a little nosy."

"Enough witty repartee. Were you ever married?"

"Don't beat around the bush."

"No time. Come on."

I shook my head. "Came close once, before Jacqueline, an MBA student at Pepperdine. After graduation she got a killer job offer with a dot-com in the Bay Area. We tried to keep it going. I racked up the air miles with Southwest. But in the end it was too much of a strain. I don't think it would have worked out."

"Why?"

"Me. I was too into myself."

"And now?"

I didn't know how to answer. How to get at the heart of what I knew but could not express: that Jacqueline had been the one. How do you explain something like that? To a near stranger?

"Another time," I said.

"I so understand."

I was glad someone did.

43

I DROVE BACK to the office, taking Sunset to Landfair. That took me past the east boundary of UCLA and the law school.

Whenever I could, I drove by the law school to remind myself of why I was doing any of this. When you get out into the working world, the law is no longer the pristine battle of ideals you once thought it was.

In school, you read the great opinions. Holmes and Cardozo, Warren and Frankfurter, Douglas and Brennan.

For that little three-year period of time you walk around in a bubble of high-mindedness and are awed by the great old volumes of law in the stacks at the library, even though everyone knows the end of the yellowed book road is supposed to lead to a pot of career gold. A few would take the academic path and stay lofty, but most of us hoped to grab the green.

I liked the lofty part. Maybe in a way I thought it was honoring the memory of my father. He died for the law. If it wasn't something worth dying for, then his death wouldn't mean that much.

I wanted it to mean that much.

So I gave a respectful look at the law building nestled among the trees and drove on to the office.

Kim brought a couriered package in for me. The envelope was card stock, about 9 × 12. Blank on the outside.

I opened it and pulled out a smaller manila envelope. Written on the outside of the envelope in black marker was one word: HUNT.

Now I knew who it was from.

I sliced open the manila envelope and pulled out one page, on which was printed the following.

Information is more valuable than a bank account.

David Townsend
Age 24
22055 Cutler Avenue #301
North Hollywood, CA

Work:
Stage Manager
NoHo Theatre Center
Lankershim Boulevard

What are you waiting for?

44

NOHO IS A one square mile community just north of Universal City. Originally called Lankershim, the city changed its name to North Hollywood in 1927 to take advantage of its more famous neighbor to the south.

It became a popular suburb post–World War II, but started showing its age in the eighties. Then the Chamber of Commerce got the bright idea of establishing an arts district, along the Lankershim Boulevard corridor and a few selected side streets. Officially called NoHo now, the district boasts twenty legit theaters, cafes, art galleries, dance studios, restaurants, and the obligatory Starbucks on the main corner of Lankershim and Magnolia.

The NoHo Theatre Center was housed in what looked like a vintage movie house. There was an old-time marquee in front, the triangular kind that met at a point over the sidewalk.

On the marquee it said, SWEENEY TODD—NOW PLAYING!

The box office had a window with a little hole in it.

On the other side of the hole sat a woman with short hair, a round face, and glasses with thick black rims. She was reading a paperback. Beckett.

"A little light reading?" I said through the hole.

She looked up. "Help you?" She kept the book open. She wore a gray hoodie with Stanford in scarlet letters across the front.

"I was just saying, Beckett. Nothing like a little pessimism to lift your spirits."

She stared at me blankly.

I said, "Maybe you're waiting for *good dough*."

A major furrow creased her forehead.

"Get it?" I said. "You're sitting in the box office . . . never mind."

"Would you like to buy a ticket?"

"I'm actually looking for David Townsend. Is he here?"

She shook her head.

"You expect him back?"

"There's a show tonight. He'll be here. You want to leave your name?"

"Vladimir."

"Excuse me?"

"You know, from *Waiting for Godot*."

No change of expression. "Funny."

"What time's the show? I was hoping to catch him."

"Curtain's at eight. You want a ticket? It's a good show." Her face did not match the words.

It was only five-thirty and I didn't feel like waiting around.

Then she said, "You might catch him at Jeremiah's."

"Who's that?"

"It's a bar. On Ventura and Tujunga."

"Thanks."

She looked back into her Samuel Beckett. The title was *Krapp's Last Tape*. All I remembered about that play was there was an old man in it who liked bananas.

"Keep smiling," I said to the girl in the window. She didn't.

45

I KNEW WHAT kind of bar Jeremiah's was the moment I walked in. A dance floor flashed colors as a mirror ball spun on the ceiling, and the music was loud for the men dancing with other men.

There were a few women, too, but the ratio was tilted toward same-sex preference.

It was happy hour, too. A hot station with mini tacos, veggies and dip, and chicken wings was set up along one wall. Around the dance floor were high, round tables with candles in the middle. A full bar with a long mirror ran almost the width of the place. Two men in white shirts and black vests performed social chemistry up and down the crowded bar.

I scanned the place for a guy in his mid-twenties who looked like he worked at a theater. That narrowed it down to about everybody. I wasn't going to go table to table asking.

A waiter with pad in hand walked by and I stopped him. "Hey, you wouldn't happen to know a David Townsend? I'm supposed to meet him."

The waiter, short and with a buzz cut over an oblong head, said, "I don't."

"Works up at the NoHo Theatre Center?"

"We get a lot of NoHo traffic. Ask Arty." He gave a nod toward the bar. "He's the one looks like Joe Pesci."

Well, maybe a little. Joe Pesci in his prime, his *My Cousin Vinny* days. There was a little bit of the Italian hit man to him, too.

"Arty?" I said when I managed to get his attention. I was at one end of the bar, near the register.

"Can I get you?" He put a small square napkin on the bar in front of me.

"I'm supposed to meet David Townsend. Waiter said you might know him."

Arty gave me a careful look. "You sure?"

"Sure I'm sure."

"I mean, maybe he doesn't know you."

"Right. I'm here to introduce myself."

He paused, some gears meshing in his head. "I don't think so."

"So you do know him."

"You ordering a drink or not?"

"Here." I took out one of my cards and handed it to Arty. "Tell him I'd like to buy him a drink and talk to him about a priest."

Arty looked at the card and frowned. "Lawyer?"

"Not that there's anything wrong with that."

The humorless barkeep said nothing.

I spread my hands. "Arty, I got nothing to hide."

"I never met a lawyer without something to hide," he said.

"Good one." I took out my wallet and got a twenty. "This transparent enough for you?"

Arty wasted no time in accepting the bill. "I can see clearly now, the rain has gone."

"I'll wait here," I said.

46

"WHAT IS THIS about?"

David Townsend had shaggy brown hair, some hanging over his eyes. The eyes themselves were grayish with light irises and small pupils. He had the look of a nervous point guard, ready to jump back or to the side the moment the ball came loose. And maybe for good reason. The left side of his face looked like it had been tenderized by a brick.

"What are you drinking?"

"I want to know what you want." He held my card and looked at it again. "Buchanan?"

"I wanted to ask you about Father Robert."

The gray eyes narrowed. "I'm not talking about that."

"I just wanted—"

"Ever again. That's over. Thanks for reminding me."

"Wait a second—"

"Who are you a lawyer for?"

"I know the father."

"Oh yeah? He molest you, too?"

"I just met him."

"Give him time."

Townsend's rage was evident but also, I thought, practiced. Like an actor going over familiar lines.

"I've also met some other people," I said. "Like Dr. Kendra Mackee."

"You know her?"

I nodded.

"Why?" he said.

"What'll you have? I won't take much of your time."

He thought about it a moment. "Kamikazi," he said.

I motioned for Arty, who was back on his step. I ordered the kamikazi for Townsend. The music was still a little loud and the place a little more crowded.

"Have an accident?" I asked, looking at the discoloration on his face.

"Why don't you get to why you tracked me down?"

"Just making some talk," I said.

"Look, I don't trust you, okay? You're a lawyer and you mentioned Father Robert, and that's two strikes against you, far as I can see. You trying to get him back into the priesthood or something?"

"He's still a priest."

"Yeah, but they got him where he can't hurt any kids again. But don't worry, he'll find a way." He took another drink and it was a good one. I was hoping it would loosen his tongue, so I said nothing.

"And if it weren't for Dr. Mackee, the scum'd still be out there."

"She help you, did she?"

"Yeah, that's right. What of it?"

I shrugged. "I just know that repressed memory stuff is controversial."

"Who you work for?"

"Is it?"

"Is it what?"

"Controversial. Because some people say it's just manipulation."

Arty put a shot glass in front of Townsend. I tossed a ten spot on the bartop.

Townsend took a sip of his drink, thought about it, then downed the rest with a pugnacious turn of the hand. "I'm only going to say this once. I was having nightmares about Father Robert for years. And Dr. Mackee, after I worked with her, after she found out why, they went away. And they haven't come back. And I don't know who you are, and that's all I'm gonna say to you."

He put the shot glass down and started away.

"What about Lorimar?" I said.

For the briefest moment he froze, as if responding to a loud noise. "I don't know what you're talking about and—"

"Davey, what if you were used?"

"Where do you get off? I'm not—"

"What I'm saying is, maybe Mackee did more than help you remember. Maybe she actually did a little creating. That's what some people think."

"Who, that witch Lea Edwards?"

"Among others."

"You have no idea."

"But what if this has some validity?" I said softly, trying to keep him talking. "What if all this resulted in an innocent man being implicated?"

"You are so full of it."

"Can you be sure?"

"I told you. What are you bothering me for?"

"Just talking, Davey—"

"My name is David. And I know yours, and if you ever say anything about me I'm going to come after you."

"Is that a threat?"

He smiled. "This is the part where I'm supposed to say, 'No, it's a promise.'"

"Is it?"

"Yeah."

"Okay, I've got one, too. I find out you made any of this stuff up, I come after you. Maybe the D.A. does, too."

He jumped me. Got his hands on my throat and I went down. Next thing I know I'm being choked by a wild-eyed stage manager. When air isn't coming to your lungs a knee-jerk reaction sets in. I threw my leg up and managed to roll him over. I outweighed him so it wasn't hard.

But he kept his death grip. I sat on his chest and grabbed his wrists and pulled them off my throat. He wasn't particularly strong, but he was wiry. His face got red, tears started spurting, and he screamed at me to get off.

About five guys were on me, pulling me off Townsend. Yelling in my ear to leave him alone, give it up, get off, get out.

On my feet I jerked my way out of the grips. Joe Pesci had arrived by this time and got his pinched face in mine and told me I better leave. I told him he should teach his regulars that attacking newcomers is bad for business. He said he didn't need my business and I left.

47

THE DEPOSITION OF Dyan Trudeau, Jonathan's ex, took place the next morning. As I was driving to Barton Walbert's office, I tuned into KNX radio for the news. What I heard set up the mood for the depo to come.

The night before, in South L.A., a man had barricaded himself in a house with a knife, his ex-wife, and his three-year-old daughter. The LAPD SWAT team had spent the night at the corner of Eighty-fifth and Hoover, negotiating with the man, to no avail.

The standoff, the reporter said, was continuing.

In Compton, a man was shot to death on the 400 block of Pear Street. That was Compton's first homicide of the year, according to the story. The year before they'd had fifty-nine.

Then there was the man stabbed on the 13100 block of South Largo Avenue in Willowbrook. He was the victim of a robbery. They caught the killer, who had managed to get the victim's wallet and all seventeen dollars the guy'd been carrying.

Another day and night in L.A., and now two lawyers were about to face off with questions and objections as weapons. That, along with a monumental mutual dislike, was a mix that just had to explode.

It did.

I started off with, "Isn't it true this whole lawsuit is a product of your hatred for you ex-husband?"

Dyan did exactly as I'd hoped. Her surgically upgraded face twitched under the Rodeo Drive makeup job. Her black hair, pulled back tight, made a glacier-like move forward before sliding back into place. I'd rippled the façade before breaking a sweat.

Dyan's blue eyes threw up a steel wall. "That is a stupid thing to ask."

"That's not an answer," I shot back.

Walbert, sheathed in a gray three piece, was sitting next to Dyan across the conference table from me. "I'm going to object to the whole tone of this, Mr. Buchanan, and I'll call this deposition off right now."

"Off the record," I told the stenographer. She put her hands in her lap. To Walbert I said, "You want to dance, let's waltz over to a judge."

"Good by me."

"You going to run your client meter? How does Mom feel about that?"

Walbert started to stand.

"Wait." Dyan put her hand on Walbert's arm. "I don't want to have to come back. Let's finish this. I can handle him."

Walbert gave it a thought, then nodded, but told me with his look that this was lodged permanently in his head. He'd probably call McDonough to complain, pull the collegiality card. Guys like Walbert and McDonough, who drank together at the California Club, made a big deal out of getting along.

Again, I surprised myself by the depth of my not caring.

"Back on the record," I said. "My question is as follows. Does not this lawsuit have its genesis in your antipathy toward your former spouse?"

"No."

"You don't exactly like your ex-husband, do you?"

"I don't think about him."

"Never?"

"Oh, something I see may bring back a bad memory. But we split up long ago."

"But you allege that he sexually abused your daughter."

"He did."

"That doesn't engender hatred, Mrs. Trudeau? That hardly seems human."

"Objection," Walbert said. An objection in a deposition isn't like one in court. A judge doesn't rule on it. It's just a way for the lawyer to make a record or, in Walbert's case, blow smoke.

"You may answer the question," I said. Walbert could direct her not to answer, and then I would decide whether to stop the deposition, go to a judge, and get a ruling. Make an argument for sanctions. That would run into money for both sides. But Dyan had indicated her desire to go on, and she and her new husband were the ones paying Walbert's costs.

He let her answer.

"I don't hate, Mr. Buchanan. That's so boring."

"Hatred is boring?"

"Your questions are boring."

"Well, let me try to make it a little more interesting for you, Mrs. Trudeau. Back when you originally filed for divorce, you did not allege any sexual abuse of Claudia by Jonathan, did you?"

"I didn't know about it."

"Instead"—I picked up a file and looked inside at some notes I'd made—"you alleged physical and psychological abuse directed at you."

"It was true."

"But when it came to custody, you changed your story."

"I did not change anything. It came to my attention, with the help of Dr. Kendra Mackee, that Claudia had been . . . touched by Jonathan."

"So you just dropped the other allegations."

"I didn't drop anything."

"No?"

"Why would I? Jonathan is a very strange man, Mr. Buchanan. He believes things about himself that aren't true. He once claimed to me that he'd been an assassin for the CIA. Can you imagine that? I mean, if you're going to make up a lie at least make it plausible. He had delusions that he was Harrison Ford or something. He's sick. I want to make sure that's on the record."

While I was glad she ran off at the mouth a little, what she said had a vague resonance with me. I hadn't been a hundred percent comfortable with Jonathan since our "hunt the meat" talk. Maybe he *was* the kind of guy who'd make up wild stories about himself, to help get him where he was. He wouldn't be the first delusional billionaire. But did that evince a man who was off the beam enough to molest his daughter? Wasn't for me to say. Getting to Dyan was my only concern.

She added, "Did he ever give you his "hunt the meat" speech?"

My lips jiggled on my teeth. "I am asking the questions, Mrs. Trudeau."

"Just wondering."

She looked like she *knew* it, like this was something B-2 spouted all the time. And the look on her face was too satisfied for my taste.

So I dropped my bomb.

48

A COUPLE OF days before the deposition, I'd had one of our investigators do a little background on Dyan Trudeau. What he unearthed was a nice little tidbit that he could not have nabbed without greasing a palm. That was fine with me. Whatever worked.

"You attempted to have an acting career at one point, did you not?"

Dyan snapped a quick look at Walbert. The lawyer opened his mouth, but Dyan turned back to me and said, "I had an acting career going but gave it up for Claudia."

"Is that right? I thought the reviews that came in—"

"How is this relevant?" Walbert said.

"No," Dyan said, "I'll explain life to Mr. Buchanan. He seems so interested. I was represented by one of the best agents in town. I had offers coming in, but my first concern was always Claudia."

"You loved Claudia that much?"

"Of course. Do you have children?"

A thought of Jacqueline shot through my head. "I'm asking the questions, thank you. Your devotion to your daughter knows no bounds?"

"None."

"Let me turn your attention, then, to a few days before you went to see Dr. Mackee, before the first of her videotaped sessions with your daughter."

Dyan shifted a little in her chair. Walbert kept his eyes locked on me.

"I believe at this time your daughter was taking acting lessons at the Stella Adler studio in Hollywood?"

"Yes. So?"

"Relevance," Walbert said.

"Oh this one's relevant, Barton," I said. "This one the jury's going to hear."

"If it's not, I'll move to strike the whole thing."

"Do what you want, this is going to come out."

"What is?" Dyan said.

"Your daughter's acting lessons," I said. "You obviously wanted to live vicariously through your daughter and—"

"That is absolutely untrue. She has talent to burn, and I only wanted her to develop that."

"I see. And didn't the acting studio arrange a showcase that Claudia was a part of?"

Dyan Trudeau looked astonished. There is nothing a trial lawyer loves more than seeing that reaction in a hostile witness.

"Yes," Dyan said.

"Which is where agents and casting directors come to watch the students do scenes, right?"

"Yes."

Suddenly, Dyan wasn't so talkative.

"And your daughter was told by a casting director that her chances of succeeding in the business weren't all that great, correct?"

"How do you know that?"

"It's true, isn't it?"

"That woman was an idiot, she was—"

"Your daughter threw a fit that night and tried to commit suicide."

Walbert shot up so fast his knees hit the bottom of the table. Through his wince he said. "Off the record right now!"

Dyan's mouth was hanging open.

For a moment I sat back and enjoyed the spectacle. Walbert losing his cool was a good one. Dyan Trudeau and her fake face, her cherished ability to control things, out the window like a flung ashtray.

Walbert told Dyan and the stenographer to leave the conference room.

When we were alone, Walbert let out a snort, like a bull in a ring. "Who do you think you are, you little snot-nosed punk? You think you can pull that stuff around me? You think—"

"Come on, Barton, you don't have to pose now." To me, he was just like that guy outside El Tapado. He was every thug with a knife, every lowlife who stained the landscape. Only his weapons were bluster and legal manipulation. I wasn't going to let him cut me.

"You don't come in here and act like that," he said. "You don't pull that dirt in my office."

"What dirt is that, Barton? You have a thing against the truth?"

"McDonough's going to hear about this."

I said, "You're scared. Because you're going to lose this case. Because Barton Walbert is going to take a dive into the toilet."

Barton Walbert had faced down a slew of great lawyers. I was being pretty reckless. But it was time somebody yanked off his gilded robes and sent him to the street in his boxers.

"You just committed professional suicide, kid," Walbert said. "You don't go around breaking rules of conduct like that."

Like I cared. I grabbed my notes and stuffed them in my briefcase. With a quick step on the chair I jumped onto the conference table. As Walbert's eyes opened wider, I did a little three-step tap dance.

"What are you doing?" he howled.

"Gene Kelly," I said.

"Get off that table!"

"This is what it's going to be like, Barton. You looking up at me from now on."

His face changed colors. Cheeks rosy like the dawn. I don't know why I did it, except that I never liked bullies. On the schoolyard or in a plush conference room.

Gerry Spence, the greatest trial lawyer of his day, was once asked on *60 Minutes* what he'd have done if he were a cowboy in the old West, facing a guy with a knife. "I'd leave him bloody on the floor," Spence said, "which is the way I try cases."

I jumped off the table and said, "See you in court, Barton. I'm going to leave you bloody on the floor."

49

OUTSIDE THE CONFERENCE room Dyan's husband, Frank Trudeau, got nose to nose with me. "You just made the wrong enemy, friend."

"Get in line," I said.

He pointed a finger at me. I had to stop myself from biting it. Trudeau's face was rectangular, with a downturned mouth that reminded me of Bill Cowher, the former coach of the Pittsburgh Steelers. If Trudeau didn't actually chew nails, he wanted you to think he could. A full head of coiled brown hair was either real or a better-than-William Shatner job.

"You ever do anything like that to my wife again . . ." he sputtered. "You ever try to hurt my family. You ever . . ."

"Finish a sentence, Frank."

He did more than that. He started screaming every curse in the book at me, even making up some anatomically impossible new ones. I thought his red face was going to explode.

I just laughed.

Walbert jumped in between us. "Relax, Frank, relax. I'm calling the State Bar about this."

"Tell 'em to spell my name right," I said. Without another word I walked out of Barton's office and into the cool January air. The weather was kind of a lead blanket on my shoulders, and I didn't want to head back to the office.

There were a couple of motions I could work on at home, but litigation was the last thing on my mind. Strange. All through law school and my early, hungry years with the firm, I was the work dog, the guy who could do anything at any time by sheer force of will. Many a time Al and I had stayed out a little late, and the next morning I'd be ready to go at my desk by the time Al, shades still on, wandered by my office muttering about life's unfairness.

Now the thought of going back to the office almost made me sick. But I went anyway, feeling like I was about to get blasted in the gut.

Didn't take long to happen. I was ordered to see McDonough the moment I stuck my face in the office.

Rose, McDonough's assistant, didn't miss a beat. "You can go right in," she said with appropriate dread in her voice. Madame Defarge in a suit.

McDonough motioned for me to sit.

"How long you been with the firm?" he said.

"Five years this August."

"You've done quality work. Really quality. Everybody thinks so."

Waiting for the blade to drop, I nodded. Pierce Patrick McDonough was the quintessential company man. Started the firm in 1977 with Steven Gunther and William D. Longyear, all Yale Law classmates who came to conquer the West. Made his way by being conservative, convivial, and most of all, smart. He was a brilliant legal mind. But he didn't go to court all that much anymore, which made me wonder if he could still do it.

Like I was sure I could.

McDonough ran his right hand down his muted blue tie. "You've also been through a tough time, a very tough time. We all know that, too."

"Thanks."

"But what you did in Barton Walbert's office is inexcusable."

Of course it was, but I wasn't in the mood to agree. "Is it?"

"Of course it is. I got a call from him."

"Don't I have the constitutional right to confront the witnesses against me?"

"You saying Walbert is lying?"

"Depends on what he said. Did I go after his sham witness? Yes. Did I hammer her? Yes. Do I have some information that helps show her motive to fund Barton Walbert for her daughter? Yes."

"That's not what I'm talking about."

"I knocked his wit to the mat, and he threw a fit."

"And you responded by jumping on his conference table?"

"Oh that."

"Did you?"

"I did not jump. I tapped."

McDonough shook his head and sat back. "Tyler, I am not able to under-stand such a stupid stunt."

"He was being an—"

"I don't care what he was!" He sat back up, like a gray tiger. "It's his *office!* And you're a lawyer representing our firm. There is no way you can justify what you did."

I put my hands up. "You're right. There's not. But Walbert thinks he can push anybody around just because he's got a big name, and I wanted to show him he couldn't do that to us. To our firm, Mr. McDonough."

"This was not the proudest moment in the history of our firm. What am I going to say when this hits the street?"

"It'll give this place some color." I smiled.

McDonough flashed an angry look.

"Face it," I said, "we're a stodgy place. That's what they think about us, the Walberts out there. We'll be all buddy buddy, reach a settlement. We've got to get a little attitude back."

"Walking on a conference table is not the way to do it."

"Maybe it's a start."

To his credit, he thought about it a moment. To his further credit, and my relief, he didn't throw me out on my elbows.

"If you will apologize to Barton, I think I can convince him to keep this quiet. He sort of intimated that on the phone."

My face burned. "He wants me to grovel, doesn't he?"

"Tyler, you have a great future here. I still believe that. And I'm willing to consider your grief as part of the explanation for what you did. But I don't want to see you throw away your legal future for a few moments of childish behavior—"

I opened my mouth. He shut it with a look.

"—*childish.* Now because of the recent severe stress in your life, I'm thinking that maybe you should be taken off the Blumberg case and get into something a little less pressing."

It wasn't the sound of the guillotine blade, but it was the rack. "Mr. Mc-Donough, I don't want . . . I've been working like crazy on this."

"My point. Crazy. You need to—"

"Please, Mr. McDonough. It won't happen again, what I did today."

"I really can't be sure of that."

"You can. If I mess up again I'll walk. I'll clean out my office."

McDonough took a long breath. "Let me talk it over with the committee. If you'll write a letter of apology to Walbert, that'll help."

Reprieve. Pierce McDonough had been my biggest booster at the firm, an early cheerleader. When I first got here I worked eighteen-hour days doing research for a big international case McDonough was handling. It was my brief that won the appeal in the Ninth Circuit. The old cliché about a second father was true with me and McDonough.

But I had the feeling I'd used up all of a son's goodwill in one moment in Barton Walbert's office. There wouldn't be another chance.

The walk back to my office felt like the last mile on Death Row. They weren't giving me the injection, so I went back to my cell to await further word.

In a lot of ways my office did feel like jail, the same way memories locked me in anguish, like when I asked Jacqueline to marry me for the third time, three months after we met.

"We hardly know each other," she said.

We were at the Getty, looking down on west Los Angeles and at the ocean. It was a clear day and it looked like you could reach out and touch Catalina. I figured there would never be a nicer spot to pop the question.

"How much more do you need to know?" I said, and then I kissed her. A soft, long kiss, as perfect as the view.

"Just a little more than that," she laughed. "Even though that's very nice."

"You know all about me. I'm a very simple guy. I work hard, I make money, and I perform legal miracles."

"You play drums."

"I *kill* on drums. What more could you want?"

She got serious then and leaned on the rail. "I do want you. This is a serious step."

"I'm a serious kind of guy."

"Are you?"

"Hey, don't let my ego fool you. I take it to court with me. I need it to win. But when I come home at night, I put it in a shoe box."

"Shoe box? Shouldn't that at least be a whole garage?"

"All right, maybe a garage. I'll move the car to the street."

A wistful smile floated across her face. I made a move to kiss her again, but she pulled back.

"That's bribing the jury," she said.

"What is it you need to know about me? I'm an open book here."

"It's not a matter of words."

"You want to spend more time with me?"

"Yes. I do. A lot."

"Done. Only tell me you'll marry me."

"Ty—"

"And we'll do it this way. We'll make marriage the default. And if I do anything to blow it, you can say, That's it."

She paused.

"I won't do anything to blow it," I said. "I know this is supposed to be."

"What about me? Don't you want to know more about me?"

"No. I mean, not to marry you. I know all I need to know."

"Marriage is supposed to be for life, you know."

"So is that a yes?"

"No!"

"So it's no?"

"Stop."

"Is it wait?"

"All right, Buchanan." She faced me full on. "We'll get married. We'll jump into it. But you and I are going to be together a lot. And we're going to talk. About a lot of things."

"That's just what I—"

She put her index finger on my lips. "But not now. Not at this moment. Now you can kiss me."

I did and made it count.

Six weeks later, she was dead.

50

BACK IN MY office I shut the door and looked out the window for a while. The view from the twentieth floor of the Stafford Building was, on a clear day, something for a booster's postcard collection. Today, with gray over the city, it was more like a sad song.

Westwood Village still looked quaint from up here, and beyond were the red tile roofs of UCLA, the original brick and cast stone buildings that went up in the twenties.

Then, up in the hills behind the campus, in the rarified oxygen of Bel-Air, was some of the most expensive real estate in the world.

But behind the wrought-iron gates and manicured lawns there were all sorts of stories being played out. Some of them were as much a part of the fabric of the city as billboards and Du-pars pancakes.

Over on Benedict Canyon, back in 1969, a pregnant Sharon Tate, wife of Roman Polanski, was stabbed sixteen times by an acid-laced Charles Manson acolyte named Susan Atkins. You could actually get maps to famous murder sites from street vendors or on the Net. They'd direct you to Leimert Park down near Crenshaw, where the body of Elizabeth Short was found, cut in half, in the infamous—and unsolved—Black Dahlia case.

Or to the address in Beverly Hills where Lana Turner's fourteen-year-old daughter stabbed Johnny Stompanato to death, or another where mobsters rubbed out Bugsy Siegel.

I didn't believe in ghosts, but there was always this shadow hanging in my mind when I looked out at the city. Things happened under the surface, sending ripples and even shock waves that you never saw coming and couldn't prepare for.

If anybody knew that now, it was me.

The phone rang. My assistant said it was Channing Westerbrook.

"I just wanted to tell you how much I enjoyed lunch the other day," she said.

"Yeah. Very nice."

"I mean, a lot. You know, I don't often get a chance to sit down with people I do stories on, so that was a really cool thing."

"Thanks."

Pause. "So how's it going?"

"It's going."

"Can we get together again?"

"You want to?"

"That's why I asked. Are you all right?"

Not in the mood for a long conversation with a reporter. "I'm a little busy right now. Can we make it another time?"

"Sure, but let's do it soon."

"Right."

"I mean, real soon. I mean, as in let's make an appointment right now."

Her tone was a little demanding and rubbed me wrong. "How about I call you?"

"Are you trying to put me off or something?"

"No, no. I had kind of a rough day today, and I—"

"Rough? How?"

"Later."

"When?"

"Let me call you."

"If you don't, I'll come looking for you." Playful now, but with an edge.

I hung up and looked back out the window. That's all I felt like doing at the moment. There was a snarl down on Wilshire, a big line of cars. I followed the line down to Veteran and saw there was an accident there. Some SUV was diagonal across the intersection with a little red hatchback—now made smaller by impact—off to the side.

Not good. Some impatient people were going to be very upset. Some were going to end up in fender benders of their own. Some things never changed.

51

AL BOUGHT ME dinner at Sagebrush Cantina in Calabasas. He thought I needed it because of the slapdown I got from McDonough. I never turn down free Mexican food. I met him at seven. A large basket of warm tortilla chips and fresh guacamole got us started. Al was already on his second Foster's. I sipped water.

"You freaking *walked* on Walbert's conference table?" Al said with a mix of mirth and admiration.

"Danced."

"Oh I wish I could have seen that. You da man."

"I'm a man on the block," I said. "Got a feeling McDonough doesn't want to back me anymore."

"You'll make partner, no prob."

"Not so sure, bud."

"Look, if it makes you feel any better, McDonough ripped me, too."

"You? Why?"

"He's got a wedgie about the Blumberg litigation. I don't think he likes me."

"Come on."

"I mean it, man. You're the fair-haired boy at Gunther. You got nothing to worry about."

"McDonough's hard to read sometimes," I said.

"All I'm saying, don't get your goodies in a knot about it. Relax. Eat. You'll feel better."

He was right, of course. Sagebrush was a good place for getting out of your head. We had a patio table, the night was pleasant. Always a good crowd here, and being with people made me think that there was an island of normalcy somewhere.

"And don't think I'm not here for a reason," Al said. "Gives me a good excuse not to go home." Al drained his beer.

"Yeah? More trouble?"

Al shrugged. "I don't know how much more I can take."

"Come on. You guys have been married, what?"

"Seven years. Wasn't there a movie about that?"

"You mean *The Seven Year Itch*?"

"Was that the one? Had Marilyn Monroe in it?"

"That's the one. But come on, you don't want to throw that away."

"Throw what away? She's . . . I don't know what she is."

"Let me give you a chip's worth of advice," I said. "Keep it. Just keep it. Grit your teeth and work through it. You don't know what you have. When it's gone, then you'll know."

"Fine for you to say. You had Jacqueline. I mean, she was perfect."

I scooped up some guac. "Adrienne's got a heck of a lot going for her."

"A lot of money."

"Don't be so cynical."

"And her old man. The *old man*. He'd have my head on a platter."

Adrienne's father was one of the big lawyers in town. He had gotten Al plugged in at Gunther, McDonough & Longyear when Al—he once admitted to me—wouldn't have made the grade on his own.

Al sighed. "Maybe I should just suck it up and stay with the kids and get something going on the side."

"Don't be a jerk."

"Why not? If life is a pool of warm spit, I should be able to choose who I swim with."

"That's just beautiful."

"Life reeks of bodies, dead on the beach."

"Now you're getting really boring. Like Bukowski."

Al looked at me with eyes starting to glaze. "Man, can you look at me and tell me, after what you've been through, that there's a point to all this? I mean we go in every day, and we try to make money and we try to figure out ways to make somebody else *lose* money and then we go home. You go home to an empty house, I go home to a house I wish was empty. Or at least had a babe waiting for me who actually wants me. Where does it say this whole life deal is a good thing? Does my life have any meaning at all?"

I thought about that for the length of time it took me to dip another chip and pop it in my mouth. I talked through the chip. "Jacqueline thought so. I never gave her much of a chance to talk to me about it. I was putting it off. I was thinking maybe I could avoid it. Maybe I was thinking she was too good for me, and if she started talking about things that matter she'd realize that."

"Interesting theory," Al said. "Everybody has to believe something, so I believe I'll have another beer. You?"

"You better take it easy."

"I have to get out of this thing."

"Shut up."

"But—"

"Just don't give me that." My voice was carrying over the din of the usual Sagebrush crowd. "You keep what you got. You got marriage. You got two kids."

"I better order two beers."

"Jerk."

"If I get drunk, will you drive me home?"

"No."

"So who's the jerk?"

"You want to get hammered? Here's what you do. You walk the half mile to Domino's, order yourself a pizza, and when they go to deliver it, ask for a ride home."

One of our fine Southern California women appeared to take our order. I opted for a chicken quesadilla and wondered when I'd ever be interested in another woman. How long is grief supposed to last?

"If I tell you something," I said, "can you keep your pie hole shut?"

"You know me."

"That's why I'm asking."

"Fire away, Charley."

"What do you think of Channing Westerbrook?"

He raised an eyebrow. "The TV reporter?"

"No, the hockey goalie."

"Yada yada. She's pretty hot."

"I mean as a reporter."

Al bobbed his eyebrows. "Does anyone care how good a reporter she is?"

"Come on, man."

"Sure. Why not? I haven't really studied her career. Why?"

"I've been talking to her."

Al leaned forward. "What's up with that?"

"She covered the accident, and then I talked to her about it. She kind of got a jones for the story."

"No way. She going to put you on the air?"

"Nah. Maybe a book. We're sort of using each other."

He thought about that one. "How far does this *use* extend?"

"Nothing like that."

"You could do worse."

"I'm not interested in doing anybody, okay?"

"That'll change."

"Shut it, why don't you?"

"You brought her up."

"You know what Al? Your life does have meaning."

He looked at me. "What is it?"

"To serve as a warning for others."

52

IT WAS ALMOST nine o'clock when I drove home.

The moon was incredibly bright. It was right out in front of me as I drove east on the 101, and I just kept thinking about how I avoided talking about deeper things with Jacqueline. I thought there would be much more time. All our lives. I'm sure after we were married, she would have said something like, *The moon is a sign of something bigger than ourselves.* I would have said, *That's great. Let's make love.*

I pulled off the freeway at Valley View, and the surface was jammed with cars. Great. The freeway had moved smoothly, but now there was a traffic jam in my own neighborhood. Sometimes L.A. was nothing but a floating gridlock game. Usually an accident. Maybe some kid had plowed into a tree or something. In fact, I could see some flashing red lights up ahead.

It would take me about ten minutes to get home from here, so I turned to classic rock. Heard Keith Moon rattling his cage. Great! Listened to Roger Daltry scream. Thought maybe that was the way to get through my days—scream like Daltry once every hour.

The flashing lights were coming from somewhere on Hamlin, my street. A cop was standing in the intersection waving cars away. He was not allowing traffic through.

I rolled down my window. "I live up there."

The cop shook his head. "Not right now. Can't get any cars in there."

"Why not?"

"Fire."

"What?"

"Move on, please."

I pulled to the right, over to the curb, parked, and got out. I ran up the hill.

And saw that it was my house.

In the night and flashes of red, the outside of the house looked like a scarred face. No flames now, but plenty of black licks smearing the cream-colored paint. Bits of smoke still rose from the east end creating hovering dark plumes.

A small crowd of neighbors stood around watching, not even noticing I was there now. A couple of firemen went about their business with calm efficiency, pulling back a long tube from the front door. From the body language the worst was apparently over.

For me it was just beginning.

I walked fast, then ran past the firemen with the tubing.

"Hey!"

"Get outta there!"

Ignoring them I got inside, smelling the wet on burned wood and chemical foam, feeling the dying emanations of heat.

The inside looked like a model of an acid stomach for some antacid commercial. Clots of foam dripping from ceiling and walls. Everything looking like burnt toast.

What I was after was in my bedroom, and I was shaking as I ran for it, slipping once on the tile. Voices behind me were yelling like crazy to get me to turn around. I didn't.

The master bedroom was more of the same. In the past I probably would have been stressing over my now melted Bose system, the plasma TV, the collection of suits. All could be replaced.

But one thing couldn't.

Almost diving into the closet, I skidded on my knees across crispy carpet and saw it in the corner. Smoke damage was obvious on my Armani and Brooks Brothers collection of clothes. But the box had not ignited.

The box with Jacqueline's journals. I took it in my arms just as a fireman entered the room.

"You idiot, get out of there. Come on."

"I'm coming."

"Don't take anything."

"I'm taking this," I said.

"You'll have time—"

"I said I'm taking this. Get out of the way."

53

"YOU'RE GOING TO have to help us," Rebson said. He'd introduced himself as a sheriff's office arson investigator. Dressed in a dark blue coat and tie, I was sitting on the curb, the box between my legs, holding a random journal, then putting it back. Numb to everything else.

"Mr. Buchanan?"

I said nothing.

"I know how you must feel, but if you could just give me a moment."

I shook my head.

"Can you think of anyone who might have a reason to do this?"

I shrugged.

"What kind of stuff are you into?"

"Nothing."

"Mr. Buchanan, that is not true. Somebody torched your house."

"That's obvious."

"So who was it? Who has a reason to do this to an upstanding citizen like yourself?"

"Maybe it was random."

"Maybe O'Reilly's humble."

"What?"

"Not bloody likely, sir. Think about it. Who have you ticked off lately?"

Should I tell him? Part of me wanted to. But most of me knew the sheriff or LAPD would want to drag me further into things. I didn't want to be dragged. Not yet. I wanted this on my terms.

"Not anything that would result in a Molotov cocktail in my house," I said.

"What line of work are you in?"

"I'm a lawyer. I tick off a lot of people."

"What kind of law do you practice?"

"Civil litigation."

"You have anything going on right now that might be a bone of contention with someone?"

"I want to be left alone right now."

"I'm not inclined to do that."

Rebson just stood there like an unwelcome guest, a guy who won't leave even after you've turned off the lights.

I stood up and faced him. "I'm not really interested in what you're inclined to do or not, now—"

A voice from behind me said, "I'll take it from here."

I turned around and almost jumped out of my shirt.

It was the guy who'd picked me up outside Mrs. Salazar's house. The guardian angel who'd held a knife to my face.

54

HE WAS DRESSED in business casual. Rebson, the arson investigator, backed off immediately. He flashed me an annoyed look before walking away.

My mouth was stuck between open and closed.

"How's your car?" the guy said.

My mind, already mashed, was sliding into a bizarre realm. "What is this?"

"Name's Cisneros," he said. He took out a leather case and flashed me a credential. I saw his picture, the name Rubén Cisneros, and United States Secret Service.

I looked back up at him. "I don't believe this."

"Let me buy you a cup of coffee."

"First tell me what's happening."

He put his hand on my shoulder. "Come on. You've had a shock."

I didn't know if he meant my house or my talking to a knife-wielding Secret Service agent.

"What are you doing here?" I said. "Homeland security or something? The president in town?"

"Hang in there," he said.

"Why doesn't anybody tell me anything?"

"Because, Mr. Buchanan, we don't want you to get hurt."

He kept it buttoned for the rest of the ride. Took me to a Denny's on Ventura. We settled in a booth in the back, and he ordered us some coffees. Good. I needed a clear head.

"This isn't about Homeland Security," Cisneros said. "Or the prez. That's what most people think of when they think of the Service. You know, Clint Eastwood running alongside the president's coach. But that's not all we do."

"Yeah, you threaten people with knives, too."

He smiled. "Just needed to get you a message. Sorry I couldn't fill you in at the time."

"Why now?"

"Because you're a target."

"I gathered that. But why?"

"Counterfeiting."

I shook my head.

"That's why the Service started, by the way," he said. "Back in 1865. To protect the integrity of the currency."

"You think I'm passing bogus money or something?"

"No, but you know somebody who is."

"You mind telling me?"

"Rudy Barocas."

"Barocas?"

"That's who you got yourself tangled up with, isn't it?"

"Where you getting your information?"

He sat back a little. "I'm the Secret Service, my man. You don't think we got sources?"

"Okay, since you got sources, why don't you stop asking me questions and just lay it all out? I'm tired and my house just burned down and I want to know why you know all about me."

The unsmiling waitress plopped a couple of coffees in thick white mugs in front of us. She pulled some creamers out of her blue apron and dropped them in the middle of the table, where they scattered. She put down a bill on receipt tape and left without ever showing a tooth. Cisneros slid the bill to his side of the table.

"You deserve to know," he said. "All right. It started with a lap dance a year ago. In Hollywood. A small-time op named Gabriel López got the action from a stripper at a club on Ivar. Two hours worth. Then she sees him reach into his sock and come out with a wad, and he peels off a couple of yards."

"Pretty expensive lap dance."

"She wasn't complaining. Then she goes backstage and smells something funny. Like vinegar. It's the bills. She tells the manager who goes out to ask the guy what's up and they fight. A bouncer the size of Montana steps on López while they call the cops."

"The bills were counterfeit?"

"He had another eleven bennies in his wad. Vinegar laced. That's to keep the dogs off 'em."

"Sniffers?"

"Right. At the border, smelling for contraband. Naturally, that interested us. What we got out of Mr. López was confirmation of something we were already working on, a counterfeiting ring down in Mexico, we think in Guadalajara. They have the same offset printing equipment as our boys in the Bureau of Engraving and Printing. And they're moving the bills up here using the same routes as the drug mules."

"There's drugs involved, too?"

"There's a guy, Carlos Ayarza-Moreno, runs a cartel that controls most of the drugs on the Mexican Pacific coast. He's partnering with the head of the counterfeit ring, a guy named Chapo Guzmán. You with me so far?"

"Hanging in there."

"Now both these guys use the same mules. One month a mule will be transporting drugs to Los Angeles or Miami, the next he's hauling counterfeit notes. Or she is."

"She?"

"Guzmán likes to use women. Less conspicuous. We caught one a few months ago walking pretty as you please across the border at San Ysidro. Let's just say she looked a little too well endowed. Turns out she had $200,000 of fake bills in her bra and underwear."

"I still don't get how this is supposed to relate to me."

"I'm getting there. We figure about eight million in fake Benjamins has come in over the last couple of months alone. So where do all these bills go, you might ask."

"I ask."

"Distribution is through street gangs. Here in L.A. and Orange County, as far north as Spokane and as far south as New Orleans. New Orleans has been hot since Katrina. That's where Barocas comes in."

"He works with Latino gangs."

"Depends what you mean by work. He's got an operation going on that looks good on the surface. We think he does a little special training on the side. But he's got himself in with the powers that be, so to speak. There's a hands-off policy at City Hall. No one wants to tee off the brown vote."

"But you guys don't care about teeing off anybody."

"All I care about is nailing him. He's the big fish. And that, in short, is what you've stumbled into."

"I didn't stumble," I said. "I wanted to find something out."

"Having to do with your fiancée?"

For what seemed like the hundredth time that night, I shook my head. "That's scary."

"We have actual computers, Mr. Buchanan. We're hooked up to the Internet and everything."

"Hilarious."

"Your story wasn't hard to trace. You went to Mrs. Salazar's to find out what you could about Ernesto Bonilla."

"Yeah."

"And what did you find out?"

"Squat."

"I'll unsquat you, if you want." He took a sip of coffee. I noticed what looked like burn marks on the back of his fingers.

I said, "Tell me."

"Bonilla had some tattoos on his neck."

"Let me guess. Three dots? *Mi vida loca?*"

"Impressive. There was another one that interested me. A 666 on the right side of his neck."

"Isn't that some sort of religious thing?"

"In Latino gang culture, it's another way to designate eighteen, for the Eighteenth Street Gang. Located in the Rampart Division of L.A."

Rampart was a name well known to me, as it was to many in Los Angeles. The big LAPD scandal out of that division's gang unit in the nineties made national news and resulted in so-called Rampart Rules that many say hamstrung the police. It wasn't a coincidence that gang activity went up after the rules went into effect. Best laid plans.

"The Eighteenth is into a lot of things, from carjacking to meth, and in the nineties some sections got in with the Mexican Mafia and drug cartels. Bonilla was arrested in that connection three years ago. He plead out to a lesser and got diverted to an honor ranch."

"Run by Rudy Barocas?"

"You got it. You thought maybe you'd go looking into Bonilla, the guy who fell on your fiancée's car, and instead you almost got yourself killed. And a firebombed house. That's why I want you to stay out of this thing. I want you to go somewhere for a while and forget about this. There's nothing more you can do."

I looked over toward the front window, where an Asian man sat alone. He had a cup in front of him but didn't hold it. Then he looked out the window at the night. That was L.A., I thought. You could be alone in a lot of well-lighted places.

"There's something you don't know," I said.

He raised his eyebrows. "Yeah?"

"Jacqueline may have been alive after Bonilla hit her car."

Cisneros held his cup at mouth level, unmoving.

"The guy who hit me at Mrs. Salazar's, I'd seen him before. He came to Jacqueline's funeral. He came up to me after and told me he'd seen a guy go down to the accident, and this guy found Jacqueline alive. And then killed her."

For a long time Cisneros said nothing. The Asian man was still looking out the window. The city seemed to be stopped on its crazy axis.

"That's very interesting," he said.

"Tell me why."

He looked down at the table. "I have to think about that."

"Think about *what*?"

"What I can say."

I put both my hands, palms down, on the table. "Why don't you just tell me? It's really simple. I'm sitting right here."

"I can't."

"Yeah you can. You just won't."

"All right then, I won't."

"Sure. You're just another company man."

"Look—"

I stood up.

"Where you going?" he said.

"I'll walk back."

"Buchanan, don't do anything stupid."

"My whole life is based on stupid now. I'm on a roll."

He grabbed my wrist and put a card in my hand. "Listen to me. Anything else happens I want you to call that number and ask for Phil."

"Phil?"

"That's it. Phil. You'll be directed from there."

I put the card in my back pocket. "Thanks for the coffee." I walked past the man who was still watching the world. When I got outside and walked past the window, I saw his face. It was a blank, as if he was waiting for something, anything, to happen.

This town pulsates with two kinds of desperation. There's the lust for the juice, the buzz, the thing —most of the time unknown and unnamed —that will keep you from looking in at the inner abyss.

Then there are those who have given up the fight, and the other kind of people who swirl around them like a human dust storm. These people sit, watch, not caring, not hoping for a jolt anymore because for some reason they don't believe it exists.

The question I had, and couldn't answer, was which kind was I?

I walked back to what remained of my house. People were still milling around—fire and sheriff's deputies, a cop, some neighbors. I spoke to no one, just got in my car, where I'd left the box with Jacqueline's things, and drove away. I called Al and asked if I could have the sofa for the night.

He seemed real happy about that. I could hear his wife yelling at him in the background.

55

AL'S HOUSE WAS still dark when I woke up.

I was on his sofa, under a blanket that Adrienne had reluctantly given me. Clearly, she was not a Benedictine.

But neither Adrienne nor Al was on my mind at the moment. I kept thinking about Cisneros and what he'd said.

Barocas. Counterfeiting. Bonilla.

Why would Bonilla shoot his wife and then himself? Maybe it had something to do with Triunfo. Maybe some kind of net was closing in around him and his wife. Or his wife had something to say and he didn't want her to say it.

Or maybe he was just a nut loaf.

But somebody had followed him. Somebody who wanted to make sure he was dead.

Somebody from Triunfo maybe? Watching him. Because Bonilla and his wife weren't being good little tchotchkes, dangling from Barocas's chain.

And the guy following slid down the hill and saw Jacqueline alive. Saw her staring at him. Maybe pleading for help with her eyes. Eyes that could identify him. He snapped her neck.

I sat up, sweating, tight breath.

Al and I breakfasted on Brown Sugar Cinnamon Pop-Tarts and coffee. Nothing better for you at seven A.M.

"Man, I am so bummed about your house," Al said. "You got insurance?"

"Of course," I said.

"Where you going to stay?"

"I'll stay with Fran, Jacqueline's mom. She's alone in this little house in Reseda."

"What started it?"

"I have no idea."

"Arson?"

"Wouldn't surprise me."

"Why not?"

My cell went off. I looked at the screen. Channing Westerbrook was up early.

"You didn't get back to me," she said.

"Sorry."

"When can we meet?"

"How about I call you next week?"

"I won't be put off, Ty." Her voice was a mix of play and threat. For some reason I thought of that line Glenn Close says in *Fatal Attraction*: "I will not be ignored!" Wonderful.

"Hey, look, I've got—"

"No, Ty. We have a deal and things are happening."

"Yeah, you don't have to tell me about things happening. Let's make it next week."

"When?"

"I don't know, I'll check—"

"Tuesday?"

She wasn't going to go away. "Wednesday," I said. "After work."

"I'll give you an address. You have something to write with?"

I grabbed a pad and pencil from an end table and wrote down the address she gave me.

"Eight o'clock," she said and clicked off.

"Trouble?" Al said.

"Westerbrook."

Al pointed at me, like a preacher making a point. "Babes, my friend. Can't live with 'em, can't kill 'em."

"You know what the word 'misogyny' means?"

"It's a Swedish thing, right? Deep tissue?"

"No, it's Greek. *Mis* meaning *you* and *gyny* meaning *jerk*."

"I didn't know you knew Greek."

"Lend me some clothes, will you?"

"Will they fit?"

"You mean because you're a pathetic physical specimen? Close enough."

I ate the last of my Pop-Tart and washed it down with coffee. "And cover for me with McDonough. Tell him I'm—"

"That your house burned down."

"No, I'll break that news to him myself."

56

BUT NOT RIGHT away.

I took the box and drove over to Fran's. She wasn't home, so I got the key out of the snail statuette she kept in the garden and let myself in. Then I called her at work. She was an assistant in the library at Cal State Northridge.

She said she'd love to have me stay with her for a while. She actually sounded happy about it.

When I hung up I went into Jacqueline's old room. Just smelling it.

In my mind, I thought I heard a voice telling me to open Jacqueline's journal.

Then thought, just my imagination. . . .

I took the journal to the big front window and sat on the window bench with it. I opened up to the first page, and heard Jacqueline again at age sixteen.

> Mr. St. John was out of control in class today. He kept talking about how there was no soul in animals or humans. We were all part of the same basic group. Different limbs on the same tree.

Of course there's a soul! You can feel it when you listen to music (except Grunge, of course).

And besides, Mr. St. John, if there is no soul life is meaningless.

Sarah and Paige brought over an old Woody Allen movie, *Annie Hall*, last Friday. They didn't like it, but I thought it was hilarious. I loved the part where the little Woody Allen character is sitting in the doctor's office with his mother and she says to the doctor he isn't doing his homework!

The doctor asks him why, and the little Woody says the universe is expanding. Someday it will blow up. So what's the point?

The doctor says that won't happen for billions of years! So let's just enjoy ourselves while we can!

That doctor could have been Mr. St. John!

A soul. Jacqueline did believe in it. We'd had one long talk about souls once. She had some sort of intuition about these matters that I didn't.

"Just give it time," she'd say. "You'll see it, too."

I closed the journal, still hearing her voice.

57

TRAFFIC TO WESTWOOD was a snarl the next morning, Friday. The Sepulveda Pass was a parking lot. KNX News said some guy had been changing a tire on the shoulder near the Skirball Center and got rammed by a pickup. That was death to the guy and death to the commuter traffic.

So I breathed steadily and tried to figure out how I was going to get through this day.

On the one hand, I had my head on the chopping block at the firm. If I didn't keep up on the Blumberg litigation, I was gone.

As far as my house, there'd be all sorts of little plates I'd have to spin, from insurance, to the arson guys, to wondering who did that to me and why.

I put in a full morning's work in one of Al's suits. At lunch I hit my favorite men's store and put a couple grand on my American Express.

I even managed some office time on Saturday and Sunday. Monday was Martin Luther King's birthday, the post office was closed, and there was an unspoken understanding at the firm that it could be a light day. So I gave myself permission to go to the beach. Alone, with a couple of Coronas and a Subway. But it was cloudy again and cold, so I ended up eating my lunch in the parking lot at Zuma, rain spattering my car.

By Tuesday I was starting to feel like maybe I could get back into the professional swing of things, even with all the hell of the last few weeks. I was feeling strong about it, too. This would show McDonough, show them all.

Yeah, right. All they were about to find out was how far a guy can fall.

58

LATE TUESDAY AFTERNOON I decided to get a closer look at our client in action. If Lea Edwards ever had to testify as a respondent, it would be a much different dynamic for her than easy interviews in my office. So I arranged to sit in on a seminar she was conducting for a group of criminal defense attorneys. If you can keep your cool in shark-filled waters, maybe you'll do okay on the stand.

It was in a ballroom at the Biltmore Hotel downtown. This was one of L.A.'s classic hotels, located across from Pershing Square. It's the place where they used to hold the Oscars back when it was a big banquet. I sat in the back so Lea wouldn't see me. Didn't want her performing for her legal counsel.

As if it would have made any difference. She filled the room like a diva. She was dressed to kill in a sleek, form-fitting black suit, like something Katharine Hepburn might have worn. She walked back and forth on the stage and spoke without notes. Her voice was head miked so she was free to gesture with her hands. And gesture she did.

"The line of attack on any eyewitness starts before you get to the memory," she said. "You start with the character because everything we think is funneled through the interior of our deepest beliefs. Our core. That's what interprets all stimuli, instantly, before it settles in to become what we recall."

The criminal defense lawyers were taking notes. They were an eclectic bunch—young, old, hairy, bald, a couple of gray ponytails, and lots of T-shirts and jeans.

"Let me give you an example. Do you think if George Bush witnessed a man shooting a gun, the picture would lodge in his brain the same way it would if Hillary Clinton saw it?"

The crowd twittered.

"I mean, you have a pro-gun, ol' boy Texan and a cultured, intellectual New Yorker. Do you think they'd process the stimuli the same way?"

Loaded question, I thought, amusing myself.

But someone was not amused. A conservatively dressed guy in the front row, the only one wearing a tie in the whole room, stood up and shouted, "You are so full of yourself!"

Lea stopped short and spun to face the man. Audience heads turned.

"Why don't you tell them about the lawsuit?" The man waved his hands. "Why don't you tell them you're being sued for being a fraud?"

Then voices rose: "Shut up! Sit down! Get him out of here."

"Tell 'em about all the guilty people who are walking the streets right now because of you!"

"Sir—" Lea started to say.

"Does the name Will Stockdale mean anything to you? Does it?"

One very large attorney, who looked like an ex-biker, stood up in the second row and started for the man in the suit.

"Tell them!"

The man saw the big attorney and immediately made for the side door. Just before he went out he flipped off the entire room.

A stunned silence clamped down on the room.

"Well," Lea Edwards said. "What do you expect from a deputy D.A.?"

The place erupted in laughter.

"Now, where was I? Oh yes, the filter of our core values. There is something I'd like you to do. Write down what our friend was wearing. Describe his face, hair, clothing. And write down exactly what he said. I'll give you a couple of minutes. And no talking to each other. This is a test!"

After a few minutes of eager scribbling, Lea called everyone back to order. "And allow me to introduce to you a friend of mine, Bart Holland."

The side door opened and Lea's accuser came back in, smiling. He joined Lea on the stage.

"Don't throw anything," Lea said. "Bart is an actor. In fact, he's in a play right now at Theater East you should all go to see. But I want you to look at him. How many of you described his tie as something other than blue?"

Several hands went sheepishly up.

"How many of you got the hair right?"

Several hands.

"So the rest of you got it wrong. How about the coat? Who got that?"

Hands.

"Bart, read your lines again."

Bart repeated his diatribe. Then Lea said, "How many of you got every word substantially correct?"

Only a small number raised their hands.

"How many of you correctly got the name Will Stockdale?"

Only three hands this time.

"How many of you three know that Will Stockdale is the name of the character in the movie *No Time for Sergeants*?"

The hands went down.

"Finally, how many of you think that my crack about Bart here being a deputy D.A. may have put you in a contentious mindset? Don't bother raising your hands. I know it's most of you. So remember. Know the eyewitness inside and out. Especially inside. Get the dope on the person's life from the cradle. It will lead you through the haze of their memory and show you where you can attack."

59

LEA MET ME in the Biltmore's oak-paneled Gallery Bar. With the golden chandeliers and fancy carved wood ceilings, it had an elegant 1920s feel. Like that bar where Jack Nicholson decides to kill his family in *The Shining*. We took a table near the back, next to a framed picture of the Biltmore from 1930. The Biltmore must have been something in her prime. Like Lea, who ordered a manhattan, was now. I had a Pellegrino.

"Do you know the name Elizabeth Short?" Lea asked.

"Sure. The Black Dahlia. I saw the movie."

"They say this is the place she had her last drink the night she was murdered."

"Imagine that. And here we are."

"You believe in omens?"

"No."

"Good. Neither do I. Not rational." She smiled.

"I thought I could use a brush-up on eyewitness testimony," I said.

"What did you think of my little demonstration?"

"It was good. I couldn't have picked up all the stuff on the guy."

"And that's the point, isn't it?"

A waitress in black served our drinks. Lea lifted her glass. It had a cherry in the amber liquid. She said, "To victory."

I clinked my glass on hers and we drank.

"And it will be victory, won't it?" she said.

"I'm going to do everything I can."

"I'm glad."

"Can I ask you a couple of questions?"

"Personal or business?"

"Business of course."

"It can be personal too, if you want. I'm in your hands."

"Mackee was involved in a case before Claudia Blumberg. A guy named David Townsend who accused a priest of molesting him when he was a kid. Do you remember that case?"

"What was the name again?"

"David Townsend."

She took a contemplative sip of her drink. "And he was Kendra's client?"

"According to the priest."

"You talked to a priest?"

"He contacted me, actually. He wanted me to know about this, thought it might be relevant."

"And is it?"

"It might be, depending. How about the name Lorimar?"

"Isn't that a film company or something?"

"It was a name the priest says Townsend used. I thought it might be another doctor or something, that maybe you knew this person."

She shook her head.

"If anything occurs to you, call me. It might be good to have you interview Townsend."

"That might be sticky. What Mackee does is a form of brainwashing. Her clients become extremely loyal, like little vampires are to Dracula."

"Now that's an image we can use in closing argument."

Lea laughed. Her red lips parted like flower petals opening to the sun. I could understand why some very powerful men had orbited around her.

A threesome of suited men at a nearby table broke out into too loud laughter, the sort that indicates a dirty joke filtered through vodka and Red Bull. One slapped his knee repeatedly. He snorted like a pig, sending his friends into another laughing jag.

I felt Lea's hand on mine. I turned around.

She said, "You realize, of course, that we're going to have an affair."

60

ON THE OLD *Honeymooners* show with Jackie Gleason, that ancient black-and-white series you can get on DVD, Gleason portrays Ralph Cramden, a bumbling, blowhard bus driver always trying to get ahead. And never does.

Sometimes he gets into an embarrassing situation. When he does, his eyes bug out and he tries to speak, but the only sound that comes out is *Habba habba habba habba . . .*

That's the sound I almost made when Lea Edwards dropped that little item across the table.

Lea kept her hand right where it was. "Didn't expect to hear that, did you?"

Habba. "Um, no."

She squeezed my hand, then removed it. "Have you ever read *Atlas Shrugged*?"

"Ayn Rand."

"Have you?"

"Never got around to *Atlas Shrugged*. Thought I'd read the Los Angeles telephone book instead. Shorter."

"It's an intellectual masterpiece. I don't know how much you know about Rand, but you ought to look into it. She was the most dazzling mind of the twentieth century. And she had this theory about love being an exchange of values, not chemistry. Love makes sense only when it's rational. And that's why you and I will end up together when the time is right."

I took a long sip of Pellegrino. The bubbles kicked the back of my throat.

"I know the time is not now," she said. "You've been through a personal tragedy. But that doesn't mean life stops for you. If we allow tragedies to stop us, then we're doomed. And I, for one, am not ready to be doomed."

She finished her manhattan. "What I want is another drink and some talk about things other than this stupid lawsuit and then we'll part until the next time."

61

WEDNESDAY NIGHT AT eight I showed up at the address Channing had given me. It was one of those nice high-rise apartment buildings on La Cienega. It was, in fact, Channing Westerbrook's apartment building. There was a fancy security guard, blue coat and gold shield and everything, sitting at a console in the very formal lobby.

I gave my name, and he picked up a phone, announcing me. He asked me to wait. I sat in a chair next to a large fern.

A few minutes later Channing, dressed in a pure white coat and black pants, greeted me. She looked like she was going out, even had a gold chain with a pearl pendant. Her hair was back and pretty, and she wore a perfume that was very nice.

In another life, I would have gone for her at the drop of a name.

"Thanks for coming all this way." She shook my hand.

"It didn't seem like I had a choice."

"Oh, let's not be all tangled about it. You're here. Come on up and let's get down to business."

The security guard looked at me like he had some idea of what the business was.

62

CHANNING'S PLACE HAD a wide open living room you had to walk down a step to get to. The room was a perfect square with a thick white carpet and cream-colored furniture with dark wood trim. A coffee table with a glass top framed by polished wood had, not surprisingly, a coffee table book on it. It said *New York,* and I figured it was the book that went with the Ric Burns documentary.

The recessed lighting gave the room a pleasant illumination. From speakers I couldn't see, cool jazz was being piped in. On the walls were some prints or paintings—I couldn't tell which—of some current art school or other. They didn't seem to represent reality. There was a surrealism about them. I'm no art critic, but these were probably worth having because everything else in the apartment seemed perfect.

"A little intimate, isn't it?" I said.

"Thought you should see how the other half lives."

"Other half?"

"TV reporters. We make up half the world now."

"I figured you live pretty nice."

"And what do you think? Fit the image?"

"Perfect."

"May I pour us some wine?" Channing said. "There's a little winery in Los Olivos that I love, and their cab is out of this world."

"Is this a business or social call?" I said.

"It's a little bit of both. Why can't two people who are working together enjoy some wine and good conversation along with everything else?"

"Sold," I said.

While she uncorked the bottle, I thumbed through the book on New York. It looked crowded. A bunched up group of gawkers on top of the Empire State Building put me in mind of Gershwin.

She came back and sat next to me on the sofa, handing me a glass while clinging to her own.

I took a sip. "Hmmm . . . conversational without being verbose."

She laughed. "So you're a wine critic."

I held the glass up to the lights in the ceiling. "Playful, without overstaying its welcome."

"Keep going."

I looked at her. "Ambitious, with the hint of ongoing mystery."

She sat back, propping her head on one hand. "You've got my number, eh?"

"You've got mine and you keep calling it. Why is it you wanted to see me?"

"I don't want the story to get away from us. I need to find out what's going on in your life. How you're dealing with the day-to-day."

My day-to-day was not a subject I was anxious to revisit. "I get up each day, and I see what I have to do, and I go do it."

"Come on," she said, pointing to her chest. "In here."

For a second I considered telling her about my house. That would certainly qualify as a little item for her book. But instead I said, "What about me? What have you got for me?"

She smiled coyly. "You might be surprised."

"Surprise me now."

"Whoa."

"I want to know what you know about Barocas and Triunfo."

She ran her index finger around the rim of the wineglass. "I do have other things I'm working on."

"But you know something."

"Wanna trade?"

"Yes. You start."

Crossing her legs and leaning back, relaxed, Channing Westerbrook looked like someone in complete control of her life and circumstances and of all who orbited around her, like me. "I know it's been looked at by some law enforcement agencies, because anytime you're a success like that you're going to get some scrutiny. But they're clean. Nothing's stuck. Barocas is one of these Teflon guys. But he has help."

"What kind of help?"

"Downtown help. You know about Leland Rich?"

"Just that he's a county supervisor and gave Barocas's book a blurb."

"Well, Rich is really investing a lot in Barocas for political reasons and kind of protects him. Everybody knows Rich wants to be mayor, and for that he needs the Latinos. But he's about as non-Latino-looking as you can get. You ever hear him try to speak Spanish?"

I shook my head.

"Hilarious. He made a speech in East L.A. once and tried to say something nice in Spanish, but it translated as "I love the bodies of your people." So he's not going to make that mistake again, and Barocas is one of his tickets to the mayor's office."

"Has anybody ever accused Barocas of being in league with drug dealers or running things from Mexico?"

"No doubt. He works with gangs, and there's some speculation about that. But he's had a lot of success turning gang kids around."

"What about—"

"Hey," she said, putting up a hand. "My turn."

"Just one more—"

"Trade, remember? I want you to tell me what's going on inside you."

I shook my head. "I don't know. I'm not Dr. Phil. What am I supposed to say?"

She took a lingering sip of wine as her eyes hovered over the glass, looking at me.

"Tell me a little about her," she said. "About Jacqueline."

That was a subject I did not want to revisit with anyone. It was a private section and I had a No Entry sign on it. "Is that really relevant?"

"Oh stop sounding like a lawyer. I want to know about the person. Would it help if I asked you questions?"

"No."

"Okay. When did you first meet?"

"Channing—"

"Love at first sight?"

"Maybe." I figured I could use terse answers like a good witness on cross, never offering more than the question demands. She'd get the message sooner or later.

"You met her where?"

"Mexican restaurant."

"And?"

"That's where we met."

She pursed her lips and looked away, and I felt bad about that. She had gone out of her way for me. I'd been the one who tracked her down in the first place.

"All right," I said. "We met that night and I was attracted to her, but really fell for her when I got to know her. She just had this inner life that pulled me in."

"Soul mate?"

"If you believe that sort of thing, then yeah."

She took another sip of wine. I had barely touched mine. She got up and went to the kitchen, came back with the bottle. Without asking she poured a little more for me and for her.

"Thank you," she said.

"For what?"

"For being vulnerable."

I shrugged.

"What was one thing about her you really loved?"

"Just one?"

"Mm."

"Her honesty. She didn't have a hypocritical bone in her body."

Channing nodded. "That's nice. What about you? What was something about you she loved?"

A faint, twisting pain was starting to grow in me. "I don't know."

"Just one."

"She liked my drumming."

"What's that?"

"I used to drum. She really liked it when I did that."

"Now that," Channing said, "is the sort of detail that will make this book come alive. Like the *pro bono* work you did for those illegals last year."

"How do you know about that?"

"Hello! Reporter! So why'd you take that up? What was it? Ten people in a one-room apartment?"

"Nine."

"Against a slum lord. Now you didn't have to do that. Why—"

"Maybe that's enough for now."

"Ty—"

"Listen."

The music was Larry Carlton. We drank some wine and listened to the music.

"Would you show me sometime?" Channing said.

"Show you?"

"Drumming. I'd like to hear you."

"I don't really do it anymore."

She leaned a little toward me. "You'll want to again. I know it."

Physiology marches to its own drummer, and right then mine started playing *Wipe Out*. Had this been any other night and any life of mine where Jacqueline Dwyer had not existed, I would have been all over Channing Westerbrook. And I knew she wanted it that way.

Which made me put the wine down and stand up and walk to the window. Because if I didn't, I thought I might do something stupid like cry or curse or throw the wineglass across the room.

It was a nice view at least. Any view of L.A. at night, if you're up high enough, has romance about it. Flickering lights are inviting when you look down on them, less so when you're on the street looking up. It was nice to be up high.

Next thing I knew Channing had her lips on mine.

63

WITH NO TIME to think I let the kiss happen, let her deepen it. It was as surreal as the paintings on a wall. This wasn't really happening.

Her arms were around my neck as she leaned her head back and smiled at me. "Nice," she said.

I gently took her wrists and pulled her arms down. "Channing, I don't want you to think—"

"I don't want to think. Neither do you."

"That's just it. I am thinking. About a lot of things, and I'm just not ready for this."

"I can make you ready."

She closed in on me again, fast. She practically threw her mouth on mine, and I smelled the cabernet on her breath and thought she might be a little drunk. And then she had her right hand clutching the back of my neck and pulled me to her.

I jerked back and her nails scratched me, hard.

"Don't," I said.

"A man's not supposed to say that."

"Come on, Channing."

"Is something wrong with you?"

"I just lost my fiancée. You're supposed to be writing about that. I don't need this right now."

"You still feel things. So do I."

I walked away from her and the window.

"Why don't we just forget that happened," I said. "In fact, why don't we forget the whole arrangement. I don't think it's working out the way we planned."

That's when she cursed at me.

"Hey," I said. "A little overreaction."

"Shut up. Just shut up." She turned her back.

"Channing—"

"Just get out, why don't you?"

One thing I never wanted, even in my days when one night was all I cared for, was a woman mad at me. Ty Buchanan, everybody's friend, the charmer.

I went to Channing and put my right hand on her shoulder. She didn't turn around.

"Can we give this a rain check?" I said. "Can you understand, in your journalistic capacity, that my head is screwed up at the moment?"

I kept my hand on her shoulder. Finally she turned around and said, "Sorry. Sorry."

"Me, too. Let me call you in a few days. Let me settle down."

Channing looked at the floor, and I thought that nine hundred ninety-nine guys out of a thousand would have been really glad to be here right now.

Maybe, given enough time, I would be, too.

64

THE SECURITY GUARD gave me the same look he'd shot me when I went upstairs. I wanted to rearrange that look for him and send him back to security guard school where all they teach you is to say, "Where you going? Go ahead."

On the street, the night was cool and wet. A fog had rolled in from the Pacific and made the streetlights fuzzy. I'd parked on the street about a block from Channing's building.

I'd only gone halfway when a voice behind me said, "Mr. Buchanan?"

I turned around to a guy about my height in a white, very expensive looking coat and open-necked red shirt. His hair was clipped close to the skull, and he sported a manicured moustache. Thirty-ish, he seemed like he could lift the back end of a car.

"You know me?" I said.

"There is a man who would like to meet you."

His eyes were black as night, his expression even. In the dim light, though, I could see a pronounced teardrop tattoo under his left eye. I said, "You follow me here?"

"It's important to us."

"Who is *us*?"

"If you'll give us a moment?" He put his hand out like a butler showing someone into the library.

"I'm not going anywhere with you," I said. A small finger of ice traced my spine.

"Mr. Barocas doesn't do this for everybody," the guy said. "You should consider yourself blessed."

"Barocas?"

"He's right over there." He pointed across the street at a Hummer limo, a thing that looked like an office building tilted on its side and fitted with wheels.

I stood there wondering all sorts of things, from how a Hummer limo could have followed me without me knowing it to visions of my demise.

As I contemplated turning and running as fast as I could toward Hollywood, the guy said, "There's been a misunderstanding somewhere. That's all. Mr. Barocas would like to clear it up."

Imagining an automatic weapon or knife or flamethrower under the guy's coat, and figuring if they could trace me here they could trace me anywhere, I thought what the heck.

"Lead the way, Chalmers," I said.

He didn't smile.

65

THE INSIDE OF the Hummer limo was a prom queen's dream on steroids.

I got let in through a rear door. The floor running down the middle was made up of lighted squares under Plexiglas. Running along the sides near the ceiling were speakers and subwoofers and who knew what else, a sound system that could have served one of those cliffside mansions in Malibu.

Below that, also running the length of the limo, were separate bar areas, maybe five on each side. These were subtly changing colors, giving the whole interior a party atmosphere. The ceiling itself was mirrored with a starlight effect. I couldn't believe this was a vehicle. It had to be a club. The only thing missing was a velvet rope.

All the way at the other end, which seemed a football field away, were two large flat-screen TVs, one on each side. A cartoon was playing on both screens.

The sound for the cartoons was jacked up, piping over the speakers. I heard the unmistakable voice of Homer J. Simpson.

"Come on down!" someone yelled from near the TVs, someone I couldn't see. The guy behind me said, "Just go on down."

I went, wondering if there was tram service from back to front.

As I got nearer, I still couldn't see anyone. Despite the flickering lights, it was fairly dark inside.

Then a face appeared as if out of nowhere. It had turned toward me.

"Have a seat, Ty," the face said. "I'm Rudy."

66

THE MOMENT I was seated next to him it was like I'd stumbled into a power grid.

Some people walk into a crowded room and suck up all the energy. I've met billionaires and U.S. senators and Mel Gibson, and all of them had this aura.

So did Barocas.

He was dressed in black, so his brown face seemed disembodied, floating around on its own. The perfect features of the man I'd seen on the cover of the book in Hollywood were even more pronounced in person.

"You seen this one?" he said, looking up at one of the TVs.

"I couldn't say," I said. "I wasn't much into *The Simpsons*."

"Oh, man, how can you not be? This is the one where Mr. Burns gets all the famous baseball players to play for his softball team. You got Jose Canseco, Darryl Strawberry, Griffey Jr., Mattingly. Is that too funny or what?"

"Hilarious." My heart was really pumping now. I had no idea how much Barocas knew about me or what I was thinking. It was like being in an old film noir where Robert Mitchum gets taken for a face to face with Mr. Big, played by Kirk Douglas or some other menacing dude. Only this was full-color L.A. and anything can happen here.

"No, I mean it," Barocas continued, like we were old friends. "You know, this show was making me laugh when there was nothing in my life to laugh about. You know who my favorite character is?"

"Not really."

"It's Mr. Burns! You know, that old guy, loves his power and his money and doesn't make any bones about it. He's no hypocrite. And that means a lot to me, not being a hypocrite. Does that mean a lot to you?"

"Can I ask why you went to all this trouble to follow me?"

"Wait, wait." Barocas was still looking at the screen. Mr. Burns was giving some sort of mixture from a bottle to one of his players. The player said, "It's like there's a party in my mouth and everyone's invited."

Barocas slapped his thighs and laughed. "I love that line! That's Ken Griffey Jr. up there. Funny thing is, this was before the juice scandal in the majors. Today if they made this episode, that would be Barry Bonds."

He lifted a remote and pressed a button, and the picture froze on the face of Mr. Burns.

"See, I came from about as low as you can get," Barocas said. "And what I have now I enjoy very much."

"You and I are from the same place," I said.

"True?"

"Miami."

"Get outta here. Isn't that something? It's a small world."

"Or a big limo."

Barocas rocked forward and laughed. "You are a funny guy. And I bet you are a very good lawyer."

"I do my best."

"And that is the key to success, my friend. Drink?"

"No thanks. I'd like to get going if you don't—"

"Hang on, hang on. You know I talk about this all the time to people. I have a system I try to teach the young guys, the bangers, but it all comes down to that one thing. The best is all you can do, but the secret is you got to do it, day after day. When you do, great things can happen. This is still the greatest country on earth."

"Where anybody can follow anybody."

He looked at me for a long time. Not with menace, but almost like he was trying to read my mind and put the information into his head for future reference.

"When you work hard and reach the top," he said, "it's kind of like climbing a mountain. You don't ever want to come down. Or get knocked down."

I didn't say anything.

"See, I help a lot of people. A lot of people depend on me. I have over three hundred good folks on the payroll. I got a camp that's full of young guys who'd be committing crimes right now if it weren't for me. That's something to respect and protect."

I stayed silent. If you can get a hostile witness to run off at the mouth, he'll sometimes say something to hang himself.

"And when you're standing at the top you've got people down below, throwing rocks. Sometimes worse. You ever been contacted by the Feds about me?"

The question had come out of left field, and I knew that everything he'd been saying to this point was a setup. Sometimes a lawyer will ask a series of questions on cross just so he can throw the witness a sucker punch and get him all flustered. Barocas had done this brilliantly.

In that brief second between his asking and my answering, I managed to stay cool. "No, why should they?"

"'Cause they want to kill me, that's why. They got guys want to bring me down because I'm a spic who's got too much power, man. I had a couple guys from the ranch get into trouble last year, and they want to pin it on me. I ask you if that's right, Mr. Buchanan. Can you tell me? A guy tries to do good and they throw it in his face?"

"Sure," I said calmly. "That's the way of the world."

"You got it. So nobody's come to you?"

"No."

"But you've come to somebody."

"Excuse me?"

"This reporter."

Even in the dim light I could see his eyes boring holes in me, and I knew he wanted me to wilt under the heat. It was a test.

"I had a drink with her," I said.

"That all?"

"Yeah."

"You got a thing goin' on with her?"

"Maybe."

"You could do a lot worse. Wait, didn't you just lose your fiancée?"

"You know about that?"

"Somebody showed me something, from the news or something. Some real freak accident, right?"

"Yeah. Freak."

"Accidents. What're you gonna do? Can't resign from life, can you? Well, I guess you can."

He paused and pressed a button and bright lights filled the limo. I squinted.

"You know, I got to control the spin," Barocas said. "News guys want to bury me, too. Hey, you'd think I was paranoid or something. But if everybody's out to get you, hey."

"Nice meeting you." I turned toward the back and saw the other guy sitting there like a jailer.

"What's wrong? Hey, you're bleeding, man. What went on up there?"

My neck. I put my hand back there and felt the stickiness.

"Rough sex?" Barocas smiled and the light bounced off his white teeth.

"Can I go now?"

"Sure, I just wanted to say hello and lay things out for you. Make sure that when you talk about me, you're informed, you know? I always like people to be informed."

"Appreciate it."

"I hope so. And one more thing."

I waited.

"If you reach for the stars, you may not quite get one. But you won't get a handful of mud either."

He winked at me. I nodded and made my way back down the dance floor where the jailer had opened the cell door. He gave me a look that was part warning, part amusement, and all attitude.

67

THURSDAY MORNING MCDONOUGH looked like the father who, after warning his kid not to smoke, calls the kid in and shows him the Marlboros he found under the bed.

"What on earth is happening?" he asked even before my rear made contact with the seat.

"Yeah, I know."

"You're some sort of lightning rod, only it's trouble you're attracting."

"It must seem that way."

"Seem? Somebody tries to burn down your house? Why is that happening?"

I sucked in some air and tried to anticipate what he'd want to hear, what would save my job.

"I really don't know," I said. "But there's arson investigators on this. I know Frank Trudeau got all Tourettes on me."

McDonough picked up a gold letter opener from his desk. He stuck the point into the pad of his left index finger and turned the letter opener back and forth. "He's not the only one."

I waited. He obviously had something more to say. He turned the letter opener a few more times. "You attacked a man in a bar," he said.

My mouth dropped open. "How did . . . What did you hear?"

"I got a call from Kendra Mackee's lawyer, Don Bascombe. He said you blustered into her office, for one thing, and then you tracked down one of her clients and threatened him."

"Mr. McDonough, that is a load of—"

"Are you denying it?"

"Every bit of it."

"You didn't track this guy to a bar in North Hollywood?"

"All right, that much is true. And I did go to see Mackee. But it's not like what some lawyer says."

McDonough raised his eyebrows. "I know Don Bascombe pretty well. He doesn't just shoot his mouth off."

"Sir, this is what happened. Mackee had this high-profile case with a guy named David Townsend a few years ago. Involved a priest and charges of molestation. I talked to the priest and I followed up on the name, and I found this guy Townsend. I wanted to see what he was about."

"How did you find him?"

"I had some help."

"From?"

I cleared my throat. "Jonathan Blumberg."

"Blumberg! What's *that* all about?"

"I don't know; he has some information networks and—"

"Ty, Blumberg is a loose cannon. If we're not careful, he's going to explode all over our case."

"He just passed me some information, and I—"

"Blumberg is about power, and he loves to throw his around, likes people to believe he worked for the CIA and was a mercenary before that. It all feeds his ego. We have to keep this guy on a very tight leash."

Shifting around on the chair, which suddenly seemed hard as cement, I said, "But his information was correct. I was able to find this Townsend."

"And so what? Attack him?"

"He attacked *me*."

"That's not what this lawyer said. And he said there was a witness who saw you take a shot at the guy."

"Oh please." I tried to contain my building rage. "I think Townsend is a fraud, and he's in on it with Mackee, and if he cracks we can nail this thing."

"Last warning," McDonough said. "You mess up again, it's over for you. And not just on the case, Ty. I won't be able to protect you. And you know what? I won't want to. You got that?"

"How could I not."

"Good. I have to talk to you this way. This is really the end of it."

"Fine."

"And I want you to clear every move you make on the Blumberg litigation with me."

'You want to micromanage me?"

"That's right."

"But how can I work like that?"

"Find a way. We clear?"

I said, "Sure."

"Don't look so hangdog. This is for your own good, Ty. I want to be part of the solution for you. No more messing around. Everything by the book, and I'm the book."

68

SO I DID my best to live by the sacred text of Pierce McDonough.

I spent the rest of the day digging into Lexis/Nexis and gathering everything I could on Dr. Kendra Mackee. Articles and professional journals and profiles and newspaper accounts. If it had her name on it, I downloaded it. There was quite a load.

I found out that Kendra Mackee had been an actress wannabe herself, back in the eighties. Interesting connection to Claudia Blumberg, but I didn't know what significance it had. Still, I jotted a note on my legal pad, *Actress connection.*

According to a background piece in the *L.A. Times* on Mackee, published in 1993, the good doctor knocked around Hollywood for a year doing actor showcases, where actors paid a fee to appear in scenes from plays or movies. Showcases were put on in Equity waiver theaters, small venues with ninety-nine or fewer seats.

The story said Kendra Mackee had done a scene from *Medea*, a play where a mother kills her children to get revenge on their father.

Naturally she became a psychotherapist in L.A.

I also found three articles that mentioned both David Townsend and Kendra Mackee, one in the *Times*, one in the *Daily News*, and one in *L.A. Weekly*. They mentioned Townsend only in passing, and all in connection with the Catholic priest controversy that was then exploding.

There was a time when it seemed every week there'd be a new story about a priest with a string of altar boy molestations in his past. It was, of course, a field day for private practitioners of the psychological arts, who descended into the pool of victims like sharks after chum. Like lawyers chasing class-action lawsuits, these doctors put the word out about their new area of specialization. And the fish swam to them.

Not that there wasn't anything to these charges. But when the waters are stirred sometimes the innocent get consumed. How many lifers have been set free because of DNA typing in the last few years?

By four o'clock or so I had a pad full of notes and an e-file of articles I'd loaded into the firm's database so it was fully indexed and searchable. It was a good, solid day of work. I'd even skipped lunch and downed a Snickers at my desk instead.

At five after, Kim told me I had a strange call, from a guy who wouldn't give his name. He'd only say it was about *a woman* and that I needed to hear it.

I punched it through.

69

"HEY, MAN, I know you." His voice was heavy, accented, and whispery, like he was someplace where he didn't want to be heard.

"Who is this?"

"You listen. I know you. I know about your woman."

I gripped the phone so hard I thought I might snap it. "So?"

"I want to tell you," he said.

"Then tell."

"No, not on the phone. Meet me."

This was pretty blatant head playing, and I wasn't going to go for it. But I still wanted to know who it was. "Forget it. I don't think you know anything. And tell whoever you're working for it's not going to get me out."

There was a slight pause, but I didn't hang up.

"OK, but she's not nice. You got to know."

What was he talking about? More to the point, who was he talking about? In the present tense it wasn't Jacqueline.

"The reporter, man," he added. "She gonna sell you out."

I waited for him to continue, but he didn't.

"So what do you want?" I said. "You're not calling me because you have some interest in my well-being."

"I got some pictures for you. Pictures of your woman. With Barocas, man."

The electricity in my body almost blew my heart up. "I want to see them."

"Five hundred."

"We've met before, haven't we?"

He said nothing.

"You kicked my head."

Another silence. Then: "No, man, not me."

"Not interested," I bluffed.

"I throw in something else for nothing."

"Yeah?"

"Sure. Picture of a guy."

"What guy?"

"Guy who killed your other woman."

In the ten seconds it took for me to answer him, my mind tried to calculate every single risk in the known universe for making this crazy transaction. All I got was a buzzing sound in my ears.

"I want to have a look at them first," I said.

"Okay, that's okay. Tonight."

"All right, you listen. I'm not going to go anywhere where I might get my head kicked again or have some low-level slime try to take me out. We're going to meet in a public place with lots of people around, and I'm going to be armed and if I decide I don't like you I may shoot you in the leg."

"Eh?"

"And if I decide I don't like the pictures, I'm not going to give you anything. If I do decide I want some for whatever reason, I'll give you two hundred dollars."

"No way—"

"Take it or leave it, man."

Pause. "Where?"

I thought it over and pulled out a business card I had in my desk. It was red with gold raised lettering. Mongoose. A club in the little enclave of Los Angeles known as Koreatown.

I gave him the address and told him eight o'clock, and to come alone.

"You come alone too, man," he said.

70

FOR ABOUT TWENTY minutes I sat there trying to calm down. Pictures? If this guy had pictures of Channing with Barocas, I didn't know what I was going to do. It would mean she lied to me, or at least concealed something she should have told me.

Could it be she was spilling her reporter's guts to Barocas? Feeding him information about me? Were they in on something together?

And what about this picture of the guy who supposedly killed Jacqueline? Could that even be possible?

Yes, this all could be another way to set me up, but I had to know, had to let this play out. So it was going to be on my terms. And that included a little insurance.

I went to Al's office. He had his feet propped on his desk and was flipping through *California Lawyer*.

"Hey, dude, what's up?" he said.

I closed his door. "You own a gun, right?"

"What's that?"

"You told me once you owned a gun."

"Yeah. I'm going to kill Adrienne with it."

"I'm not kidding around. I need to borrow it."

Al pulled his feet off the desk, got up, came around, and put his hand on my shoulder. "What have you got going on, man?"

"I can't tell you right now. Can you let me borrow it?"

"No way."

"Please."

"You know what would happen if McDonough found out you were, as they used to say, packing heat?"

"Why should he know?"

"Because if you shoot someone I think he's going to hear about it."

"It's for my protection."

Al shook his head and puffed some air. "Do you even know how to use a pistol?"

"Pull the trigger."

"And shoot your toe off. Do you realize you can't carry without a permit?"

"Of course. So when can I pick it up?"

"Maybe over the weekend, you can come to the range with me and I'll show you—"

"No," I said, "I need it tonight."

"Can I say something, pal?"

"No."

"This is not exactly lawyerly behavior, I got to tell you."

"Will you trust me this one time?" I said. "Will you just trust me that I really, really need this favor?"

Al's usually fun-filled face got serious. "My friend, I am worried about you. Please—"

"Don't be. Just do me this favor."

"You sound like Don Corleone now."

"I don't care who I sound like."

"Have you thought what would happen if you did actually fire my gun into some joker? That maybe I could get in trouble, too?"

"So what's your answer?"

Al rolled his eyes. "I know I'm going to hate myself in the morning."

71

KOREATOWN IS IN the middle of Los Angeles, a couple square miles of city near the mid-Wilshire District. I took Wilshire to Normandie and turned left, heading into the heart of K-Town. I was told once you can tell Korean script from Chinese because it's mostly straight lines—sticks—and O's. And that's what you have here, up and down the corridor.

For some reason they like clubs in this neighborhood, and at night the liquor flows and the people roam and you get a feel that's a little like New York, only without the chip on its shoulder.

Mongoose I knew because I'd been to it a few times before with an associate from O'Melveny named Ted Pak. We met when Ted was at Southwestern Law, which was just a legal brief's throw from the club. Mongoose was half a block off Normandie. I found a spot on the street to park, an omen of good luck.

Or so I thought at the time.

I sat in the car for a moment, looking around to see if anyone was watching me. Didn't look that way. So I slipped my hand under the towel on the passenger seat and took hold of Al's gun.

Al had loaded the thing for me after another attempt to talk me out of it. He explained it was an eight and one, which added up to nine, which was how many rounds it held. Showed me how to cock it with the slide and de-cock it so I wouldn't shoot my toe off.

But if I had to shoot, just pull the trigger all the way back and fire. Just make sure the gun is pointed at the guy you want to shoot, and if you are ever fool enough to do that, Al said, don't get caught because you'll end up in the slam.

Holding the weapon was not like I expected. I expected to be nervous. Maybe I was, a little, but it was more like the anticipation I used to feel before playing a big game in high school. The stands are packed as you run out on the court, the hot steamy feel of the gym, the opposing team shooting layups on the other side of the line and getting ready to do the most damage they can to your team.

We all take a stand on one side of the line or the other, and sometimes the ones on the other side want to put some hurt on you. I wasn't going to wait for that to be done to me anymore. If it came down to it, I would be the one laying on the hurt. It was a weird feeling, but as real as the hip-hop vibration from the club across the street. It was pounding deep inside me now and I could let it out, turn up the volume if I had to, and I wouldn't think twice until the deed was done. Having a gun was a deadlier form of having an elbow ready on the basketball court. Animal instinct would unloose it. But unloose it I would if I had to.

I knew I was a different Ty Buchanan from the one who started law school a decade earlier, when the law was all bound up in books and high-flying rhetoric and the noble pursuit of justice. That was all a naïve lifetime ago.

I watched the Mongoose doorman in my rearview mirror for a while, observing his patdown technique. Open your coat, then down the sides, that was it. I leaned forward and stuck the gun in the back of my pants like I'd seen them do it in the movies.

Then I took a deep breath and got out of the car.

72

THE BAR HAD a retro, Rat Pack vibe. It was a popular place for after-work suits to hang. It also wouldn't be hard for me to spot a Latino messenger, even though the Latino population had grown in K-Town over the last decade. But they had their own clubs farther east.

The crowd tonight was mostly Asian with a good mix of white clubbers.

I took a table where I could keep watch on the front door. Mongoose had a couple of jukes, three plasma TVs on the wall, and a dartboard. Upstairs were several rooms with multiple screens for "serious karaoke," but I have never been able to put *serious* and *karaoke* into a sentence without laughing out loud.

A cocktail waitress in a red silk blouse with a gold mongoose stitched on the front threw a square napkin on my table and asked what I wanted. I ordered a Coke. I wanted a clear head. She smiled with practiced courtesy and went off to get it.

As I waited I looked around and watched a couple of guys darting it out with all the seriousness of bomb defusers. Nobody looked like they were looking for me, but I had this vision of McDonough walking in. He'd see me and come over without a smile and say, *What are you doing here, Ty?* And I'd say *I'm waiting for a guy and I have a gun in my pants. Can I buy you a drink?*

The waitress came back with the Coke. It was eight-thirty-five.

At eight-fifty a cute A-girl stopped at my table and said with a lilt, "You come here often, baby?"

She had short black hair and wore a tight black dress. Her eyes were dark and her lips red and playful. It had been a long time since I'd been picked up. The attempt was sort of nice, reminding me that I was still human.

"Not exactly," I said.

"You don't look it."

"Look what?"

"Like you come here often."

"Good call." I took a sip of Coke.

She didn't move. "Dancing?"

"Not tonight, thanks."

"Drinking?"

"Alone."

"Aw, poor baby."

"Poor baby," I said. "That's me."

"Don't have to be."

I said nothing. She pulled a chair next to me and sat down.

"Really," I said. "Not tonight."

"Don't like what you see?"

Now I started to wonder if she was a pro. "I like it fine," I said. "I'm just waiting for someone."

She winked. "Don't believe you. You look like you could use good company."

"Persistent little minx, aren't you?" Sounding like Bill Murray in *Ghostbusters*.

She slid closer.

"Is this where I buy you a drink?" I said.

"Thank you."

"Please. Don't take this personally, but I'm really meeting someone for business and—"

"Good," she said. "After business, pleasure."

She slipped her hand down my back and stopped when she felt the gun. Her face changed from playful to surprised; then a frown line split her forehead. "Where you at, honey?"

"Told you," I said. "Business."

She stood up quickly and I grabbed her wrist. "Just between us, right?"

"Let go of me."

"Right?"

She slapped me with her other hand. I didn't let go. "What happened to pleasure?" I said.

She tried to slap me again, but I caught it with my left hand. "I mean it," I said. "Just leave now and be quiet about it and everything'll be fine."

She struggled in my grip, and that's when a hand with steel fingers grabbed my shoulder.

I let go of the girl. She cursed and said to the hand, "Get him out."

"Come on," the hand said. I looked up into a wide, cinder-block face with chiseled features. Even his lips seemed to have muscles.

"I'm meeting somebody."

"Not here you're not."

He grabbed a handful of my coat and pulled me up. I knocked his hand away. He showed remarkable restraint in not pushing my face into my brain. But he looked like he'd do it at the next sign of resistance.

"I'm walking out," I said. The girl watched me with the satisfaction of a pro scorned.

Mr. Cinder Block escorted me to the door as a few of the clubbers applauded. I was the evening's best entertainment so far, I guessed. Even better than karaoke.

The bouncer watched to make sure I headed away from the club. I went about twenty yards at a slow clip, then leaned against the wall. Hip-hop was still pounding away, making me want to rip out somebody's lungs and use them to muffle the speakers.

I heard a retching sound and saw a kid on his knees in front of a store with a locked grill. That, I thought, was a perfect metaphor for the night I was having. When the kid was finished he stood up, rocked a little unsteadily in his grunge togs, then saw me looking at him.

"What up?" he said. At least that's what it sounded like, then he walked on down the street looking for more adventures in fine living.

I stood there for another fifteen minutes or so, making sure people walking by could see me and I them. But nobody with any pictures showed up.

Somebody'd just played me, making me dance like a puppet. Maybe he was watching me from a car right now, laughing.

I got back to my car and made a U and got back on Normandie. I drove up to Hollywood Boulevard and hung a left and just drove, thinking, wondering what I could do with Al's gun. Now I was in the mood to shoot something.

Maybe the marquee at the Pantages, or the Kodak. Or maybe the Triunfo place. I turned left on Vine and drove past it. It was locked up for the night, dark. But I had the feeling somebody was inside all the time, looking out, maybe seeing my face right now.

Instead of shooting out the windows I continued down to where Vine turns into Rossmore and intersects Wilshire. I drove west and just kept on going.

A long night drive to clear my head. It didn't work.

73

AL WAS ALL over me the next morning, wanting to know what happened at the "Gunfight at OK Corral."

"A big fat nothing," I said. "But thanks for the loan anyway."

"I'm very disappointed," Al said. We were in my office. A hint of rain outside. That would bring trouble, because people just don't know how to drive in L.A. in the rain. It freaks them out and makes them crazier than they already are.

But who was I to talk about crazy?

"Where'd you stow it?" Al said.

"At Jacqueline's mother's house. You can have it anytime you want."

"Good. Adrienne's right on the edge."

"Quit joking about that, will you?" I put my head back on the chair and looked at the ceiling.

"You going to tell me what's going on now? Why you think you need to play Mel Gibson?"

"It's better you don't know. It's better you help me stay sane and keep my job."

"This sounds like a serious call for a pitcher of maggies—"

"Not tonight," I said.

"Soon then."

"Sure."

Al paused then said, "You sure you're okay?"

"Someday I will tell all."

Kim buzzed and said, in a breathless way over the speaker, that two Los Angeles police detectives wanted to see me.

Al looked at me. "You sure you didn't shoot somebody?"

"What is this about?" I mumbled, getting up and starting for the door.

"Make 'em read you your rights," Al said.

"Shut up."

The two detectives—one about my height, the other shorter by a head—were standing at Kim's cubicle just outside my door. Pierce Patrick McDonough stood with them, his arms folded.

"This is Tyler Buchanan," McDonough said to the detectives.

"I'm Ben Sayer," the tall one said. He had salt-and-pepper hair, a matching moustache, and a serious chest. "This is Mike Bloch. We're with Wilshire Division. Is there somewhere we can talk?"

"Take the conference room," McDonough offered. His eyes offered me something else. A thorough clock cleaning.

Kim brought in three Styrofoam cups of office joe. She looked worried. I told her *Thanks* in a way that tried to give her a comfort I did not enjoy.

When we were all settled in like a Bible study, Detective Sayer asked, "What kind of law you practice, Mr. Buchanan?"

"Civil litigation mostly," I said.

"Ever do any criminal work?"

"No."

"Good. That's not a specialty we particularly warm to."

Detective Bloch, who was younger than Sayer and a little on the Pillsbury Doughboy side, said, "I like the civil guys much better, too. My brother-in-law, he's a defense lawyer out in Riverside, and I don't like him at all. Makes Thanksgiving a little difficult."

I said, "What is it I can help you with?"

"We're investigating a homicide."

"Homicide? What's that have to do with me?"

"Do you know Channing Westerbrook, sir?"

74

I MANAGED TO say, "No way."

"You denying you knew her?" Sayer said.

"No—"

"So you did know her?"

"Well, yeah. Sort of. I can't believe—"

"How well did you know her?"

My mind was shrinking down to a size that could only repeat a loop showing Channing Westerbrook alive. I couldn't get myself to believe she was dead.

"What was the nature of your relationship?" Sayer said.

"It was purely professional," I said. "She did a news story about my fiancée's death, and that's how I met her."

"You weren't romantically involved?"

I thought about her kiss and her eyes. "No."

"When was the last time you saw her?"

"Wednesday."

"What time?"

"Around eight or so."

"Eight at night?"

"Yes."

"Where?"

As I answered I could sense the skepticism starting to build in the cops, and I couldn't blame them. "I went to her apartment."

"For business?"

"Hey, guys, I'm not a suspect in this thing, am I?"

The detectives looked at each other, then back at me, like synchronized swimmers. "We're just here to ask some questions."

Sweat started to bead my armpits. "I didn't kill Channing Westerbrook."

"Nobody's saying you did," said Sayer.

I didn't believe that for a second. This was beyond unbelievable, a nightmare. Somebody murdered Channing. It probably had something to do with me. But these detectives had the wrong idea. How was I going to convince them of that when I'd been up in her apartment only a couple of nights ago?

Detective Sayer said, "Would you mind telling us where you were last night?"

"What time?"

"Say from seven on."

"Well, I had a meeting around eight o'clock. But the guy never showed."

"Who was this meeting with?"

"Is that really relevant?"

" If you'll let us ask our questions and answer them fully, we can wrap this up and let you get back to your business."

"All right, let me try to explain," I said.

"That would be nice."

"Channing Westerbrook and I were working on a book together. What I mean is, she wanted to write a book about me. She wanted to write about how I was dealing with my fiancée's death. A human interest kind of thing, I guess. I said she could do that if she would help me out, too."

"Help you out how?"

"I think somebody might have killed Jacqueline. It was supposed to have been a freak accident, but I got some information, and I followed up on that and some things started happening to me."

"What kind of things?"

"Have you ever heard of Rudy Barocas?"

"Sure, he works with gang kids."

"What if I told you he followed me to Channing's apartment on Wednesday? And he was waiting to talk to me when I came out?"

"Is that what you're telling me?"

"Yes. And I would put him on your list of people to talk to."

Bloch was taking notes and wrote something down. Then his cell went off, and he stood up and walked to the other side of the conference room to take the call.

Sayer said, "So you were in Channing Westerbrook's apartment on Wednesday?"

"Yeah, we were talking about the book."

"At her apartment?"

"She requested it."

"Let's finish up about last night. Where were you having your meeting?"

"At a club."

"Where?"

"Koreatown."

"A little off your track, isn't it?"

"A place I know. Mongoose."

"Anybody see you there?"

"I got tossed out by the bouncer."

Sayer frowned. "What time was that?"

"I don't know, maybe around nine."

"Can you account for your time after that?"

"I went driving."

"Where?"

"Nowhere in particular. I was mad. I was—" I looked at both of them. "Set up."

Sayer said, "What's that mean?"

"I got a call from a guy, said he had pictures of Channing with Rudy Barocas and so I wanted to see them. She didn't tell me she was meeting with him."

"Should she have?"

"We were supposed to be working together, and she wasn't telling me something."

"Allegedly."

"Yeah, allegedly."

"So you might have been a little angry with Ms. Westerbrook, is that safe to say?"

I glanced at Bloch who was still listening on his phone, holding his off hand over the other ear. He was looking back at me.

"No, I didn't have enough time to get mad at her," I said.

"So you'd say that your relationship with her was, what did you say, purely professional? Nothing else?"

"That's right. Nothing else."

I was watching Sayer's eyes, reading doubt there, when I became aware that Bloch was standing directly behind me. I whipped around in my chair. "Hey."

"Ask you a question, Mr. Buchanan?" Bloch said.

"Sure."

"How'd you get that mean looking scratch on your neck?"

"What scratch is that?" Sayer asked.

"Back of the neck," Bloch said.

My face got hot, and the place on my neck where the scratch was burned hotter. I must have looked guilty as sin, back when people still believed in it.

"Now I'm a suspect," I said. "Now I better talk to a lawyer."

"You're not under arrest, Mr. Buchanan," Bloch said.

"You're accusing me."

"We haven't," Bloch said. "Still asking questions. Do you want us to stop?"

"You'll find out anyway. Channing scratched me. She was trying to kiss me and I pulled away."

Sayer squinted. "I thought you said it was purely professional?"

"We had some wine, she got a little playful. I told her I wasn't interested."

"So for that she attacked you?"

"I didn't say *attacked*."

"She's quite a looker," Bloch said.

"Was," Sayer said.

"What's your blood type, Mr. Buchanan?" Bloch asked.

"What's that have to do with anything?"

"You refusing to answer?"

"B positive."

Bloch looked at Sayer and nodded. Then back at me. "By the way, her body was found five minutes away."

"Five minutes away from what?" I said.

"From where you were that night. Little park on Ardmore."

My throat went dry. "That's it." I stood up. "This interview's over."

"Is it over?" Sayer said to his partner, not to me.

"Let's do it," Bloch said.

"You're under arrest, Mr. Buchanan. Put your hands behind your back, please, while I sing that good old Miranda song."

Sayer read me the rights as Bloch put metal cuffs on me. They paraded me out of the office with everybody looking.

Kim almost started crying.

McDonough turned his back and walked the other way.

Al fell in step with us and said, "Don't say anything to anybody. I'll call a lawyer. The best in L.A."

"No such thing," Bloch said, and smiled.

75

AT WILSHIRE DIVISION they took all my personal effects, printed and photographed me, entered me into the system. They gave me a phone call, and I decided to use it to call Fran. I didn't want her hearing about this on the evening news.

There was no easy way to do it.

"How you doin', kid?" I said.

"Baking," she said. "I thought you might like some of my famous corn-meal muffins. Maybe some chili to go with—"

"Fran, about that. I'm not going to make it."

"Oh? You have to work?"

"Listen to me for a second and promise me something. Will you do that? Will you promise?"

"What's wrong?"

"Promise me you won't get upset because I'm not. I'm just fine." What a practiced liar I was.

"Are you hurt? Are you in the hospital?"

"Fran, there's been a big misunderstanding. You know that TV reporter who covered Jacqueline's accident?"

"Channing Westerbrook. Yes, I like her."

"Something's happened, Fran. They found her. She's dead."

"What?"

"And I'd been seeing her. She wanted to do a story on me. Well, now that she's dead they think I might have had something to do with that, and they're talking to me about it."

"Who? The police?"

"Yeah. Now would—"

"Oh Ty—"

"Listen Fran. Just listen. Call Al Bradshaw." I gave her the number. "He'll give you more info."

"Ty—"

"All right?"

"Yes, Ty."

"And try not to worry. I'm not guilty of this. I'll be out in no time."

Sure.

They parked me in a cell. It was a little like the Old West, these cells were. About a dozen of them, I guessed, steel bars so everybody could see everybody else. A bunk that smelled like old bread and ammonia.

76

NEXT MORNING THEY cuffed me and loaded me on a sheriff's bus, drove me and a few other accused felons to the men's central jail, which was between Chinatown and Union Station. Many well-known defendants had been housed here, including O.J. and Robert Blake. Both walked out free men.

But I never won a Heisman Trophy or had a hit TV series. My hole cards weren't too hot.

They herded us off the bus in a line, into a booking area where I was told to strip. All the way. Then they handed me a T-shirt, boxers, and orange scrubs, the latest fashion statement in municipal incarceration. Actually, I was told, this was because I'd been designated as a *keep away.*

Later I learned that was the vernacular for a K-10, which is a prisoner they want to keep away from the other inmates, either because they are high-power dangerous, or were involved in a big case, like I was. Channing Westerbrook had been murdered, and it was all over the news.

I was being kept away for my own protection. Inmates could improve their reps by taking out someone like me.

O.J. and Blake were both keep aways, so I was in good company.

They also gave me a pair of black Vans tennis shoes, without laces, and flip-flops for the shower, a bedroll, and a towel. They put a plastic wristband on me with my name and number. And then, all shackled up, the nice deputy walked me to my cell, my home away from home.

It was a small box with a toilet, a table and a bunk, white walls, and a smell like moldy oranges. When they locked the door on me, I thought about how much we take privacy for granted. The deputies watched us from a thick steel and glass enclosure out beyond the railing.

Later, when they turned down the lights, the screaming started. Somebody was up and wanted everybody to know about it. He screamed, and he rapped, and he did jam poetry, and he screamed some more.

All night long.

77

NEXT MORNING THEY served up powdered eggs and warm bread and an orange. Then I was told I got an hour of roof time, which was their idea of outdoor exercise. It was like a cement playground, only the chain link was over the top of the yard, with razor wire around the edges. There were a couple of basketball hoops and a handball wall. On another wall were stainless steel toilets and pay phones.

But none of that was for me. The K-10s got put in a sort of cage, with a pull-up bar in it.

I did twenty pull-ups before my arms started to burn. Then I sat and looked at the sky through the chain link.

A deputy named Reynal came up and said I had a visitor. He put the bracelets on me and brought me down to the attorney interview room, sat me on a stool at the end of the row, unshackled my hands, and put them in the set of cuffs fastened to the table.

"Wait here," he said. Jailhouse humor.

A moment later a man I'd seen only on TV walked in and sat across from me.

Martin Latourette was known around town as the Silver Bullet. Silver because of his hair, full and white and worn long. Bullet because he was the desperate defendant's last shot and very often the winning one.

Like a lot of successful criminal defense lawyers, Latourette had started in the D.A.'s office, gaining valuable trial experience and an insider's view of the system. He went out on his own and had a good ten years of defense work under his belt when the case that made him a legal superstar came calling.

That was the Ben Soledad murder case. Soledad, the TV star from the eighties, was accused of murdering his model girlfriend, Stacy Regis, in the parking lot of the Sherman Oaks Galleria late one night. Public opinion and late-night comedians had Soledad in San Quentin from the start. But then Latourette took over.

He was everywhere. Latourette was on talk shows and outside the courtroom, wherever there was a camera. And then he went to court and actually got Soledad acquitted.

Now this legal magician was sitting across from me in the attorney room at L.A. County Jail and asking if I'd like him to be my lawyer.

"I don't have your kind of money," I said. "Even after I sell my real estate and tap all my accounts."

"What if I told you money was not a concern?"

"I'd ask why."

"Let's not jump the gun here. I haven't said I'd take the case yet."

I shook my head.

"I'm only asking at this point if you'd be interested in discussing it further."

"Yeah, I would," I said. "I shouldn't be here."

Latourette smiled and nodded. "Then tell me exactly what happened. Tell me as if you were talking to a jury in the courtroom. I'm going to listen to you. I may ask a question or two. When you're finished, I'll tell you if I can take you on as a client, and if I do, you won't have to worry about the money aspect."

With a shrug, I told him everything, and he just sat there with this intense concentration. It was a little disconcerting at times, like he was able to climb in my head and root around for information I wasn't giving. I talked while he opened drawers and looked under beds and scavenged in the closet.

When I was finished he folded his hands. "Quick arrest," he said. "They must have something more on you."

"What could they possibly have? I didn't do it."

"That's what they all say."

"Hey, don't you—"

"I'll take your case, Tyler."

"Just like that?"

"That's right."

"Without a retainer?"

"Right."

"This is all a little sudden."

"Like a guy asking a girl to marry him on the first date."

"Something like that."

Latourette said, "Let me take you through arraignment and bail hearing."

"You think I might get bail?"

"If the prosecutor doesn't allege special, and I don't think they will. That's the good news. The bad news—bail schedule says a mil."

"Hey, no problem. Pocket change."

"I'll try to knock it down. You have something you can put up for a bond?"

I started to shake my head, then said, "I own some land. Used to have a house on it. But the land itself is worth that much."

"All right. Let me try to get you out of here. If I do, you can keep me. If I don't, you can fire me. I won't mind. Any questions?"

"Yeah. One. Why are you doing this?"

He stood up. "Ego. Pure ego. I'm one of the few lawyers who'll admit that. I love to win and I hate to lose, and I'll fight for you like nobody's business. Because your case is high profile and so am I, and I like appearing on *Larry King*. Oh yeah, and one other thing. I'm convinced you're not guilty. It would be nice for a change to represent someone I think is innocent."

"What about Ben Soledad?" I said. "Didn't you think he was innocent?"

The Silver Bullet smiled and winked at me, and left without another word.

78

A COUPLE OF hours after my meeting with Marty Latourette I was told I had another visitor, one I had not expected.

Father Bob was sitting on the other side of the glass and asked through the handset, "How you doin'?"

"I've been better."

"I hear you."

I said, "What brings you down here?"

"Came to see you."

"Why?"

"Suffering is wasted if we suffer entirely alone."

I just looked at him.

"Thomas Merton said that."

"Who?"

"Merton. A Trappist monk. He wrote that in *No Man Is an Island*."

"Oh yeah?"

Father Bob nodded.

"Easy for him to say." I paused. "No offense."

"You can't offend me," Father Bob said.

"You haven't heard me try."

"You want to?"

I shook my head. "Thanks for coming. I mean, that was real nice of you. But if you're here to save my soul or something like that, that's not exactly on my plate right now."

"I didn't say anything about your soul. But anytime . . ."

"Right."

"Merton also said that only the man who has had to face despair can be truly free."

"What did this guy do, sit around all day saying things?"

"He lived in a hermitage. He had lots of time."

"Like me."

"Is there anything I can do for you?"

"Sure. Bring me one of your holy fruitcakes with a file in it."

Father Bob laughed. He apparently appreciated gallows humor. "You'll be out of here soon enough."

"Not if the prosecutor has anything to say about it. They actually think I did it."

"So does half the city."

"Thank you."

"But I don't."

I studied his face. It was a good face, the kind you'd want around if you were looking for faces to comfort you. "Why not?" I said, suddenly interested.

"It's just an instinct. I've spent a lot of years looking people in the eyes. Some can fool you. I don't think you're one of those people."

"If it matters, I really didn't do it."

"I believe you."

"Great. That makes three of us. You, me, and my lawyer. Now if I can just get you on the jury."

"Do you have representation?" he asked.

"Marty Latourette."

"The Silver Bullet?"

Now I laughed. "I guess you've really arrived when the Catholic Church knows your nickname."

Father Bob said, "If you need anything when you get out, you know where to find me. I don't often venture this far."

"How'd you get here?"

"Sister Mary Veritas. She's the best driver we have."

"All right," I said.

"Hm?"

"You and the good sister can do me a favor."

"Name it."

"Send up some prayers."

"Ah. So maybe you do believe in God."

"Let's just say I want to cover all my bases."

Father Bob smiled. "You know, when Constantine was a Roman general, he faced off against a rival, Macentius, at the battle of Milvain Bridge. Had a vision of Jesus, so the story goes, and came up with a Christian symbol to put on his men's shields. He was a pagan, but he was also covering all his bases. He won the battle, and came to power as emperor and made Christianity the official religion of Rome."

"Order me a toga," I said. "Preferably one without stripes."

79

BACK IN MY cell I kept trying to think about what Father Bob said about despair and being free. Sitting on the stainless steel can, looking at three walls and a door, I found it hard to believe.

What I really found out was how easy it was to go crazy. They used to call prisons penitentiaries. They'd stick you in your box and have you sit there alone, thinking of your sins, until you repented.

Most of the time prisoners went nuts.

Because your mind doesn't click off. It starts playing games with you. It gets the idea that now that you haven't got anything to concentrate on, no work to do, it can come out and pretty much zigzag wherever it wants.

And if it zigs to a place you don't want it to go it laughs and keeps on going there, like to Jacqueline's face the time we had our first blowout.

We were at her apartment and she was making dinner for me. Italian. Sausages and sauce and pasta. I'd come from the office after a particularly bad day. One of our clients had screamed and yelled about a contrary ruling on a motion. McDonough was the one who'd signed off on it, but I'd done the bulk of the research and writing, and McDonough let me take most of the heat.

So I was in a foul mood, and Jacqueline was happy because her fifth graders had all behaved themselves on a field trip to the Gene Autry Western Museum. She wanted to tell me all about it, and I didn't want to hear.

She kissed me and said it couldn't be all that bad, and I said it was, and she said listen to what Armand said about the stuffed horse, and I said I didn't care what Armand said about the stuffed horse.

And Jacqueline stepped back and looked at me like she didn't know me.

I kept jabbing at her and eventually it made her cry and she fought back and then we made up.

But it was her look saying that she didn't know me that I kept seeing in my mind as I lay there in the cell. It was worse than the crying face, because I didn't want Jacqueline to not know me.

That would be my idea of hell.

Her face just kept coming back, though, until I screamed and hit the wall with my fist. The pain helped. For about ten minutes.

80

ON SUNDAYS THE K-10's get forty minutes for a single visitor if any-body wants to see them. I wasn't expecting anybody. My arraignment was set for the next day, Monday, and Marty Latourette would meet me at the courthouse.

But then I got the word that I had a visitor. As I wasn't going anywhere, I let them chain me up and take me down to the visiting room.

Seated on the other side of the Plexiglas was Agent Rubén Cisneros. I picked up the handset.

"What are you doing in there?" he said.

"I'm having a little disagreement with the prosecutor and somebody who is setting me up for murder, but other than that, everything's cool."

"Setting you up? Like who?"

"I wouldn't want to mention any names, like Rudy Barocas, so I won't."

"What a coincidence," Cisneros said. "That's the very name I wanted to talk to you about."

"I got nothing but time."

"Imagine my surprise to learn that you had been arrested for murdering a popular television reporter. You don't seem the type. But now you're big news."

"I haven't been keeping up on myself lately."

"Oh yeah. You're the next big thing in celebrity defendants."

"Great. When do I get a book deal?"

"When you're acquitted. If you're convicted, they won't let you collect any money on a book. Some First Amendment we got, huh?"

"For what it's worth, I didn't do it. I didn't kill her."

"You get representation?"

"Marty Latourette."

Cisneros smiled broadly. "Now this case has everything. Sexy victim, am-bitious young lawyer, and the Silver Bullet."

"I can do without any of it. I just want to get out of here and away from everything and never come out again."

"That's what prison'll do."

"Thanks."

"Tell me what happened."

Well, I guessed it wouldn't hurt to have the Secret Service looking into this. I said, "I think maybe Channing Westerbrook was looking at Rudy Barocas a little too closely. Like I was. I think Barocas figured out a way to get rid of two annoyances. And here I sit."

"That would have to be a pretty elaborate setup."

"Anything is possible in America. Isn't that what Barocas is always spouting about?"

Cisneros nodded.

"He followed me to Channing's apartment the other night," I said. "I went to see her, to talk about the story we were working on, and—"

"Followed you?"

"I came out and one of his guys was standing there, waiting for me."

"What'd this guy look like?"

"Nice clothes, about thirty or so, strong, clipped moustache."

"Vargas," Cisneros said. "Enrique Vargas. Barocas's bodyguard. Used to run with the Lobos crew out of Eagle Rock. Very bad dude."

"Another one of Barocas's success stories?"

"If you believe the press releases. So what else makes you think Barocas had Channing Westerbrook killed?"

"He had somebody call me up and set up a meeting, and I was stupid enough to fall for it. So I'm sitting waiting for nobody at the same time they're killing Channing and leaving her body to be found."

"There's the little matter of the blood."

I stared at him a moment. "What blood? The detectives said she died of asphyxiation."

"I talked to the D.A.'s office. Talked to 'em within an hour of when I heard you'd been popped. I may be telling you something your lawyer doesn't even know yet."

"Tell me."

"They found blood on a blouse in her apartment. You know anything about that?"

The back of my neck heated up again. "She gave me a good scratch Wednesday night. I don't believe this! Is that my blood?"

"If they match the DNA, you know what that means. The CSI effect."

The visitor's room got real cold all of a sudden. "You mean a jury is going to think it's a slam dunk against me because of DNA, just like on TV?"

"That's it." Cisneros leaned a little closer to the glass. "I don't think you did this. I know Barocas, and I know he could have set this up without much effort at all. The only problem is proving it."

"You have any ideas, I'm open."

"Why I came down here. I got some people might be able to look into some things. But I don't want you to say anything to anybody, not even your lawyer. Not yet. Think you can do that?"

"Not talk to a lawyer? Yeah, I think I can do that."

81

EARLY MONDAY MORNING they put several of us on the sheriff's shuttle to the criminal courts building on Temple Street, then took us up by private elevator to the fourth floor. The fourth held no courtrooms and allowed no public. It was a custodial floor. They held incarcerated defendants here before they appeared in court. The others on the ride got a community cell. I got an isolated as befit my *keep away* status. It was about four by eight, with an aluminum toilet and sink, dim, with a metal mesh over the lights. The walls were industrial green, dulled by time. Gang symbols and initials were scratched into the walls.

They had the air-conditioning cranked up, as if we had to be preserved like meat before our appearances. The gate was plain jail bars, with a waist-high opening for stuff to pass through.

The only thing that passed through it was air. At some point a deputy sheriff opened the gate and attached my shackles and took me to a stairway and up one floor. He passed me through a thick door and into the box of Division 30, the felony arraignment court.

I felt like Liza Minnelli making another comeback. The courtroom gallery was full, and I could tell immediately that a cordoned section was for reporters. This bevy started scratching and mumbling as soon as they saw me. A TV camera had its eye aimed at me.

The box was where a jury would have sat if this were a trial court. But it wasn't, and this box was like a bullpen. There were nine wooden benches, worn down by countless criminal butts over the years. Plexiglas with a chin-high opening for lawyer chats spread across the front of the box.

I shouldn't have been surprised. This was the hot story in town.

I sat on one of the benches—I was alone in the pen—and looked at the two long tables facing each other in the center of the courtroom. Behind each were lawyers and paralegals for the public defender's and D.A.'s offices. There were computer monitors and printers on each desk, and papers strewn all over.

The Silver Bullet was nowhere to be seen. Probably waiting to make a grand entrance.

There was no one on the bench. I stared at the sign on the opposite wall.

Communication With Custodies is Forbidden by Law
La Ley Prohibe Communicarse Con Las Presos (4570 P.C.)

82

A LITTLE BEFORE nine by the clock on the back wall, my lawyer strode into the courtroom. He caused a stir like Springsteen entering a concert stage. At least the attention was turned away from me for the moment.

He had an amazing presence, seeming to hold title to the courthouse. He was dressed in a black suit, the better to offset his hair.

Behind him was a woman who looked like she'd stepped off the UCLA cheerleading squad and into a dark blue pinstripe suit. She had long dusky hair and brown eyes, and it was clear she was associated with Marty.

After Marty gave the glad hand to a couple of the lawyers, he came to the pen and motioned me over.

"How you doing?" he said.

"I'd rather be in Philadelphia."

"No you wouldn't. I tried a case in Philadelphia once. Lost. They don't know what they're doing out there. This is L.A. Here we win." He looked at my jail scrubs. "Sorry about the uni. I requested plain clothes but got turned down. Commissioner K is in a foul mood this morning."

I looked at the woman.

"This is Gabrielle Galloway," Marty said. "My assistant."

"Hi," I said.

She nodded, all business.

Marty said, "From now on you'll be in a good suit. Today, just keep your head up like you've got nothing to be sorry about."

I looked over his shoulder and saw a formidable looking woman in a gray power suit looking at a file. "Is that the prosecutor?"

Marty nodded without turning to see. "Usually they have an arraignment deputy for these things. But not when Marie Antoinette Rocha is on the case."

I'd heard of her. She had a nickname. The Dragon Lady. Terrific. The Dragon Lady and the Silver Bullet. I felt like I was in a comic book. Two superheroes about to face off with fire flying from their mouths.

They were opposites. Where Marty Latourette was tall with white hair slicked back, Marie Antoinette Rocha was short with her black hair coiffed high. But she looked like she could take up the whole courtroom if she wanted to. Expando Woman.

Marty explained a few things to me about what was going to happen and what I should say and how I should act. Then he said, "Just leave everything else to me."

A moment later the commissioner came in looking like he would rather have been in Philadelphia, too.

Kenneth Khachatoorian was his name. He looked twenty years old. Arraignment court is not exactly a plum assignment, and more experienced judges avoid it. It's left to the new kids on the block, usually lawyers employed by the county as commissioners, sort of judges lite.

Commissioner K had olive skin and dark hair and eyebrows like feather dusters. He sat in the leather chair beneath the Great Seal of the State of California mounted on the wall.

"Case number BA-361626, People v. Tyler Buchanan," he intoned.

Marty took two steps to keep in line with the TV camera. "Martin Latourette for the defendant, Your Honor. We will waive a reading of the complaint and statement of rights and are ready to enter a plea."

Commissioner K looked at the Dragon Lady. "Is there any reason why a plea should not be taken at this time, Ms. Rocha?"

"No, your honor," the Dragon Lady said with a theatrical tone.

"Mr. Buchanan, has your lawyer explained to you the charge and your constitutional rights?"

"Yes, your honor," I said.

"And do you understand those rights?"

"Yes I do."

"Do you waive your right to have this court explain them to you?"

"Yes."

"Are you ready to enter a plea?"

"Yes."

"You are charged with violation of Penal Code section 187, murder, one count. To this charge how do you plead?"

"Not guilty."

"Very well," said the commissioner. "Do we have an agreeable date for preliminary hearing?"

"We'd like waive time," Marty Latourette said. News to me.

"Mr. Buchanan, you understand you have the right to a preliminary hearing within ten days?"

"Sure."

"Do you waive that right?"

"How many rights am I waiving today?" I said, generating some twitters in the gallery. But I was serious.

Marty leaned toward me and whispered, "Just say Yes."

I whispered back, "I don't want to sit in the can for who knows how long."

"Don't worry, I'm getting you out."

"Mr. Buchanan," Commissioner K said. "Do you waive your right to a statutory prelim?"

"Might as well," I said.

"Is that a Yes?"

"Yes."

"Counsel join?"

"Yes," Marty said.

"Now was that so hard? How does May 8 sound for coming back here to set a prelim?"

Gabrielle looked at her PDA, tapped it a couple of times with a stylus, then nodded at Marty.

"That works for us," he said.

"Ms. Rocha?"

"Good for us, too," she said.

"Mr. Latourette, do you want to be heard on the matter of bail?"

"You bet I do," Marty said.

"As you know, the presumptive bail is a million dollars. Do your best, Mr. Latourette."

"Your honor, this is a murder accusation," Marty said, "and I fully understand that substantial bail must be applied. That's what we are ready to comply with. A million is too much, of course, but a good quarter of that is more than enough to ensure my client's presence at trial, in addition to my own persuasive powers."

"Legendary as they are," Commissioner K said.

"Need I say more?"

"Some mitigation would be nice."

"It's quite clear, your honor. Mr. Buchanan has substantial ties to the community. He's been employed for five years by a prestigious law firm. He has no record, so there is no reason to suppose any future violent conduct. He also owns a residential property. He is certainly no flight risk. If this were not a murder charge, O.R. would be almost automatic."

"Well, why don't we let Ms. Rocha give it her best shot, as long as she's made the effort to be here."

Marty bowed slightly and backed up to the pen. I thought I was in the first row of a dinner theater.

And now it was the Dragon Lady's turn before the camera.

"This is quite extraordinary, Your Honor. Mr. Latourette apparently believes his powers of persuasion are enough to offset the bail schedule and the heinous nature of the crime. I'm sure the court will pardon the People of the State of California if we take a different view. That view is that this will be treated as a first degree murder and that the defendant has the resources to make him a flight risk. He is not married, and he no longer resides at his home, because it burned down recently. We would ask that bail be denied."

"And so we have gridlock," Commissioner Khachatoorian said. "I'm going to split the baby and make it five hundred thousand. Anything else? No? Good." He hurried off the bench as if he had to go to the bathroom.

Marty said, "Hang in there, pal."

"What else have I got to do?" I said.

Nothing except take the ride back to county, jangling shackles and all.

83

THE BOND, SECURED by my real property, was posted at ten the next morning, Tuesday, and I was back on the street by noon. In Marty Latourette's Mercedes. Silver of course.

His assistant sat in the back, taking notes.

"Let's go over the time line," Marty said, "and assume the worst. According to the police report they've got the blood on Miss Westerbrook's blouse, which is yours."

"Of course. They wouldn't use Rudy's."

"And you got the scratch on your neck on Wednesday evening?"

"Yes."

"So Channing Westerbrook gets a little of your blood on her blouse."

"How bad is this?"

"Blood is a complex puppy and a lot more fickle than we think. Unless you leave a big splotch on the floor."

"So what's that mean?"

Marty turned his head slightly and spoke behind him. "Gabe, give Matsumoto a call. Set up a meeting." Then to me: "Serologist, testified for me before. He'll have Rocha tied up in little knots."

That was good. I wanted her in knots. And from the Blumberg case I knew the value of good expert testimony. Like most of America, I was all over the O. J. Simpson murder case, when Barry Scheck, the DNA expert, beat a poor technician named Fung like a bongo drum. It had an effect.

"Oh, and another thing," Marty said. "You will not say anything to anybody about the case, okay? I don't want you pulling a Scott Peterson on me. You remember that?"

I did. Peterson, accused of murdering his pregnant wife and unborn child, thought he could go on national TV with Diane Sawyer and make a case for himself. He muffed it badly. It was the eyes. You could tell he was lying just by watching his eyes.

"No, I want to keep things quiet," I said.

"Good. I love a quiet client. We're going to get along just fine. Anything you need?"

"Some answers," I said. "Who's your investigator?"

"Murray Jones. He's good. Very good."

"He's going to have to be."

"And don't worry so much. What's the worst that could happen? This goes to a jury? That's where I shine."

84

FRAN SNIFFLED AS she made me dinner. I watched the news. Of course, I popped up on KTLA, Channing's station. They had an "investigative reporter" giving updates, and they kept replaying the picture of me tromping into the arraignment court in my orange scrubs. Orange shouts guilty. And that's what KTLA wanted to show the jury pool every night.

So when I drove to the office the next morning, as if nothing was changed, I knew I was stuffing my head in the ground.

Two news crews were waiting at the entrance to the parking garage. As soon as I pulled in I was recognized and up came the cameras and mikes. Nobody ever looks good not talking to a reporter. It was once Geraldo's greatest weapon, as he'd chase people down the street shouting questions.

Even as I swiped my security card and got into the garage, I knew the news would have a nice set of pictures for the evening broadcast.

The office I entered was not the same one I left. It was cold. I could almost feel the ice forming on the walls. The looks were of the dead man walking variety.

I didn't have to be told that McDonough wanted to see me. But Kim told me anyway with red-rimmed eyes. I kissed her cheek and told her I was like a cat and always landed on my feet, but I didn't get a smile out of her.

The first words out of McDonough's mouth were, "I'm sorry."

"Would it help if I told you I'm not guilty?"

"No."

"Hey, that's just great, Pierce. I'm glad the presumption of innocence is honored at good old Gunther, McDonough."

"Sarcasm isn't going to help you, Ty."

"Is anything?"

"I'm afraid not."

"Ah. There's another great trait, Pierce. Your open-mindedness, your—"

"Insults won't help either."

"Call somebody who cares." I stood and picked up his phone and held it out to him. He shook his head, like someone witnessing the mental decline of a beloved family member. He wasn't that far off.

"Put that down and end this like a professional," McDonough said.

I slammed the phone down. "Don't hand me that. I don't want anything to do with your kind of professionalism. You don't care who you get in bed with, Pierce, as long as it doesn't tarnish your reputation on the cigar and martini circuit—"

"Enough—"

"You called me in here to can me. You're going to hear what I have to say. Thank you. Yeah, thanks. Because I might not have left on my own, but now I see it's the only thing I could have done that would have saved me. If I stayed here, I'd end up like you. I'd end up compromising just to keep my position in life. I wouldn't take any more risks. And I'd be working for things that don't really matter much. I can't do that anymore. I don't see things the same and I don't want to. So thanks, Pierce. This works out best for both of us."

I turned to walk out with a grand theatrical style and bumped into a chair.

85

KIM BROUGHT ME a few boxes so I could clean out my office. It wasn't the easiest task I ever performed. McDonough had the office security guard and our IT guy standing in there, preventing me from taking the computer or CDs or anything like that.

Al helped me lug the boxes to my car. It took an hour to get everything loaded up.

And then we were there, in the garage, and all that was left for me to do was get in the car and go.

"Call me," Al said.

I nodded. And then he had his arms around me, pounding my back.

When we broke I said, "Let me keep your gun awhile."

"That's the sweetest thing anybody's ever said to me."

"Okay?"

86

SO I WAS sprung. From jail. From Gunther, McDonough. Damaged goods.

But there was an odd sense of freedom. Like I really wasn't going to miss the firm. Or even practicing law. At least their kind of law.

What was that barf-inducing quote they had in the sixties? Something about if you love something, let it go and if it doesn't come back it was never yours? They were always coming up with stuff like that back then.

But now, heading out of the garage, ignoring the press, I sort of felt that way. The law as practiced by Gunther, McDonough was flying away, and I wasn't trying to get it back. Didn't want it back. It didn't seem all that important anymore.

I called Latourette's office from the car and was put through to Gabrielle. She said she was glad I called and could I meet with their investigator in the afternoon. I told her I didn't exactly have a full plate of social obligations. She laughed and said maybe the two of us could remedy that sometime.

Newly sprung and hit on.

I told myself to let it go, and if it came back, duck.

87

I SPENT HALF a day recovering as much stuff as I could from the remains of my home. Technically it was red tagged, and I shouldn't have been in there alone. Technically, I didn't give a rip.

I unloaded the rented van at Fran's house, half filling her small garage with the flotsam of my life. On a wall of the garage was a girl's bike. Jacqueline's no doubt. Pink, with faded tassels hanging from the handgrips. It had been here all these years, waiting, perhaps, for the grandchild Fran would never have.

When all that was done, I showered and dressed and joined Fran on the back porch. She was reclining on a chaise lounge looking at the one tree in the middle of the modest lawn. I took a white plastic chair.

"Jacqueline used to sit out here for hours sometimes," she said. "She liked to watch the weather. When it was cold, she'd put a blanket around herself and just sit, right here. Almost like she was looking for something."

I imagined the little girl with the blanket around her.

"I want you to know something," I said. "I want you to know I loved your daughter more than anything else in my life."

Fran, looking straight ahead, nodded.

"Something else," I said. "I want you to look in my eyes as I tell you this." She turned to me.

"I did not kill Channing Westerbrook—"

"I believe you, Ty."

"—and I don't want you to believe anything you hear on TV about this case."

"I won't."

"We're clear on that?"

"Perfectly."

"All right, then another thing. We move on. We've mourned Jacqueline and that's as it should be. But she would not have wanted us to stay there. So we won't. We start tonight and we move on. Are you with me?"

She gave me a long look, her face showing the signs of what was going on inside. Thinking it over. Wondering if she could do this.

I took her hands in mine. "Okay?"

She nodded.

"And the first thing, I'm going to cook you a great big steak dinner with baked potatoes and peas and cherry pie for dessert."

"Ty—"

"Because what they feed you at the jail isn't on any food list known to man—"

"It's late—"

"And I won't take no for an answer."

"Whatever gave you the idea I wanted to say no?"

88

WITH SHADES AND a Dodgers cap on, I walked the aisles at Albertson's and picked out the makings for dinner. A couple of healthy-looking T-bones for the main course. I even threw in a box of Cap'n Crunch for myself. As long as I had the prospect of permanent incarceration hovering over me, I was going to eat what I wanted when I wanted. For as long as it lasted.

A skinny, earnest-looking kid bagged the food. I got out of there with no one recognizing me, though the kid kept giving me the eye. Maybe he thought I was a Dodger out slumming.

Driving back to Fran's I was starting to feel a little normal. For a minute or two it was like I was alive again, in the old way, everything good about to happen. I was going to cook a great dinner and share it with someone and tomorrow I'd get up and go about my business. Somewhere there'd be an office waiting for me because not to have me practice law would be a waste.

I think I actually whistled as I got out of the car and carried the shopping bags toward the front door. That stopped when somebody jumped me from behind.

The bags fell under me as I went down. A potato jammed me below the ribs. I lost breath, fought for air as two fists started in on the sides of my head. The guy was sitting on my back, working me.

I tried to breathe. It wasn't easy with the weight on me. The guy muffled curses between breaths. I managed to get my hands to the sides of my head, trying to hang on.

The fists flew. I was barely breathing. I wheezed and sucked in grass and coughed. Then the weight on me lifted a little. I thought maybe the worst was over.

It wasn't.

The hands pulled at my shirt and rolled me over on my back.

Looking up, I saw only an outline. The sky above it was full of stars. Maybe some of them were behind my eyes.

The hands went around my neck.

Now I really couldn't breathe.

The guy said, "If they don't do it, I will."

I couldn't ask him who "they" were, or what they were going to do. My head was losing oxygen. All I could do was flail my legs. The guy on me didn't budge.

Then I knew he wasn't going to wait for *them*. He was going to do the job himself, and the job was death.

Still kicking out with my legs I managed to get my right hand into my pants pocket. Then I played possum. I went completely limp. I wasn't far from being limp for real and for good.

For a second I didn't think it was going to work. The thumbs kept pressure on my windpipe. Looking back, I think I had maybe ten seconds of life left in me.

The countdown started.

Eight . . . seven . . . six . . .

His grip started to loosen.

. . . five . . . four . . .

The thumbs came off.

My hand came out. In it was my cell phone. It was the old Danny Sullivan trick to take the give out of the fingers. In one motion I pulled my shoulder back and shot the fist up. Caught him flush on the chin.

I rolled away, gasping for air, got to my knees.

The guy was on his side, groaning.

I crawled to him. Gave him another shot to the side of the face.

For a minute I watched him as my lungs got back to working order.

With the air came the rage. I got up ready to kill him. I'd do it by kicking or maybe with a loose brick if I could find one.

I stood over him and lined up his face.

Then the light went on. The porch light.

Fran stuck her head out. "Ty?" Then she said, "My God, what's happened?"

The light was enough to see the guy's face. He looked familiar. I didn't place him at first. Then it hit me.

"Open the door, Fran," I said. "I'm bringing him inside."

Channing's cameraman looked like he'd had his brains scrambled. I managed to plop him on the big blue chair in the living room.

"Shall I call the police?" Fran asked.

"Not yet," I said. I went to Jacqueline's room and got Al's gun, which I'd stashed under the bed. When I got back to the living room, Muscles was groaning, his eyes rolling around a little.

"What's that?" Fran said, looking at the gun.

"Don't worry," I said. "It's registered. Just not to me."

"What are you going to—"

"Fran, let me talk to him alone."

"You're not going to shoot him, are you?"

"Do I look like Clint Eastwood?"

"Please—"

"A few minutes. Please."

Fran nodded tentatively, then left.

I looked at the guy I called Muscles. He seemed aware now. When I held up the gun he came around even more.

"Don't try anything stupid," I said.

He said nothing.

"You come near me again and I'll do something inhuman and ugly and painful, and your body will make the evening news. Only you won't be filming it. I have a witness who saw you here, waiting for me, trying to kill me. Self-defense won't be hard to prove."

"Just wanted to—"

"Shut up. You're going to listen. I didn't kill Channing. There's somebody setting me up for it. You've got the wrong guy. Okay, I understand your devotion. Commendable. But wrong, and you're stupid to do something like this."

"Why should I believe you?"

"Because you're still breathing."

He thought about it.

"What's your name?" I said.

"Greg."

"Greg *what*?"

"Beck."

"So what do we do now, Greg? Want me to call the cops?"

"No."

"You need some ice for your face?"

"What'd you hit me with?"

"Does it matter?"

He rubbed the side of his face.

"Hang on," I said. I called to Fran and had her fill a Ziploc with ice and give it to Beck.

"Go on home," I said. "Just know that I want to find out who did Channing as much as you. More."

But I don't think he believed me.

89

NEXT MORNING I left the house early. It was almost like I had to hit commuter traffic in order to stay in the flow of existence. If I didn't get up and get out and do something I'd be conceding defeat. I'd be waiting for the next attack.

But out here in the city people were eagerly planning my demise, legally or otherwise.

Greg Beck. Would I have to worry about him? Probably. He'd heal up and start thinking about last night and get mad again. If I was acquitted, he'd still be there to dispense his own brand of justice.

If I got acquitted.

I took the 405 to Sunset, and Sunset to La Cienega. Found a meter on the street. That was a good omen in L.A.

When I walked into the lobby of Channing's apartment building, the security guy almost jumped out of his blazer. For a second it looked like his mouth was trying to move but wouldn't.

"Don't worry about it," I said. "I'm not armed and dangerous."

His mouth still wouldn't work. Then his head took over, and he put on his security guard frown. He stood a little taller behind the horseshoe-shaped console. He made sure I could see the badge pinned to his left coat pocket, a badge that meant absolutely nothing.

"I'm going to have to ask you to leave, sir."

"Why is that? You don't even know why I'm here."

"Sir, you'll have to leave."

"What's your name?" I asked.

"Please leave sir."

"Pete. Is that your name?"

He picked up a phone and stuck it to his ear.

"Okay, I'll call you Pete," I said. "Pete, you're withholding evidence, and that's a crime."

Pete lowered the phone. "What are you talking about?"

"You know who I am."

"Yeah I do. And—"

"And you know Channing invited me up to her apartment a week ago and I left after that. I think you know even more. I think you watched me after I left."

It was a guess but apparently a good one because he put the phone back.

"You saw me talking to a guy, didn't you?" I said.

"I'm not interested in you or anything you say."

"What did you tell the cops? What did you tell Detective Sayer? Did you mention that I was talking to a guy? Did you mention the Hummer sitting right across the street?"

"I don't know about any Hummer."

"I don't think you're being up front with me, Pete."

"Stop calling me Pete."

"What do you prefer?"

"That you get out."

"I didn't kill her. Look at me. I did not kill her."

"I don't know what you did. But I'm not gonna talk to you about it."

"Just tell me what you saw. If you saw what you saw, it's just a fact, right? I don't care if you tell the cops or the D.A. or *Good Morning, America*."

"I didn't see anything. This is a private building. You have to leave now."

"I'm not ready to leave yet. I—"

The elevator in the lobby opened then, and an older woman in a running suit and blue baseball cap stepped out. She looked about seventy or so. She paused outside the doors and an even older woman emerged. This one also wore running togs and carried a cane.

They linked arms and walked toward us.

"Good morning, Samuel," the younger older woman said.

"Good morning," the security guard formerly known as Pete said.

The older woman nodded at him.

The younger smiled at me and was about to say something when she frowned, as if she recognized me.

"Good morning," I said.

"New tenant?" she asked.

Samuel jumped in. "I'm dealing with it, Mrs. Morrison."

"Dealing with what?" the older woman asked.

Mrs. Morrison turned to the older and said, "It's nothing, Mother."

"Out for a run?" I asked.

"Wait a second," Samuel interrupted. "You talk to me, not them."

"Samuel, what's the matter?" Mrs. Morrison said.

"What's wrong?" the mother asked.

"Nothing's wrong, Mother."

"Who is that?"

"A new tenant."

Samuel said, "He's not a new tenant, Mrs. Morrison. Shall I get the door for you?"

"I'll get it," I said and before Samuel could emerge from his horseshoe I headed for the entrance.

"What a nice young man," the mother said.

I opened the door and the two shuffled past me. I followed them out to the sidewalk.

"Going for a little exercise?" I said.

"Oh yes," Mrs. Morrison said.

"Would you mind if I asked you something?"

"When are you moving in?"

Samuel was at the door now. "You don't have to talk to him, Mrs. Morrison."

She gave him a hard look. "That's not the way to treat the new tenants, Samuel."

"He's not—"

"Go on." Mrs. Morrison waved him away. He slunk back inside.

"He gets a little snippy," she explained.

"He's rude," Mother added. "And he needs a woman."

Mrs. Morrison shook her head.

90

THE MID-AFTERNOON TRAFFIC was light on La Cienega. The sun was out. Good time for a stroll, but the ladies didn't seem anxious to get on with it. I think I was a novelty for them.

"You'll like this building," said Mrs. Morrison. She had an elfin face that must have made Mr. Morrison very happy at one time. I wondered what had happened to him. You could see the mother in the daughter, too.

"I'm not moving in," I said.

"What's that?"

"I want to ask you about Channing Westerbrook."

A short silence passed, then the mother piped in, "She was murdered!"

I nodded.

"They arrested a man," Mrs. Morrison said. "A lawyer."

"Saw it on the TV," Mom said. "I hope they hang him."

Mrs. Morrison whispered, "Mother believes in the death penalty, but I don't."

"I'm glad to hear that," I said.

"Did you know Miss Westerbrook?"

"I did, actually."

"Lovely girl. She needed a good man. I didn't care for some of the men."

"Did you see her with many men?"

Daughter looked at mother, then back at me. "She wasn't a loose woman, if that's what you mean."

"Oh, I don't know," Mom said.

"She wasn't!" Mrs. Morrison shook her head at her mother, then came back to me. "How well did you know her?"

"Just starting," I said.

"Did you have the hots for her?" Mom said with a wry smile.

"Professional," I answered. "I was helping her with a story. But maybe one of those men can help me. Can you describe any of them?"

"Oh, I don't know," said Mrs. Morrison. "I'm not a snoop."

"Curly hair," Mom said.

I looked at her. "How's that?"

She wiggled wrinkled fingers over her head. "Curly. One of 'em had curly hair. I saw him once."

Her daughter shook her head, annoyed.

"He came out of her place," Mom insisted.

"Anything else?" I said.

"Hanky panky," Mom said.

"You don't know that," Mrs. Morrison said.

"I could tell."

"Anything besides curly hair?" I asked. "Color?"

Mom said, "Brown, I think. Or maybe blond."

"We need to go," Mrs. Morrison said. "Very nice meeting you Mr. . . ."

"Call me Ty," I said.

"Good-bye, Mr. Ty," Mrs. Morrison said.

"Come back and see us anytime," Mom said.

Not likely. They were nice enough but of no help. Curly hair of uncertain color. A million guys in the city could fit that. For some reason, though, I thought of one in particular. Because, depending on your interpretation of *curly*, you might be able to get away with saying that Frank Trudeau had a head like that. I had a distinct picture of it in my mind from the day he went nose to nose with me after Dyan's deposition. He sure had a killer look in his eye that day.

When I got back to Fran's, I drove up on some bad news—the News.

There was a little media camp outside Fran's house. A couple of vans, two guys with cameras.

One of them being Greg Beck.

When they spotted me in the car, the cameras turned and the reporters, one man and one woman, started running toward me.

Instead of pulling to the curb as I'd intended, I shot straight past them and kept going.

I saw the cameras pointing at me in the rearview mirror.

Now what?

In L.A. some people live in their cars. Even lawyers. I remembered reading about a homeless lawyer who'd managed to get a case to the Supreme Court, all while living out of his ten-year-old Caddie. If I holed up in my Cabriolet, I could just consider it a studio apartment.

Right.

I called Fran and told her to stay inside. Then I drove up Reseda Boulevard, headed absolutely nowhere. I could see the Santa Susana Mountains to the north, it was a clear day. Clear enough to present a solution to my immediate problems.

91

SISTER MARY VERITAS looked up from the Mac laptop on the antique desk and almost jumped out of her habit.

"Mr. Buchanan," she said.

"Hi."

"Um, welcome."

"You sure about that?"

"I'm sorry." She stood up and came around the desk. "I didn't expect to see you."

"Why not?"

"Your troubles have been widely reported."

"You're following my case?"

She gave a nod to the Mac. "I keep up with what's happening in the city. It's part of my service."

"The crime beat?"

"The heartbeat. If we're going to be any earthly good to the community, we need to take the pulse, don't you think?"

"Sure."

"And right now you're big news."

"Guilty," I said. "No, let me rephrase—"

"No need. The presumption of innocence does not contravene Catholic teaching."

An inner door opened and a woman in her mid-fifties stepped in. She held a sheaf of papers in her hand and was already speaking. "Sister Mary, I thought the quarterly report for—"

She saw me and stopped. She was dressed in a plain white blouse and brown slacks and what my grandmother would have called sensible shoes. Her face was grim and had no make-up. I figured her for some sort of controller or accountant.

But then Sister Mary Veritas said, "This is Mr. Buchanan. Mr. Buchanan, our congregational leader, Sister Hildegarde."

Sister? She was out of uniform.

"May I help you?" Sister Hildegarde said.

"I was wondering if I might see Father Robert."

"Is there anything I can help you with?"

"I think so."

"And that is?"

"Father Bob, Robert, was telling me about your fine order." I tried hard not to sound like Eddie Haskell. "And your dedication to hospitality."

At that the leader looked at Sister Mary, like both of them knew exactly what was coming.

"I have the need for a place to stay," I said. "And that's why I'm here."

Sister Hildegarde frowned as wheels turned in her head.

Sister Mary Veritas immediately said, "That is our calling, Mr. Buchanan. You are welcome here."

At which the leader glowered, then said, "Summon Father Robert."

Sister Mary headed for the door.

92

"I NEED TO kind of lay low for a while," I told Father Bob. "Isn't this place like a sanctuary?"

He smiled. "You mean like in *The Hunchback of Notre Dame?*"

"Whatever works."

"Those days are gone, my friend. Cops can even grab our private papers now. Forget the priest–penitent privilege. If they want to prosecute a priest, anything goes."

We were standing outside his trailer. The smell of sage from the hills was strong on the warm north wind. Father Bob was dressed for the weather, in a black T-shirt and blue jeans. "So what do I do? They rent out rooms here or anything?"

He paused a moment. "See that trailer? That used to be where Father Maximilian lived. He's now running a drug rehab program in San Francisco. It's open. Would that do?"

"I think it might do just fine."

"Then it's yours. There is no charge."

93

WHEN I WAS a kid I had a friend, Tony Paige, who lived with his mom in a trailer in a little park with a lot of other trailers with old people in them. We were friends from school and I never knew why his dad had run off or what his mom did to keep food on the table. When you're eight, you don't think about those things as much as you do about bikes and firecrackers and spit wads. But I do remember being in there once when Tony's mom was out and he was making a mustard sandwich and the smell of the mustard filled the trailer. I felt like it was the smallest place in the world all of a sudden. How could anybody live there, let alone a kid and his mother? I suddenly got very sad, for Tony and his mom and anybody who had to live in a trailer, because you couldn't get away from the smell of the mustard or the walls. I remember thinking if I ever had to live in a place like this I'd feel like I was in jail.

All that came back to me as I sat in the trailer that was now my temporary home. It had nothing but faded flower curtains on the small window and a plain mattress on the bed that looked like it had come from Alcatraz.

It was almost funny. Well-off lawyer with a nice house and beautiful fiancée, in the space of a couple of months is reduced to an unfurnished trailer in the hills above L.A. Among the Catholics yet.

There had to be a comedy in this somewhere.

A knock on the door sounded like a fist hitting cardboard. It was Father Bob with some items in his arms.

"Thought you might need some essentials," he said. He came in and put the things on the Formica table. Two bottles of water, a couple of cans of chili, and a big blue can with a blue plastic cap. He held the blue can up. "This will get you through many a night, if you're careful with it and don't stuff yourself."

I took the can. It said Trader Joe's Rosencrunch and Guildenpop gourmet sweet popcorn, almond and pecan clusters.

"Try it if you don't believe me," Father Bob said.

I pulled off the plastic cap and peeled back the sealed top by the ring. I offered him the first take, but he nodded at me. "You first."

It was nice of him to do this, but I didn't expect anything sensational. I was wrong.

"I can see by your face you approve," Father Bob said. "See what I mean?"

"Good," I said.

"Just the right balance of butter, sugar, and salt. A tango of crunch. Nut and popcorn across the dance floor of the tongue. It's a symphony in the mouth, is it not?"

"It's Beethoven," I said.

"Gershwin."

"Tell me if I'm safe here."

Father Bob finished his crunch. He nodded slowly. "I think so. No one goes searching monasteries these days."

"Who runs this place? Who was that Sister Hildegarde?"

"She is the Superior."

"Superior to what?"

"Everybody else."

"Why doesn't she dress like a nun?"

With a wry smile, he said, "Sister Hildegarde is of my generation, the Baby Boomers. Among the Benedictines, many of the nuns grabbed hold of Vatican II and sixties social movements and started trying to be, how should I put it, *relevant*. The old nuns' habits were a relic of the past. They decided to be a little more *now*."

"But Sister Mary, she's a young one and wears the whole thing."

"Ah, but this new generation wants to go back to the good ways. They actually want to be Catholic. They want to be like the nuns before Vatican II. They call those nuns the Greatest Generation."

I shook my head. "Whatever, I'm glad you're here. I'm glad I'm here. I'm going to need to sort things out without getting found."

"You are welcome in the place, my friend. You have clothes?"

"Just some gym stuff in my trunk."

"I can get you fixed with some basics. We have a little thrift store down the hill."

"So if I talk to you, I want you to consider it privileged."

Father Bob nodded. "You don't even have to ask."

"Maybe your set of eyes and ears can help me."

"Glad to try."

I stood up as if I were going to address a judge in court. "All right. My fiancée is driving down the freeway when a freak thing happens. A body falls on her car. That is pure chance, pure accident. But she's alive. Someone gets to her almost immediately. It's raining and people are confused, so no one gets out of their cars and no one reports seeing this man. Except a strange little guy who looks like a rat. He comes to see me at Jacqueline's funeral. Are you getting this?"

"I was with you up to the rat."

I explained to him as best I could. "I don't know what his connection is, but I do think there's a link to a group called Triunfo and the guy who runs it, Rudy Barocas. The man who shot himself and fell on Jacqueline's car was part of this group, and the guy who got to the car was, too. He wanted to make sure the dead guy was really dead. Maybe he had something on the group that they didn't want to get out. Then he found Jacqueline alive and killed her so she couldn't ID him."

Father Bob didn't say anything, but his cogs were turning.

"A reporter, Channing Westerbrook, was on the scene, so I contact her and convince her there's something going on. She sees me as a story to follow and wants to turn it into a book maybe. So we strike up a bit of a deal. Exchange information. She also decides to make a play for me one night."

"A play?"

"Who knows why. She had a little to drink. She ends up scratching my neck. Outside I find Rudy Barocas waiting for me. In a big old limo. I think maybe Channing had started sniffing around Triunfo and Barocas wanted it to stop. He wanted me to stop, too. So he sets it up to kill Channing and put it all on me. My blood is on her blouse. How convenient is that?"

"Sounds almost too good to be true, if you're the district attorney."

"That's what I think."

"You didn't kill this woman, did you?" He said it as if he believed in me, not like he was cross-examining.

"No."

"Then we have to try to figure out who did."

"We?"

"I haven't got that much else to do. Say mass, solve murders. All in a day's work."

"All respect, Father, but I don't want you to get yourself in any trouble."

"Life is trouble," he said. "Only death is not."

"Thomas Merton?"

"Zorba the Greek."

At that we paused for a handful of Rosencrunch. Then I said, "I talked to David Townsend."

The look in Father Bob's eyes almost cracked my chest. It was a mixture of such loss and sadness that I thought he might fall into it and never come out. But then he blinked it away and asked, "What happened?"

"Nothing much," I said, "except he put up a hard line and then tried to choke me."

"Choke you?"

"He looked a little nuts. Also scared."

"Why?"

"Somebody did some work on his face."

"Like plastic surgery?"

"Like with knuckles."

"Beat up?"

"Could be anything. Mugging. Lover's quarrel. Or maybe he just fell down the stairs. I don't know, but I had a feeling there was a connection between his face and my questions. That's why he was scared."

Father Bob shook his head slowly. "Poor kid."

"Poor kid? He lied about you. He got you booted."

"He's in the grip."

"Grip?"

"We're all in the grip, Ty. The world, the flesh, and the devil. Until we let God loosen the fingers. Davey is still in the grip of his lie, and that's not a good place to be."

"I would have thought you'd like to work on his face yourself, after what he did to you."

"That's not my calling, son."

94

I WOKE UP the next day to a familiar sound.

A basketball drumming asphalt, short silence, then the sound of iron rim. Repeat. Repeat.

I twisted out of bed and looked through one of the porthole windows of the trailer. There was a basketball court about fifty yards away. Somebody in gray sweats was shooting hoops. Alone.

Sister Mary Veritas.

Making some very good moves. And she could shoot.

I threw on some shorts and shoes and a T-shirt, which amounted to about half my wardrobe at the moment, and went out to the court.

Sister Mary hit one from the foul line.

"Very nice shot," I said.

"Thanks."

"You played some ball."

"In high school." She dribbled in place. Her hair was nut color, short.

"Shouldn't you be praying or something?"

"The body is the temple of our Lord. It's our duty to take care of it. So I pray, play, pray, and eat. That's my morning. Do you play?"

"Some. Almost got my nose broken the last time."

"Don't worry," she said. "I don't throw elbows. Unless you come into my house."

I almost laughed at the thought of this little nun, who came about to my chin, trying to body me out of the post. "Is that a challenge?"

"Anytime," she said.

"I may take you up on it. I actually have a favor to ask."

She took a shot from the side of the key, banked it in. "Sure."

"Your car. I wonder if I can borrow it."

"You want to borrow the Abbey car?"

"If I may."

She looked over at my Cabriolet, parked behind Father Bob's trailer. "You have a nice ride."

"That's the thing. I need to be a little less noticeable."

"You figure to help yourself out?" she asked.

"You know what I'm talking about?"

"Of course. I googled the whole thing last night."

"Nuns google?"

"Remember our computers?"

"Ah."

"It's a little dangerous, what you're doing."

"I haven't done anything yet," I said.

"Maybe you should just stick here."

She shot again. I moved under the basket and caught the ball when it came through the net. I twirled it on my finger. "Thanks for the advice. May I borrow the car? I'll let you drive the Cab. You'll be the envy of all the other nuns."

"Envy's a sin, Mr. Buchanan."

"So is denying a man a favor, isn't it?"

She shook her head, smiled. "I'll play you Around the World for it."

"What?"

"Around the World. You win and the car is yours."

"Isn't that gambling? Isn't that a sin?"

"It's not gambling at all."

"How so?"

"Because I know I'll win."

Getting smack talked by a nun on a basketball court was surreal. Also irresistible. "You can go first," I said.

"You'll be sorry."

I was.

She didn't miss. Went all the way around and hit the final two. It was one of the most amazing displays I'd ever seen, and I saw Magic, Jordan, and Bird.

"All you have to do is make 'em all," she said, "and you'll tie. I'll give you the car on a tie."

She was like a little gremlin now, and I was hacked off. She needed to be taken to school, but I wasn't going to be the one. My first shot clanked off the rim.

Humbled by a nun. Not my best guy moment.

"You can use the car," she said.

"But—"

"Mercy is a virtue, Mr. Buchanan. And anytime you want a rematch . . ."

"Count on it," I said.

She bounced the ball triumphantly. "May I offer a suggestion?"

"Now that you've thoroughly shamed me, go ahead."

"Follow the sin."

"Excuse me?"

"You'll find the answer there."

"Can you be a little more specific?"

"Do you know the seven deadly sins?"

"Let's see. Lust?"

"Check," she said.

"Daytime television?"

"Close. Lust, gluttony, avarice, sloth, wrath, envy, and pride. Somewhere in there is the motive for every crime."

"Gluttony? The crime of overeating?"

Sister Mary smiled at my apparent ignorance. "The classical view of gluttony is overindulgence or excess in something you put into the body. Drugs and alcohol would fall into that category. There are drug crimes, are there not? And crimes done under the influence?"

"You have a point."

"Follow the sin, Mr. Buchanan. If I had to hazard a guess, I'd look to lust, avarice, or wrath. These seem to be the biggies these days."

"Thanks for the tip. Now can I ask you a favor?"

"Shoot."

"You're the computer maven at this operation, am I right?"

"I like the way you put that. It sounds cool."

"Are you?" I asked.

"I suppose I am."

"I need to track down a man named Frank Trudeau."

"Is he a friend?"

"Hardly, he—"

"Wait a second," she said. "That name has something to do with your case. It came up in one of the stories."

"He's married to a woman formerly named Dyan Blumberg. She's the mother of Claudia Blumberg who is suing Dr. Lea Edwards."

"Uh-huh. So why do you want to see this Frank?"

"Are you a cop all of a sudden?"

"Just curious."

"Mind if I keep it to myself?"

"Play you Around the World for it."

"No thanks."

"Mr. Buchanan, I want to help you. If you're not guilty of this charge, I'd like to do what I can—"

"Suppose I am guilty?"

She looked at me, holding the ball in her hands now. "Then I will pray for you."

"I'll take it."

"But I'd still like to know why you need to talk to this man."

"Give me the ball."

I took it to the top of the key. "This is for the info," I said, and shot. This time I hit nothing but net.

Sister Mary gathered the ball and dribbled to where I was standing. As she took her position to shoot I said, "No pressure."

She ignored me, took the shot. It rimmed out.

"I believe in mercy, too," I said. "I think Trudeau may have helped set me up. I want to have a word with him."

"Give me an hour," she said.

I waited in the trailer. And thought how being a monk might drive a guy crazy. Or closer to God, if that was the only other alternative.

Maybe that was the whole point. You sit in silence and God's the only alternative to hearing the voices in your head.

Like the ones telling me I would never get out of this, never. Somebody this determined to get you had his mallards all in a row. So why not stay here? Claim sanctuary?

Monks had their sacred text, and I had mine—Jacqueline's journals. I got the box from the trunk of my car and brought it into the trailer.

It surprised me to realize I'd been avoiding the journals. I guess I was thinking that once I'd been through them all, that would be it. There would be no new discoveries about her. She'd be gone then, truly.

But now it was like I needed her more than ever. This was the end of the world and I had no companion.

I took up a journal with a green cover. The date put her a year out of high school, the summer after her first year of college at Cal State Northridge.

> *The world is too much with us; late and soon,*
> *Getting and spending, we lay waste our powers:*
> *Little we see in Nature that is ours—*
>
> —Wordsworth

He got it right, did Wordsworth! I can't believe the beehive of pointless activity going on around me. Everyone seems to be moving, head down, toward some goal that involves real estate and BMWs, and they never look up except to watch—-

—the sordid unfolding story of a President who couldn't keep it zipped and some tramp stamp intern who kept a dress stained with his seed and didn't send it out to be cleaned. THAT is what we are fixated on!

I just sat in the backyard tonight and looked at the moon. For an hour, just the moon and the stars. The occasional plane flew overhead, blinking toward Burbank or LAX. I wondered about the people on the planes. Did they even bother to look out and see the moon? Or were they, too, thinking about real estate and Presidents who lie?

We'll keep missing what's most important as long as we don't look up.

A knock on the door. Sister Mary, in her habit.

"He works at a PR firm in West Hollywood," she said. "I have the address."

"You are good," I said.

"I'd agree with you," she said. "But pride is the great sin."

95

THE TAURUS HAD seen its best days when Clinton was in the White House. Probably purchased around Monicagate, and that just gave everything I was about to do a harmonic resonance.

Maybe things were lining up for me for a change.

Sister Mary kept the car neat. The interior was vintage nineties, and I could smell the ArmorAll. The only stuff in the car was a box in the backseat and a black cloth. The box was for fruitcake, the pride of St. Monica's. The cloth, I guessed, was for a nun's head. But I wasn't sure. I wasn't sure about nuns anymore. I'd seen a nun in sweats shooting baskets, and a mother superior who didn't wear a habit, but slacks and a blouse that might have come from Wal-Mart.

It wasn't a world I was familiar with.

The car drove pretty nice, especially for having 112,852 miles on it. Where did these nuns drive, anyway? Road trips? That must be a hoot.

I took the 118 to the Hollywood Freeway and caught the 101. Trudeau worked out of West Hollywood. It was early yet, so I decided to start my day by taking a look at Triunfo headquarters for a while.

I found a spot on Vine across from the location, sat back, and played surveillance.

The same woman who'd greeted me the last time was doing PR on the street. The book rack was visible in the alcove. At this hour it was still a little early for a lot of pedestrians. But a few regulars happened by.

The woman ignored a black man who staggered by and waved both hands at her. Nothing in Triunfo for winos I guess. She scanned the street, answered a call on her cell phone, and then went back to trolling for dollars.

What was I expecting to find here? I didn't know, but it was better than sitting in a hermitage waiting for something to break. And I figured my luck had to change. Something had to swing my way. If there was any hope of a God being in the universe, if Jacqueline had been onto something, there had to be some sort of yin to the yang I'd been dished.

An hour later, no yang had come my way, but my bladder was inflated. I got out and pushed a quarter in the meter and went looking for a head.

There was a Starbucks on Hollywood. I ordered a drip and was about to leave when a voice said, "Hey."

I turned around. A guy in his late forties or so was smiling at me from a table. He wore a camouflage jacket with a faded blue T-shirt underneath. He had a salt-and-pepper ponytail and L.A. eyes—trying to look cool and detached and hungry for money.

"You're the guy," he said.

"Excuse me?"

"Dude, you are the man. Hey, sit down a second."

"Thanks anyway." I turned. I heard his chair scrape across the floor. When I got to the door, I knew he was behind me.

Outside, I said, "I don't want to talk to you."

"Wait, man, you got me wrong." He still had that plastic smile on his face. It made me want to keep a hand on my wallet. "I'm on your side."

"I don't need anyone on my side, but thanks for the thought."

Again I tried to walk away. He stayed with me.

"Dude, wait, I just want an autograph."

I stopped. "What?"

"That's all. I sit in there and see a few minor leaguers. Bruce Jenner comes in now and then. Kathie Lee Gifford once. But never Phil Spector or O. J. Simpson."

"You want an autograph because I'm a defendant?"

"You're *the* defendant right now. Man, I can't believe this. This is so cool talking to you."

"I don't give autographs or interviews or have my picture taken with tourists, all right? You can go down to the Kodak and have fat Elvis sign for you."

He followed me to the corner. "Come on, you need friends. I might even land on your jury. How cool would that be? I'll guarantee you an acquittal or a hung. But I need that auto—"

"Look pal, the answer is no, and if you keep following me I'm going to get mad."

His smile finally faded. "That's no way to talk."

"You hearing me?"

He took a step back and reached in his jacket pocket.

Gun, I thought. *Guy's gonna kill me.*

For the half second it took for that thought to flash, I froze.

Then I saw a cell phone in his hand.

He flicked it open. Held it up.

And took my picture.

I unfroze. I dropped my Starbucks cup and lunged at him, caught his wrist, and grabbed the cell phone out of his hand.

I opened it and snapped it in two.

He turned around and whined, "Hey!" He sounded like Alfalfa from the old Little Rascals movies.

A couple of people, street people I guessed, had stopped to watch. But this being the big city they did nothing else.

"You're crazy!" Ponytail screeched.

He was right. "Boogah boogah," I said, then dropped the cell phone pieces on the sidewalk and gave them two big stamps with my heel. I kicked them down the sidewalk, past a few stars on the Walk of Fame.

He went one way and I went the other. But he managed to foul the morning air with some choice words, leaving off with, "I hope they find you guilty! I hope you fry in hell!"

96

I FRIED IN the Taurus.

I was a celeb now. There were no more anonymous defendants. With 24/7 news and Net, with picture and videophones and worldwide distribution, everybody could know everything about anybody. Just about. No more anonymity. Maybe that was as good a definition of hell as there was.

Sunglasses alone weren't doing it for me. If I was going to go out on the street, I'd need at least a modest getup. If Pitt and Cruise went out with fedoras and fake moustaches, maybe I could, too.

The only thing in the car was that black cloth.

I looked about as inconspicuous as Depp in *Pirates of the Caribbean*. But I kept reminding myself this was L.A., home of freaks and geeks and everything in between. A place where individuality was advertised as a shortcut to significance. Be different, get discovered. And if you don't get discovered, you can always pay for a billboard and put yourself on it, like that Angeline chick did years ago. She got famous for trying to be famous. It was the ultimate.

So walking around like Depp could be a new look for me, normal in Hollywood terms.

A guy in a leather jacket came by and put something under a windshield wiper of Sister Mary's car. He had a stack of papers in his hand. He didn't see me, or didn't bother to look.

I fished the thing off the window. It was a pamphlet, a tri-folded piece of paper with tight, single-spaced writing. The top of the page said that the Messiah was alive and living in Arizona. He was about to announce the beginning of the true Millennium—the last one was apparently a huge, Satanic lie —and it would only include followers of the Messiah and his prophet, the Divine Earl. Apparently the Divine Earl had been given a vision by the Messiah, and it included a description of the New Earth. The Divine Earl said the New Earth would be made up of those who had not taken the Mark of the Beast, which was some sort of stamp that related to one's social security number.

Illegal aliens would probably be in good shape, I thought.

I didn't read the rest. Thought Sister Mary or Father Bob would be interested, and tossed it on the seat. Went back to watching Triunfo.

The girl was gone, replaced by a young man with a big smile for all the people. He tried to talk to a lady walking a poodle, but she wanted nothing to do with him. The poodle yipped at his ankle. He smiled at the poodle.

I stayed another forty-five minutes. Nothing much happened. It was getting on toward eleven and I thought about driving through Burger King for a Whopper, then trying to see what I could dredge up at Frank Trudeau's office. See if he was meeting anyone for lunch, maybe follow him.

But just before I started the car I saw someone come out of Triunfo and start bopping up the street like he'd just won free Lakers tickets.

Then I recognized him. It was my good friend Ratso.

97

I GOT OUT of the car and followed him from a distance of half a block. He went to the Vine Street Metro Station, past the replica of the Brown Derby, and down the escalator.

He was going to take the train.

I was going to take him.

A few others separated Ratso and me. He was still dancing to some inner tune. He didn't have ear buds, so I could only assume he was happy about something.

Something I wanted to find out about.

He passed the ticket machine. Maybe he had a pass. I quickly bought a ticket just in case. The Metro rail ran on fear. If they did a ticket check and you didn't have one, it was a couple hundred bucks.

I got to the platform just as a Union Station train pulled in. I saw Ratso heading toward one of the middle cars. You can't switch cars on the line, so I hustled down and got on the same one at the other end.

The doors closed. Ratso found a seat at the far end of the car.

I stood at my end holding a pole.

Ratso moved his lips and head, singing to himself. Maybe he was high. He was certainly satisfied with life. That was a good thing. He was into himself and not looking too carefully at the people around him.

Not like a few others, who were looking at me.

Faces turned to me, looked away, and I wondered if I was violating some gang color rule in my crazy getup. If I got challenged on it, I could always claim I was an Oakland Raiders fan and that would probably do the trick. Raiders fans were known to be nuts and could therefore get away with pretty much anything.

We continued on. Stops at Hollywood / Western, then the Vermont stops, and down to MacArthur Park. That's where Ratso got off.

I followed him up the stairs, almost plowing over a guy sitting on the steps with an empty cup.

The Mac Park station was clean. And except for a mosaic on one wall, pretty nondescript. You could almost get a sense of repose here.

And then you take the escalators to the outside world.

MacArthur Park was directly across the street. As I emerged, still keeping Ratso in view, I could hear the simultaneous sounds of car horns, a jackhammer, and steel drums. That was the city all right. Anger, demolition, and music.

Ratso turned left, toward Seventh. It also happened to be where my favorite deli in the city, Langer's, was located. My chops lusted after a hot pastrami, but my feet kept me behind Ratso.

He took a left on Seventh and kept walking, finally turning into a little strip mall and a Hispanic market. I took a seat on a low block wall and pretended to be watching the traffic.

I sat there maybe ten minutes waiting for him to come out. No doubt he was taking his sweet time gyrating up and down the aisles looking for something to drink or eat or maybe smoke. When he came out, he had a little brown bag in his hand and continued a couple more blocks, finally turning right to go down two more streets.

I had to hang back because there weren't many people outside, and I didn't want him to see me. I followed from the other side of the street and saw him disappear into an old building with a fading sign—Huntington Hotel. Not much to look at. But better than a freeway underpass.

I ran to the hotel and entered. The lobby was full of old men sitting in old chairs watching a TV bolted to a corner. Soap opera. A couple of the old guys gave me a look. I saw the elevator doors close and went to it and watched. The lights told me it stopped at the fourth floor.

There was a front desk, encased in Plexiglas with sound holes. Nobody watching the store. I took the stairs.

At the fourth floor I entered a urine-smelling corridor. Walked it, listening. Heard babies crying and rap behind one door. A TV tuned loud, playing a commercial for DeVry University behind another. This was going to be door roulette. There were a dozen or so to choose from.

So, I thought, start spinning.

I ruled out the baby and rap door, and DeVry. I listened at a couple of others and heard nothing.

Finally, I knocked on a door at random. A scuffling sound and then a woman's voice, "What?"

"Triunfo," I said.

"What?"

"Triunfo?"

"Who's that?"

"Is Triunfo in there?"

"Ain't no Triunfo."

"Sorry."

Tried the door across the hall. Knock, no answer. I heard a TV or radio going, knocked again. Nothing. Maybe the person was out of it. Or had peeped me through the hole and didn't want any. Maybe it was Ratso.

"Triunfo," I said to the door. The rap music was loud enough from down the hall that I had to shout.

Nothing.

Went next door. This time it flew open after I knocked.

A man who looked like Shaquille O'Neal's larger brother filled the space. "Yeah?"

"Triunfo," I said.

His eyes were bloodshot. "Hell you talkin' about?"

"Looking for my buddy," I said. "Thought this was his place."

"I look like your friend?"

"Not exactly. He's about this tall, Hispanic."

"Oh yeah. 403." He jerked a thumb. "He owe you?"

"Just a friend."

"Too bad."

"What's too bad?"

"Thought maybe you was a dealer and you'd smoke 'im. I don't like 'im. Gives the place a bad smell. And you can tell 'im I said so."

"Sure." I wasn't about to deny this good citizen his wish.

At the end of the corridor, under a dirty window, was a metal trash container, the kind with the swinging top. I grabbed it and put it down in front of Ratso's door. I pounded on his door once with my fist. Then slid back to the wall, a few yards away.

A long moment passed. I thought he wouldn't bite.

Then the door opened.

I heard him say, "Hey."

His head popped out looking right, then left. At me.

I turned toward him, approached with my finger to my lips. Counted on him not recognizing me right away.

He frowned. "What's this?"

"It's OK, man," I whispered.

"What's this doin—"

Several things happened at once.

I saw his face change to recognition or fear. As he stepped back into the room, I lunged forward. Knocked the trash can over as my shoulder impacted the closing door. Drove with my feet. The door opened, slammed against the inside wall.

Ratso scurried back into his nest.

I slammed the door behind me.

The place was like a big yellow stain. Directly in front of me was a kitchenette with a yellow shade pulled over the window. A smell like Dumpster Alley bit my nostrils.

Ratso was not in the kitchenette.

To the right was a room that shouldn't have had the word *living* attached to it. It was a larger version of the trash can outside. It was a homeless camp inside four walls, down to a wire shopping cart overstuffed with items for survival on the street.

But Ratso wasn't here either.

I turned just in time.

Ratso took a Barry Bonds swing at me with a baseball bat. I ducked. The bat slammed into the inner doorjamb.

I stumbled backward into the homeless camp. Hit the shopping cart. Saw Ratso get ready for another swing.

Spinning, I whipped around to the other side of the cart as the bat whammed down on the cart stuffings. It made a sound like a fist hitting a pillow. A big fist.

I could keep the cart between me and Barry Bonds now. Like kids playing tag around a car. But that couldn't last forever.

Ratso's eyes gleamed like a rabid vermin wanting to bite something.

I needed a weapon. There was some furniture in the place. Old sofa. Tattered chair. An end table, scuffed and ancient. But with four legs.

"You die now," Ratso said.

"You don't want to do this," I said.

"Yeah I do." He smiled, and again I thought he might be high. Or just crazy.

"Put it down and we talk about it," I said.

"You not leaving with your head," he said.

He started tapping the bat on the edge of the cart. *Chank chank chank.*

I took a step back, put my right foot on the side of the cart, and drove it into Ratso's middle. If he hadn't slipped on something and gone down, I wouldn't have made it to the end table.

But he did slip. And I got the table. I held it up to him like a lion tamer. Or rat handler.

His eyes widened a little, then narrowed. "You got nothin', white boy." He laughed. "Fat white boy, you don't know how to fight."

I stared at him, not moving.

"What you say, white boy?"

Nothing.

"Say something!"

"I'm not fat," I said.

I charged, table up.

He sidestepped, but I anticipated that, guessing which side. He went to my left and drew back the bat.

I went left and high with the table. Caught his right cheek full on with a table leg.

He swung the bat but without anything behind it. It hit my shoulder but only enough for a dribbler up the first base line.

He screamed in pain.

Shoving with the table, I got him back against the wall, pinning him.

He kicked and almost got me flush between the legs.

I brought the table back and shot it forward again. This time I got him with a leg just below the right eye.

He cried out and his hands went to his face. He dropped the bat.

I slammed the table on top of his head, holding back about twenty-five percent. I didn't want him dead.

Not yet.

He crumpled to the floor like an old sleeping bag.

I picked up the bat and let him writhe a little. Then I poked him in his back with the knob end.

"Get up."

He put his hand behind him, rubbing the spot where I'd jabbed him.

I kicked his hand. He screamed again. I was glad about the rap thumping in the hallway. It would make it harder to hear him. "Get up or I take out a knee," I said.

"Who you think you are, man?"

"I'm a lawyer. Deal with it."

I poked him again. He struggled to his hands and knees.

"Sit there," I said, pointing to the couch.

He pulled himself onto the couch, rubbing his head. A nice gash was open on his right cheek. Blood trickled down and spotted his T-shirt. He looked at his hand, saw the blood, and screamed again.

I gave the outside of his left knee a healthy whap with the bat. His scream upgraded to a sharp wail.

I pointed the bat at his face. "Shut up. Shut up now."

He did. Backed up against the couch as if trying to go through it, he put his hands up. *No más.*

There was an old shirt in the spilled out mess from the shopping cart. I got it and tossed it to Ratso. "Put that on your cheek."

He did.

"You get to talk to me now," I said. "I want to know your connection to Triunfo."

"What?"

"Triunfo."

"What's that?"

I whacked his knee in the same place.

He shrieked. "Man, that hurts!"

"Talk."

"They gonna kill you, man."

"How did they get to you?" I thought a moment. "Or you to them? Was that it? You came to shake me down, then you went to them? Are they paying for this place?"

He didn't answer. But his eyes rolled around his sockets. I'd scored something, like in pinball.

"What were you doing in Bonilla's house?" I said. "You were looking for something. You blew up a car. A diversion. Do you know you almost killed a little girl?"

Another score. He shook his head slowly.

"What were you looking for?"

When he said nothing, I raised the bat. He waved his hands in front

226 JAMES SCOTT BELL

of his face. "He had stuff they want," Ratso said. "He was gonna take it somewhere."

"What stuff?"

"Stuff his wife wrote down."

"What, notes of some kind?"

He nodded. It looked defensive to me. "Is that why he killed her?" I said.

"I don't know! I don't talk to the guy. I look for what they want."

"You find anything?"

Ratso shook his head.

"So you started doing dirt for Triunfo, told them all about me, did you?"

"Don't hit me."

"I'm just getting warmed up."

"Come on!"

"I'm looking into your eyes," I said. "If I don't like what I see I'm gonna break some bone. *Comprende?*"

"I'm bleeding, man!"

"More to come, unless you talk straight." There were two Buchanans in that room. The one with the bat I hardly knew. "You know who killed Channing Westerbrook?"

"No, man. I never heard that name!"

"The reporter. You ever hear talk about a reporter?"

"No. Honest, man."

I thought he was telling the truth about that. He was low level for Triunfo, a useful idiot. But there was one thing I knew he had details on.

"Listen real careful to this," I said. "The killing on the freeway. You saw who did it. You knew it was a Triunfo guy who killed the woman. Right?"

Silence.

"Talk," I said.

"Don't hit me."

"Talk now."

"They kill me."

"So will I." It came out almost effortlessly.

"Please, man."

I held up the bat.

"I don't know!"

Like an old-time cop with his billy, I slapped the bat in my hand a couple of times. "I don't think you're being up front with me."

"All I know, I swear."

"You know the name Frank Trudeau?"

He shook his head.

"A guy with curly hair," I said. "Anglo, about ten years older than me."

"I told you everything, man. Come on, take off, okay?"

"Barocas's guy, Vargas. Enrique Vargas, the guy with the teardrop under his left eye. Know him?"

"Everybody knows him," he said.

"Is he the one? Killed my woman?"

"I don't know, I never see him up close."

"Don't lie to me."

"Come on, man!"

98

"GET ON THE floor," I said.

"Huh?"

I slammed the couch with the bat. "On the floor, on your face."

"Oh, man!" He slipped off the couch onto the floor. "Just don't hit me."

"Facedown."

"You've got nothing to worry about if you just stay still." I rolled the shopping cart back a little and dumped the contents on him. Clothes and rags and plastic bags full of who knew what.

"Hey!"

"Don't worry," I said. "This is just a precaution."

"A *what*?"

I turned the empty shopping cart upside down and positioned it on top of the stuff on top of Ratso.

"That's heavy, man," he said. "What up?"

I knelt, got close to his face. "If that cart moves, I have to get all in your face again. So just be cool."

"What you doing?"

228 JAMES SCOTT BELL

"Gonna search your place. You try to move, you're gone. I find those notes, I'm gonna get mad that you didn't tell me. I might go a little *loco* in my *cabeza*."

I slammed the bat hard on the floor, just missing his head. "Like that."

"Okay!"

"Okay *what*?"

"There. There!" He indicated with his head. "Under the freakin' bed, man!"

Watching him, I went to the mattress and lifted it up. There was a black binder underneath.

"You take it," Ratso said. "Let 'em kill you. They gonna kill me."

"What is it?"

"It's over, man."

"Tell me what it is."

"Just kill me now. Or take this off me."

"Not yet. Not till you tell me what this is."

"Just take it and go."

I thought about it. "You got something on Triunfo in here."

Ratso groaned.

"You and me," I said. "I'm taking you in."

"What?"

"You got to talk to the man."

"No cops! Triunfo will cut me up."

"Then talk to me. You tell me what this is."

"Get this off me."

"Talk first."

"No!"

I took out my phone and faked punching in a number. Waited, then said, "Is Detective Fernández in?"

"Okay!" Ratso screamed.

"For real?"

Ratso nodded.

I closed the phone and kicked the cart off him. "Stay on the floor," I said. "And start talking."

"I don't know what's in there, man. I just know it's hot."

"How do you know?"

"She told me."

"Who?"

"Alejandra, man."

"Alejandra Bonilla? The woman who got shot?"

"Yeah, you stupid—"

"You knew her?"

"Yeah yeah."

"How?"

"She was my sister, man."

99

RATSO SAT BACK against the wall, holding his head. "They killed her. Ernesto pulled the trigger, but they did it."

I sat on the edge of the overturned cart, holding the bat, waiting for him to go on. He didn't at first, then I saw he was crying softly.

"What's your name?" I said.

"Gustavo." He sniffed

"Where you from?"

"Guatemala. We got ten in our house. Pigs in the yard. All we got is pigs. Alejandra, she get me here. She get me in with Triunfo. And this"—he looked around—"is all they give me."

"That why you tried to shake me down?"

"I got to make money, man."

"Playing both sides will get you dead."

"Like Alejandra. Man, I tell her she's crazy. But she is crazy for him."

"Who?"

"Barocas, man."

"She was sleeping with Rudy Barocas?"

Gustavo nodded. "She work for him like a, you know—" he made a writing motion.

"Bookkeeper?"

"Yeah. Like that. But he got tired of her, and she got mad. In my family, we get mad."

"I noticed."

"She tell me if anything happen to her, she has that in the floor. She say it will be like, you know, when you get money if somebody die?"

"Insurance?"

"Yeah. She say that."

"So you blew up a car on the street so you could get in and find it, is that right?"

Gustavo shrugged.

"You know you"—some rusty cogs whined in my head—"you torched my house, didn't you? You're the firebug."

"I have to do what they say!"

I banged the bat on the floor. "How'd you happen to be under the freeway overpass when Ernesto shot himself?"

"Oh man."

I hit the wall above his head with the bat.

"Okay!" Gustavo said. "I wasn't under no pass. I was in a car."

"What?"

"We were watching the house. Ernesto was supposed to bring Alejandra in, you know. Barocas want to talk to her. Next thing, Ernesto is getting in his car and driving. We follow him. That's when he does it."

Gustavo put a finger gun in his mouth and wagged his thumb.

"Who followed?" I said, starting to sweat. "Who was in the car with you?"

Gustavo shook his head.

"Who went down?" My voice was stretching thin. "Vargas?"

Gustavo said nothing. I threw the bat down and pulled him up by the shirt, held him against the wall. I didn't see that he had grabbed something on the way up. But I felt it. He got me on the back of the neck.

100

THE BLOW—IT was a bottle—put me on my knees. I heard scattering behind me. I turned in time to see the door open and Gustavo run out.

I got up and shot to the door. He was already gone. The guy was faster than a ferret.

I was reeling. I grabbed the binder and got out to the street. Saw no one. And wondered if Gustavo would be scared enough to run back to Guatemala.

I made it back to Vine and saw Sister Mary's car had a parking ticket. Wonderful way to cap the day.

I gave a glance over at Triunfo headquarters. Maybe I'd see Rudy Barocas. Maybe I could find a bat and talk to him.

Or maybe I'd see a pig fly overhead. That was what it was going to take. A flying pig who could talk and tell me what was going on.

I was just getting on the freeway when I got a call from Fran. Hysterical.

"There was a man here asking about you," she said.

"What did—"

"I thought he was going to kill me."

"Fran, why—"

"I'm so scared. Please come. I don't know if he's still out there."

"Did he threaten you?"

"I don't know what to do. Please hurry."

"Are you locked in?"

"Yes, yes."

"I'll be right there."

It took me fifteen minutes. I drove up and down her street a couple of times, didn't see anybody watching the place.

Fran was looking like she might have a stroke.

I put my arms around her frail body and said, "Take it easy, Fran. I'm here. Nobody is going to hurt you."

"Who was that?"

"Tell me what he looked like."

"He was a Mexican man, young."

"Did he happen to have a tattoo on his face?"

"I don't know. I don't remember. I was scared. I shouldn't have opened the door."

"You did fine. You did what a normal person used to be able to do in this town."

I walked her to the sofa and got her a glass of ice water.

She said, "Who are these people? What do they want?"

"Just blowing smoke. Nothing's going to happen."

"I can always tell when you don't believe what you say."

"Isn't that just like a lawyer?" I smiled.

"I know you like a son," she said.

"Your neighbor, the guy who was Army?"

"Mr. Gardner. Yes."

"I'll go next door and ask him to keep an eye out. Don't worry yourself. They don't want you, they want me."

"But I worry about you."

I sat next to her. "You're a wonderful woman, Fran. I consider you family, okay?"

"I'm glad."

"Me, too."

101

IT WAS DARK when I got back to St. Monica's. Quiet on the grounds. A couple of nuns walking near the parking lot gave me a curious look. The retreat's car, but not Sister Mary behind the wheel. They no doubt knew I was the guy living in the trailer, but I hadn't exactly been sociable.

I looked for Sister Mary in the main office, but no one was there. I decided to give her the news about being a scofflaw in person.

Back at the trailer I unfolded the notebook I took from Gustavo. It had a pad inside covered with writing, in Spanish. Probably a woman's handwriting. Probably Alejandra Bonilla, if it came from the house where she was shot by Ernesto.

In the pocket of the front cover was a diskette. Who used diskettes anymore? My Mac laptop, one of the few technical devices I had with me, didn't have a disk drive.

So I was holding something that was either explosive or worthless, and I had no way of knowing which.

I tried reading a few of the pages, just to see if I could pick up a random word. I managed to see *Barocas* a couple of times and *Triunfo* a few.

Maybe one of the nuns could translate for me.

A knock on the door. Father Bob, paying a neighborly visit. "How you doing?" he said.

"I beat up a guy today," I said.

Father Bob, to his credit, didn't flinch. Didn't look like he was passing judgment.

"How'd it happen?" he asked.

"It was just one of those things that comes up."

"You want to talk about it?"

"Not really."

"I'm listening if you do. Why don't you come out and sit awhile?"

There were a couple of lawn chairs behind the trailers. You could see the dark outline of the hills and the sky and stars above that. I gave Father Bob the short version of what happened.

"How'd that make you feel?" Father Bob said.

"I don't really want to analyze it," I said.

"We are all made for community," he said. "Not good to hold back."

"That's a little odd coming from you, isn't it?"

"Why?"

"Because you live here. Alone. In a trailer."

"What makes you think I'm alone?"

"All right. If I wasn't here, right now, then you'd be alone."

He shook his head. "Not even then."

"I guess it's an advantage to believe in God sometimes. At least it keeps you warm at night."

"God always has room for one more."

"Thanks anyway."

"So you going to tell me how you felt opening up a can of whoopin' on that guy?"

"What does it matter? I did it. I did it because I thought I had to."

"Not what I asked you."

"Who asked you to ask me anything?"

He paused. "Occupational imperative, I guess. Don't mean to be nosy."

"Forget it. If anybody's supposed to be nosy, I guess it's you. Tell you what. If I ever want to talk about it, you'll be the first to know."

"The second," he said.

"Whatever, dude. Father."

102

NEXT MORNING I looked for Sister Mary shooting hoops, but she skipped it this time. I took a lukewarm shower in my trailer and shaved. Then I walked to the main building.

I was met by Sister Hildegarde, who still didn't look like she was entirely on board with St. Benedict's hospitality idea. At least where I was concerned.

"Are you getting along all right?" she asked.

"Just fine."

"Staying long with us?"

"I'm very happy to be here. Thanks for having me. St. Benedict is a new hero of mine."

She nodded. Unsmiling. "And you plan to stay how long?"

"Sister. Mother?"

"Sister is fine."

"I have some problems I'm working out down below, I guess you could say."

"I know all about that."

Sister Mary came in through a side door. She looked at her superior like she knew exactly what she'd been saying.

"I have to go downtown today," Hildegarde said to the young nun. "I trust the car has a full tank of gas?"

She said that to both of us.

"Gotta confess," I said. "I mean, you know, come clean. I didn't fill it. I'm a little short on cash at the moment, but I'd be happy—"

"Never mind," Hildegarde said. "Perhaps you can work with Sister Mary on a plan for your departure."

She started to leave.

"Oh," I said. "Here." I fished the keys from my pocket and handed them over. Hildegarde nodded sharply, left.

"Not one of the warm people, is she?" I said.

"Sister Hidegarde prefers the life of the mind," Sister Mary said. "And politics. We are all gifted in different ways."

"She got the ice gift."

"Mr. Buchanan, I would prefer you not talk that way about my Superior."

"Lake Superior."

"Hey—"

"Got it."

"She has the responsibility for this place, and despite a different view of religious matters, my duty is to help her. Plus our ovens are in bad need of replacing."

"For fruitcake?"

"For fruitcake."

I whispered, "Maybe you should take this as a sign from God and just—"

"Mr. Buchanan, did the car run all right for you?"

"Oh yeah, the car was just great. Um . . ."

"Something wrong?"

"I managed to get a parking ticket."

She looked at me, shook her head, and started laughing. Laughed so hard she turned her back.

"I'm glad you find it amusing," I said. "I'll pay for it."

She turned back around. "You can work it off."

"Huh?"

"We have things that need doing. We will be happy to have you—"

"Look, I—"

"—help us out."

"Yes. Fine. Whatever you want. Now can you help me?"

She waited.

"Can you find out what's on this disk?"

She took it. "No problem." She sat at the desk and woke up the computer. Slipped in the disk. I came around the desk and looked at the screen.

"Yeesh," she said as a bunch of unreadable code came up.

"Not good," I said.

"Let me play with it."

"Think you can do anything?"

"Jesus raised Lazarus from the dead. Gimme a shot."

103

MY LAWYER GAVE me an earful.

"I will have to pull out every IOU I have with the D.A. to keep you out of jail," he said.

"Sorry."

"Sorry? You can't go around breaking people's cell phones and expect—"

"He got in *my* face."

"I don't care about faces. Just tell me you won't do anything like this again."

"Fine."

"Where are you?"

"I'd rather not say."

"This is ridiculous. You have to trust me. You do, don't you?"

I didn't really know. He'd come into my case unannounced and unpaid. He was doing this for the publicity. That didn't mean he wouldn't do a good job. His ego demanded that he win.

"What are my chances?" I said. "Realistically."

"That's something a criminal lawyer never guesses at."

"Guess," I said.

"Ty." He took on the tone of an understanding uncle. "This thing is most likely going to trial. That's when I will finally get to plead this case to a jury. That's where I shine. And I will continue to have my investigators and forensics lab do everything they can, every day, to establish a reasonable doubt. I will do this because I believe you are innocent."

"That makes two of us," I said. "I'll be in touch."

"Ty—"

I clicked off. When he tried to call me back I didn't answer.

Sister Mary came knocking a few minutes later. She had the disk and some papers in hand. "That disk, it was an old spreadsheet program, primitive," she said. "I was able to translate it."

She handed me the sheets. It was a list of names and addresses all over Southern California, some in Nevada and Arizona. Fifty in all.

"That was all," she said. "No title on the spreadsheet. Just this."

"Well done," I said. "You are Xena, Warrior Nun."

She shook her head.

104

AT FOUR, LATOURETTE called me again. This time I answered. "Your bail has been revoked," he said.

"What? I thought you—"

"The Dragon Lady didn't go for it. You have to come in. The judge has issued a bench warrant."

I said, "No."

"Excuse me?"

"No."

"What do you mean, *No*? You have no choice."

"Let 'em try to find me."

"Are you insane?"

"I'm not going back in. If I do, I'm never getting out."

"You let me handle—"

"I'll be in touch."

"Ty!"

I put my cell on silent mode and sat with my head in my hands for a while. This was bad. Very bad. Because I'd been stupid with a jerk on the street, a judge wanted me back in jail. But I meant what I said. Somehow, if I went in

I was done. The case against me was too strong. Even with Latourette arguing for me, unless we got some actual evidence to show someone else may have killed Channing, there was no way to defend me. You couldn't present an alternative theory without some basis. A judge would never allow it.

I needed time to think. I went outside to the basketball court and sat on a bench, as if some time in the sun would shed a little light on my situation. It didn't. But Sister Mary found me sitting there.

She said, "Not good, huh?"

"I'm officially a fugitive from justice. They revoked my bail. There's a warrant out for me."

"Well," she said, "then it's a good thing you're here."

"I'm going to need a few things. Hair dye. And some clothes."

"Disguise?"

"It's a time-honored move for people on the run from the law."

"I hope you know what you're doing," she said. "It sounds reckless and dangerous."

I nodded.

"So," she added, "you want me to pick those things up for you?"

105

A DAY LATER I had dark brown hair and the clothes of a factory worker. And at 1:30 I had a driver. Sister Mary didn't think it was a good idea for me to take the car alone. Sister Hildegarde wouldn't exactly find that wise. But she did say she'd take me anywhere I wanted to go.

A little company would probably do me some good, I thought. You stay enclosed in your own thoughts long enough, especially with the law after you, and it's crazy time. I couldn't imagine being locked up in prison for a crime you didn't commit.

I also knew it happened all the time, and I could be next.

I called KTLA and got their recording, punched 0 for an operator, asked for Greg Beck. Got his voicemail and said, "I have a name to give you, maybe involved with Channing."

He called back after twenty minutes.

"Everybody in this city is looking for you," he said.

"I just want to see you," I said. "Trade information. You have anything for me?"

"I might. But—"

"But what?"

"I want an exclusive interview."

Everybody wants to be a star. "If I get out of this thing, I'll throw in an autographed picture."

"You know I can turn you in."

"You want to?"

"No."

"Then show up alone. I'll be watching."

I told him to meet me at the corner of Devonshire and Topanga in the Valley. On the southeast corner. Then I had Sister Mary drive me down to the 7-Eleven on the opposite corner so I could watch for him.

"I never expected to be in this position," I said. "Sitting with a nun in a 7-Eleven parking lot."

"Me neither," Sister Mary said. "Isn't this aiding and abetting a fugitive?"

"Scared?"

"It's a little *Bonnie and Clyde*."

"You've seen *Bonnie and Clyde*?"

"Hello. Video generation."

"It just didn't seem to go together with . . ." I indicated her habit, then felt stupid and quickly added, "Slurpee?"

"Hm, and does that seem to go with . . . ?"

"Perfectly."

"Good call," she said.

I got us a couple of the blue kind. As she sipped hers, I could see her in the stands at a high school football game, an All-American girl.

"Where'd you grow up?" I asked.

"Oklahoma City."

"Country girl?"

"Ha. What do you have in mind? Dust bowl? Okies? Wheat stalks in the mouth?"

"I mean, Oklahoma."

"We have real cities and everything. Malls and movies theaters. Cars! Imagine that!"

"What? No Pony Express?"

"You're a real snob, aren't you?"

"Slurpees bring out the best in me."

"Look, I grew up in north OKC. Private school. Dad's a lawyer, too."

"Yeah? Does he take cows for a fee sometimes?"

"You want Slurpee all over you?"

"I'll stop. I couldn't resist."

"I admit I wanted to get out of there as soon as I could. I mean, it was fine growing up in OK. My grandparents had a farm in Okmulgee. Salt of the earth sort of people. I appreciate that. But if I never hear another gush about OU football, it'll be too soon."

"You're in Bruin country now."

"I thought the Trojans owned this town."

"University of Spoiled Children? Only temporarily."

I slurped, then said, "So what made you want to become a nun?"

"I fell in love with God."

"But the whole withdrawing from the world thing, I don't quite get it."

"You were in love with your fiancée. Jacqueline, wasn't it?"

I nodded.

"Didn't you feel," she said, "that you would gladly give up a lot of things to marry her?"

"Yes. Anything."

"Same with me."

"So it's like you've married God."

"Why do you put it that way?"

"I saw *Heaven Knows, Mr. Allison*," I said. "The Robert Mitchum movie."

"Do you learn all your doctrine from Hollywood movies?"

"Deborah Kerr played a nun. She was going to get a gold wedding ring."

"She was talking about taking her solemn profession."

"What's that mean?"

"It's the final vow. Right now I'm in a sort of intermediate period. A time of testing. To see if this life is truly what I am called to."

"You mean you can still opt out?"

"I wouldn't exactly put it that way, but yes."

"I admire you," I said.

"You do?"

"You're going for something, all out. Too many people pull their punches these days. Or commit themselves to nothing. They get more upset about celebrity breakups than the great questions. We've become a pretty surface-level culture."

"You've thought that through a little."

"Jacqueline was like that. She was searching for something."

"Maybe you'll find it for her."

We talked for about an hour as I watched the other side of the street from the car. Talked about a lot of things. Even philosophy. I told her about a professor I had in college, John LaValley, who turned me onto the subject. Sister Mary had gone through the Great Books program at St. John's College in Annapolis. She knew more than I did by about a factor of five.

But it was good to think about things other than my own sorry station in life.

Finally, a Jetta turned off of Topanga and pulled to the curb. Greg Beck got out and sat on the hood, looking around.

"You mind waiting?" I asked Sister Mary.

"Just call if you need me, Clyde."

106

I CROSSED THE street and joined Beck. He didn't recognize me at first. Then said, "What's with the hair?"

"Let's get in," I said.

In the car, Beck said, "If you're not guilty, how come you jumped bail?"

"I didn't. A guy tried to take my picture with his phone and I took it away from him. The court didn't like that."

Beck smiled. "I probably would have done the same thing."

"So I'm getting pretty desperate here."

"You know, Scott Peterson changed his hair color once."

"I just love being compared to Scott Peterson. Only he was guilty. I'm not."

"I think I might be starting to believe you."

"Did Channing ever mention a guy named Frank Trudeau?"

He reached to the backseat, brought back a file folder. "I found this on her desk after she was reported dead. I kind of took it for myself. Thought maybe I could find something to use against you. But there's nothing bad about you in there."

"Can I see it?"

He handed me the file. I started looking at the notes. Saw my name on there a few times, with dates. The times we talked. She wasn't taking down things verbatim. One entry said, *He seems hurt inside and I try to get him to talk. Male reticence. Make this a subtheme.*

"So I was a subtheme," I said.

"Hm?"

"I guess she used everything as fodder."

"Fodder?"

"You know, what they feed animals."

"I don't follow you."

"It's all right. I don't like to be followed." I went back to the notes. She'd done a web diagram, a sketch of possible relationships. My name was in the center of the diagram, with spokes going out to Triunfo, Lea Edwards, Kendra Mackee, Claudia Blumberg, Law Office, David Townsend.

So she'd found Townsend, too. I never told her about him. She was killed before I could. She was doing that investigative reporter thing behind my back, delving into areas without telling me. Now I started to wonder. Did her interest in Triunfo get her killed? Had she asked one question too many of the wrong people?

"She ever talk to you about doing a story on Triunfo?" I asked.

Beck shook his head. "Never mentioned it to me. She always had two or three projects going."

"Did she have any other files? Maybe computer files?"

"I didn't get her computer stuff. The station took all that over."

"Maybe I can get my lawyer to subpoena all that," I said. "Could be something exculpatory in there."

"I hope you're telling me the truth," Beck said.

"About not killing Channing?"

He nodded.

"I'm not a killer," I said. I cleared my throat. "I mean, I could never kill anybody in cold blood."

Hot blood maybe.

I scanned the rest of the notes. Beck waited patiently, softly drumming the steering wheel. Made me think about going back in time, playing drums for Jacqueline. Going back and telling her not to get on the freeway that day. Getting in a car with her and driving someplace together, anyplace, and getting married, like they used to do in those old movies in the thirties. Clark Gable and Claudette Colbert. Us. Alive.

On the last page I saw the word "Law" again and some scribbles below it that didn't seem to mean much. But then I saw something that must have made my face pinch.

"What is it?" Beck said.

"I have to run a little errand. Thanks for showing up."

"What about the interview?"

"You'll get it, if I can get out of this."

"What if you don't get out of it?"

"I'll give you the interview from prison."

107

"KIM?"

"Mr. Buchanan!"

"Not so loud."

"I'm sorry."

"Did anybody hear you?"

Pause. Low voice: "I don't think so."

"How are you?"

"Gosh, how are *you*? Where are you?"

"I'm out and about."

"I've been so worried."

"I need you to do something for me."

"Yes. Of course. Anything."

"Is Al in?"

"You want me to put you through?"

"No. Just tell me if he's in. Don't let anybody know. Especially Al."

"I'll put you on hold."

Sister Mary waited patiently as I made the call. Kim came back on and told me my friend Al Bradshaw was in a conference until 4:30.

"Thanks, Kim."

"What are you going to do?"

"I'm going to stay out of trouble if I can. I'll be in touch."

To Sister Mary I said, "If I promise to take really good extra special care of this fine automobile, and pay for a full tank of gas, and—"

"You don't want me to drive you?"

"This one I better do alone. I'll give you a ride back."

"Would you do me a favor first?"

"Yes."

"Look at me and tell me that you're not guilty."

I looked straight into her blue eyes. "Sister Mary Veritas, I am not guilty. I did not kill Channing Westerbrook."

She nodded. "I know."

108

AL LIVED IN a nice neighborhood in Calabasas. It was an enclave for the upwardly mobile and family set, a burg of Mercedes SUVs and Priuses. Clean and smoke free. It was the first township in the United States to pass an ordinance banning smoking in public. What was next? Vote Democrat or be banished?

I parked the Taurus at the curb of the house next door and waited for Al to come home.

If I knew his pattern, and I did, he would stop for a couple of happy hour drinks and then, reluctantly, head back to what he called the belly of the beast. The beast being his wife, Adrienne. But he had two kids he doted on.

And one friend he had lied to.

I waited for two hours, until the sun was down and the neighborhood dark. It was almost seven-thirty when Al's car came around the corner and turned into his driveway.

When he climbed out I flashed my lights at him. He turned toward me and I flashed the lights again. I got out and said, "Al. Over here."

"Ty?"

"Come here, will you?"

He did. "What are you doing here?"

"I wanted to talk to you."

"Sure, just let me—"

"Hop in."

We got in the Taurus and he saw me by the interior light. "What's with your hair?"

"I'm disappointed in you, friend."

"Huh?"

"You lied to me."

"What are you talking about?"

"Remember when I was asking you about Channing Westerbrook? You said she looked good on TV?"

"Yeah."

"Wondered what she looked like up close?"

He said nothing.

I said, "Why, then, did she have notes of a face interview with you on January 10?"

"What do you mean, interview?"

"I saw her notes. So what were you telling Channing Westerbrook about me?"

"She was doing some background on you."

"Why didn't you tell me?"

"It was supposed to be confidential."

I reached out and grabbed his shirt. "What are you holding back?"

"Hey—"

"I trusted you, man. I mean, I would have trusted you with my life."

He pushed my hands away. "I'm sorry," he said. "But we have to do what we have to do. McDonough wants me to steer clear of you. Maybe someday we can start up again."

"That's it? That's all you're going to say?"

"Good luck, Ty. I hope you get out of this."

I told Al exactly where he could go.

109

I DROVE TO the NoHo Theater Center and found a place on the street. It was eight-forty-five. The show, *Sweeney Todd*, would be well under way.

The back of the theater edged up to an alley where a few cars were parked. That's where I waited. And waited. It was dark and foggy in North Hollywood that night. The streetlights gave the fog a fuzzy luminescence. Cotton balls with lightbulbs. A kid's dream. Or nightmare. It could go either way.

At nine-twenty the back doors came open and a few people streamed out, a couple lighting immediate cigarettes. Intermission.

One of them was David Townsend.

He took a few steps away from the door, lit up, lost in thought. He never saw me come up from behind. "Hi, David," I said.

He jumped and spun around. "Hey!"

"Easy," I said.

"What do you want?"

"Remember me, Davey? From Jeremiah's?"

"Geez, man, what are you doing?"

"I need your help."

"Forget it, man, I—" He started to move past me, but I stepped in front of him.

"David, I have one question for you. Who is Lorimar?"

He said nothing.

"Tell me who he is, David. And what did you tell Channing Westerbrook?"

"Man, I can't—"

"Listen to me. I'm not going to use it against you. I just want to find out what's going on. I want to know why Channing talked to you. And I want to know about Lorimar. And I'm freaking nuts right now so I'm not sure what I might do."

He looked up at the night sky and then at me. "God, I hate you guys. All of you."

"All of who?"

"All of *you.*"

"Lorimar?"

"Lattimore, jerk. His name's Lattimore. I hope he gets you, too."

"Who is this guy?"

"I hate all of you."

"Why is he messing you up?"

"Why else? To keep me quiet."

"Quiet about what?"

"If I tell you then I'm not being quiet, am I?"

"Tell me!"

He stepped back. "What are you going to do, beat it out of me? You're scum like the rest of them."

Standing there, rage coursing through me, I thought he was right.

Then he took off running. Back to the theater. There was no way to run after him without a big public spectacle.

I stood there a moment, feeling like Elmer Fudd after he's just run off a cliff. Looks around. Realizes he's standing on air. A big wrapper with *Sucker* covers his head. It's nothing but down from there.

110

I CALLED MY lawyer from an all-night diner in Studio City, left a message. Had to wait out two cups of coffee before he called back.

"Where are you?" he said.

"You always want to know that," I said.

"Ty, you have to come in. This is ridiculous."

"I have a name to give you. Lattimore."

"What are you talking about?"

"I don't know what I'm talking about. All I know is a guy named David

Townsend. Works at the NoHo Theater. I think there's a connection with Channing Westerbrook somehow. He says a guy named Lattimore has been beating him up to keep him quiet about something."

"Like what?"

"I don't know."

"Ty, you're talking crazy."

"That's right! I am talking crazy! I got nothing else!"

"Calm down."

"This is as close as I get!"

"Listen to me," Latourette said. "I want you to come in. I want you to come quietly to my office tomorrow at ten. All right? Nice and quiet and we'll talk about this."

"You gonna have the cops waiting?"

"I wouldn't do that to you."

"How do I know that?"

"Trust me, I told—"

"Here's some news. I don't trust anybody."

I slept in the car on a road in the Hollywood Hills. Maybe slept is the wrong word. Did the washing machine thing, tossing around all night.

Was hoping when I got up that something would coalesce in my mind. That I'd have the whole picture. And that I'd be free.

Not.

A haze hung over Hollywood like a wet sheet. Couldn't see much besides a Scientology sign and the murky shadows of cars haunting the freeway.

I felt like Courtney Love's ashtray. Clothes crusty with dried sweat. And knew at once I better go see the Silver Bullet. There was no way I was going to figure things out on my own. I needed a team, needed as many people on my side as I could get.

But I wasn't going back to jail.

I breakfasted at the Burger King on Highland. Ah yes, so fine. Fugitives can live like princes.

At nine-forty-five I entered the underground parking at the Silver Bullet's building in Century City. Nice digs for a criminal lawyer. Big-time. I almost felt good about my chances as I took a spot on level two. What happens when a white-collar guy gets nabbed by the FBI or police? He gets the most expensive mouthpiece he can, and a mouthpiece only gets expensive by winning a lot.

And the Silver Bullet was a winner, I thought, as I got out of the Taurus and started for the elevators.

Then stopped.

A guy in a leather jacket who did not look like he belonged was heading my way. Looking at me. He had his right hand in his jacket pocket.

I started walking again, in a direction to make a wide arc around the guy.

He started leaning my way. Studying me.

"Mr. Buchanan?" he said.

Maybe he was somebody who worked for Latourette. Knew my name, but was hesistant because of the new hair color.

Or maybe he was a reporter, in which case my cover—such as it was—was blown.

So I pretended like I didn't hear him.

"Mr. Buchanan." More insistent.

I tried to keep walking but he cut me off.

"Excuse me," I said.

"Mr. Barocas wants to see you," he said.

I looked him up and down. "How many days have you been scoping this place?"

"Let's go," the guy said.

"Tell him to send me an e-mail."

He shook his head. Made a *come on* motion to somebody. A moment later a red Thunderbird squealed up. There was no one else down here.

"Get in," the jacket guy said.

The driver, I now noticed, was holding what I took to be an assault weapon. Balancing it on the window, smiling.

"What about my car?" I said.

"Leave it."

"It'll get towed."

"Not my problem."

"You Catholic?"

He just looked at me.

"You're gonna really hack off the church if you do this."

My cell played *Flight of the Valkeries*. Before I knew it Jacket Man snatched it off my belt and tossed it under a Civic.

"That's just mean," I said.

Jacket Man showed me the handgun he had in his pocket and said, "Get in."

111

"SO YOU GUYS work for Rudy Barocas," I said.

No response.

"He made you respectable, did he?"

"Shut up, why don't you?" the guy next to me said.

"No need to be embarrassed about it," I said. "You're a great American success story. Former gangbanger. Gone straight. That about it?"

Silence. They had their order to bring me to Barocas. They wouldn't mess me up, I was sure. I should have been more deferential, if I wanted to keep all my teeth. But there was a river of ice in me all of a sudden. Like I'd used up all my fear.

My legal specialty, even though it's not recognized by the state bar, is knocking witnesses off balance, getting them to talk when they shouldn't. Maybe I could get something out of these guys.

I said, "And now all you do is spread love to the world, right?"

The driver said, "Shut up."

"Your vocabulary could use a little work," I said. "*Please do not discourse further.* Try that."

"How 'bout I break your face?" my backseat companion said.

"Now there, you see that? Going back to the old ways. You're a functioning member of society now. You go on *Oprah* and talk like that, she'll slap you."

"Not Oprah, man," the driver said. "She give us a new car maybe."

"Let me tell you about Oprah," I said. "She had a guy on who wrote a book about his life. A real heart tugger it was, about how he got his life together after being on drugs and all that. Sold a whole bunch of copies. Only problem, he made most of it up. When Oprah found out, she made him come back on the show and ripped him on national TV."

"So?" the driver said.

"So don't pretend to be something you're not. Somebody's gonna find out."

Backseat laughed.

"Tell me how he does it," I said. "How he takes you guys off the street and turns you into the fine, upstanding citizens you are today."

"He gonna show you, man," the driver said with a smile. "He gonna show you good."

112

THE TRIUNFO RANCH was located somewhere north of Lancaster, off the 14 Highway. It's in the Antelope Valley of L.A. County, though the antelope don't roam on this parched, dusty chunk of the Mojave Desert. While the Lancaster area has boomed in recent years—young couples looking for affordable housing—the outlying areas are still best left to gila monsters.

Or private facilities for the rehab of gangbangers. If you were looking for a tougher place to whip bad boys into shape, you'd be hard-pressed to find it.

The ranch was actually at the foot of some hills that would have been a great location for a fifties' movie about Mars. It was marked with a simple sign and a locked gate. The backseat guy got out and unlocked the gate. The car came through. He locked the gate and got back in.

We drove up a flat, dusty, windy road. The hills to the right had nothing growing on them. The grounds had nothing but dirt and rocks. And everything was being baked by a sun that seemed a million miles closer to the earth out here. It was an Al Gore dreamscape.

Finally, we got to a dirt parking area that had three or four pickups scattered around. On three sides were white, ranch-style buildings. The main building was a pretty good-looking, two-story job. Didn't look more than ten years old. The buildings on the sides were bunkhouses or dorms. No doubt for the tender little kiddies who came here to get their lives turned around by Rudy Barocas.

My two hosts led me into the main building. In the lobby was a reception area done up in Mexican flag colors. A large poster of a glaring guy in a sombrero was framed above the reception desk.

"Not very friendly," I said to my driver and nodded at the poster.

"That's Zapata, man," he said.

"Emiliano Zapata," Backseat said.

"Doesn't look anything like Brando," I said.

The two said nothing.

"It was a movie," I said. "Marlon Brando. You guys like Brando?"

Apparently not. They pushed me along a corridor, past double doors with windows that looked into a mess hall.

A couple of teenagers with 'tude passed us coming the other way. Everybody grunted at each other. They were like the humans in *Planet of the Apes*. At the end of the corridor the driver knocked on a door and somebody said, "Come in."

It was a pretty fancy office for such an out of the way place. Especially for a guy with that teardrop tattoo under his left eye.

"Welcome to Triunfo Ranch," Teardrop said.

"Vargas, isn't it?" I said.

He blinked. "That's good. You do homework."

"Kills time."

"Mr. Barocas thought it would be good for you to take a look at what he does for the community."

I said nothing. Vargas nodded for my hosts to leave. They obeyed like a pair of Cub Scouts.

"Two years ago," Vargas said, "those guys were running with the Second Streeters in Pacoima. Very bad. Cousins. It was a two for one deal. Court sent 'em here, and look at 'em now."

"Yeah," I said. "They handle guns real nice."

"Guns? What guns? We don't allow that." He smiled. "Mr. Barocas, he took a personal interest in them. In two months out here they were straight. No drugs. Nothin' but hard work."

"What a great story for the papers."

"Come on, I show you more."

He stood up and came around the desk. He was dressed in a pullover black shirt, tight on his muscled body, and jeans and boots. He opened the door, motioned me out.

For the moment I had no other choice but to play along. I had no idea if I'd ever get any other choice. If I did, I knew I'd take it. Without question.

We went out a back door into a large courtyard. Across the yard were a couple of barns, doors wide open. No hay in the barns. Or cows.

Cars. And a couple of pickups, young men working on them. It was a garage outfit.

"Strong automotive program here," Vargas said. "A lot of our boys go to good jobs the first day they're out. You own a car, Mr. Buchanan?"

"I look like I don't?"

"What kind?"

"An old Ford."

"You bring it out here, we fix it up nice for you."

"I'll remember that."

I followed him to the first open barn, which had a concrete floor and hydraulic lifts. A full-service garage. A kid in greasy overalls was working under a Firebird. His legs stuck out. Vargas tapped him on the feet with his boot. The kid shimmied out on a roller and stood up like he'd been ordered to.

He looked me up and down.

"How long you been here?" Vargas asked.

"Four months," the kid said. He was about sixteen.

"What would you be doing now if you weren't here?"

"Bustin' it up."

"You here because of that?"

"*Vato loco.*" He smiled.

"When you get out, what're you gonna do?"

The kid jerked his thumb toward the car.

Vargas nodded. "You gonna run with the same crowd?"

Kid shook his head.

"Why not?"

"Family is destiny."

"Who told you that?"

"Mr. Barocas."

Vargas put his fist out, and the kid tapped it with his. Then Vargas indicated I follow him farther on.

He paused at a workbench and picked up a large crescent wrench. Hefted it. "Somebody could do a lot of damage with this," he said. "You know, one of our boys could say he didn't like the way he was looked at, take this, and bam—" He slammed the edge on the workbench. It echoed throughout the garage.

"Very impressive," I said.

"Everything Rudy Barocas does is very impressive, don't you think?"

"I haven't seen everything."

"Maybe you will. Come on."

In back of the barn-garages was a bungalow, one that was almost hidden from the rest of the ranch. Unless you were looking for it you'd miss it. Vargas went up the wooden steps and opened the door. I stayed where I was.

"Come on," he said.

"I've seen enough. Where's Barocas?"

"Matter, you don't trust me?"

"Have him come out here."

"It's hot out here, man. Come on in where it's cool."

I didn't move. Then the door opened some more, and Rudy Barocas himself stepped out. He was dressed in business casual by way of GQ and Brite Smile. He even winked at me. "How you doing, Buchanan? Come on up."

Behind me, something moved. Turning, I saw the kid from the garage, staring at us. Sending a vibe. I wasn't to go anywhere.

Except into the bungalow.

113

"YOU WENT TO a lot of trouble to get me out here," I said, looking around. The place was wood paneled and set up as an office with a desk and a couple of chairs. The walls had a number of framed pictures. From what I could tell they were all Rudy Barocas shaking someone's hand.

"There's me with Magic Johnson," Barocas said. "And you see who that is?"

I looked. "George W. Bush."

"George Freaking W. Bush! Back in '04. And he's shaking the hand of a kid who escaped from Cuba and made good. Doesn't that make you feel great?"

Funny, his book jacket said he was born in Miami. "You could have sent me your press clippings. Why drag me out here?"

"No substitute for the real thing."

"I can't do you any good. I'm not good ROI."

"Return on investment! I got that in my book. Let me show you something."

He went to his desk and turned around a Mac laptop. It was some website. I recognized the seal of Los Angeles. The one they took the cross off of a couple years back because it offended the ACLU and four other people in the county.

"This is an official page about Triunfo. The page is sponsored by a Los Angeles County supervisor. Think about that."

"Leland Rich?"

"Hey, you know! You're a pretty smart guy. How'd you get into so much trouble?"

"Maybe you could help me out a little on that."

"Now." Barocas wagged his finger at me. "I think maybe you have a wrong idea. I think maybe you think I had something to do with killing that reporter."

"The thought's crossed my mind."

"If I did, you think you'd be breathing right now?"

"I always try to breathe."

"I don't go around killing people. You don't do that and get ahead in America."

"That's not what Michael Corleone thought."

He waved his hand. "That's the movies. Movies about wops don't do it for me. So I'm telling you, I had nothing to do with the death of that reporter."

"Had she contacted you?"

"I think maybe you turned her onto me. You said some things to her maybe and got her going after a hot story or something."

"Why should that worry you? You're such a great success."

"Did I say I was worried? No, my friend. That's not what worries me. What worries me is people like you, all tight inside, confused. I'd like to try to help you. You could become a Triunfo success story."

"Yeah?"

"Sure."

"And then maybe do commercials for you, like Kirstie Alley does Jennie Craig."

He smiled a little too broadly. "Now you're talking."

Vargas just stood there. Stone face. I kept thinking what it would be like to blow that face up. Dynamite it like Mount Rushmore.

"Hey, can I get you something?" Barocas said. "Coke? Beer?"

"I'm fine."

"No," he said. "I don't think you are. I think you got a lot of anger and worry, and you're sweating just being here, aren't you?"

"What do you want me to say? You yank me out here. Guy with a gun threatens me."

"Guy with a gun?"

I chuffed.

"What I need to tell you, Buchanan, is you can't do anything to me or Triunfo. It's all too big, too important. We do good work. And if you say things like some guy with a gun made you get in a car and come out here, well that's just not gonna fly with anybody. You're all alone, is what I'm saying."

"Okay. I'm alone. Can I go now?"

"Not just yet. Listen. What the mind of man can conceive and believe, the mind of man can achieve."

I just looked at him.

"Do you believe that?" he said.

"No."

"That's your problem. That's why you're there, accused of murder, and I'm here, making life better for kids and young men and living in a big house with a view. It's why you're small. You haven't got it up here. I'd like to help you change that."

"How are you going to help me there, Rudy?"

He smiled. "I'm going to show you how we do it out here, when we first get a *vato* who has an attitude problem, and that's all of them. A little discipline. That's all you need. That's why I'm your best friend."

It was only then I noticed that Vargas was still holding the crescent wrench. I guess I'd forgotten all about it. Maybe he'd had it up his sleeve all this time, waiting.

"That's it?" I said. "You're going to beat some sense into me?"

"Why should I do that?" Barocas asked. "All you need to do is tell me a couple of things."

"Okay."

He looked surprised.

I said, "The capital of North Dakota is Bismarck. And studies show if your parents didn't have children, you won't either."

Barocas stopped smiling. "Buchanan, don't make this hard on yourself. One of the big secrets to success is always to treat with respect those who can help you. Or hurt you. I can do either one."

"Cats have thirty-two muscles in each ear."

Barocas sighed and nodded at Vargas. He lunged. I flinched. My left leg went out from under me, pain exploding just below the back of my knee.

I hit the floor. A river of liquid fire spread up and down my leg.

"Not so hard," Barocas said in mock rebuke. "You have to use a little love in your discipline."

I made no move to get up. Didn't see the point in it.

"Now Buchanan, I think you've been talking to some of the wrong people, and I'd like to know about that. Here at the ranch we tell our boys to always speak the truth. At least to me."

Vargas grunted what sounded like a laugh.

"Get him up," Barocas said.

Vargas pulled me up by my shirt with one hand, as easily as he would a mattress. Barocas indicated a chair. I can't remember if I sat or Vargas pushed me onto it. I was thinking only about killing them both.

"You doing okay now?" Barocas said. "You want to make another joke now? We got all night."

I said nothing. Imagined what my leg would look like in many colors.

"So I understand you've talked to *federales*," Barocas said. "Maybe you think there's something going on that shouldn't under the Triunfo umbrella."

I shook my head.

"Maybe you think drugs or some other kind of bad stuff, huh?"

Said nothing.

"Tell me what you think, Mr. Buchanan."

Silent. But I watched his eyes. They flicked to Vargas again. He hit me in the face. It was his fist, but it felt like cinder block. He must have been holding the crescent wrench in that hand.

Tiny flares in my head. The right side of my face felt caved in. I thought about dying and didn't care that I thought about it. I just wanted to take these two with me.

"You need to be more forthcoming, friend," Barocas said. "Trust is earned, not given."

"I got a question for you first," I said.

"Go ahead."

"Why'd he have to kill her?"

Barocas didn't change expression. "Who killed who?"

"Your boy here. Why'd he have to kill the girl?"

"You know what he's talking about?" Barocas said to Vargas.

"No way," Vargas said.

"You think we go around killing people?" Barocas said.

"Have it your way," I said.

"I always do. You want to tell me what you know now?"

"Sure," I said. "Buddy Rich was the greatest drummer of all time."

Barocas shook his head, made a motion to Vargas.

He whacked me on the other side of the face.

"Now?" Barocas said.

I said nothing.

"You have something belongs to me maybe," Barocas said. "You know Gustavo."

"Who?"

"You've met him a couple times."

"I meet a lot of people."

"People are your greatest natural resource," Barocas said. "But you got to dig your well before you're thirsty."

"I'll tell you one thing, you got the clichés down real nice."

Vargas slapped the back of my head.

"Talk, Mr. Buchanan," Barocas said.

"Inch by inch anything's a cinch," I said.

"Well," Barocas said, "I tried."

That's when the fun began.

114

NEXT THING I remember I was bouncing in a box in the dark. The trunk of a car. I couldn't remember blacking out. My body reminded me.

Vargas had worked me, starting with the ribs. He drew back just enough not to crack bone. He was trying to inflict pain and keep me from passing out.

It didn't work. At some point I passed over into black.

Now, almost suffocating, all I knew was I was being transported.

My hands were tied in front of me. My nose was stuffed, probably with dried blood. My head felt two sizes larger. I didn't know if my eyes were open, or could open.

Then I saw a crack of faint light. Had no idea what time it was. Only was sure of one thing, that I wasn't being delivered anywhere. I would soon be dead.

My body told my mind not to stress about that. Just give it up, it's time, what are you doing hanging around here? You can't win against people like this. There's too many of them, and they're too powerful. Living here isn't what you thought it'd be. Try dying. Maybe you'll find that white light. Maybe Jacqueline will be there waiting for you.

My mind didn't fight back.

I may have blacked out again.

The trunk popped and orange light fell in. A figure was silhouetted there. I knew it was Vargas even before he told me to get out.

I didn't move. Didn't know if I could. Heard myself groan.

He grabbed me by the shirt and pulled me to the lip of the trunk, hanging me over it like a bag of clothes. He got his hands on my pants and jerked, and I rolled over and hit the ground on my back.

The last of the air left my lungs. Before I could suck in more Vargas kicked me in the side and told me, once more, to get up. I rolled on my side, drawing breath through my mouth, getting some dirt, coughing. I had no idea where we were, but the ground was hot.

Slowly I got to my knees.

Vargas said, "You got one more chance to talk."

All I could do was wheeze.

"Or you stay here," he said. "I got no problem either way. I think maybe leaving you out here's best thing. Get *up*."

He booted me in the ribs, the air went away, and I thudded in the dirt again.

I didn't wait for him to order me up again. Somehow I made it to my feet, wobbly. I focused as best I could, saw nothing but desert all around. Mountains off in the distance.

Vargas stepped in front of me. My head was hanging and I saw his hands. And what looked like a knife. Only the blade wasn't steel. It looked like stone.

I thought I might be going out of my mind.

"Tell you somethin'," he said. "You listenin'?"

I said nothing. Watched the stone blade.

"Look at me," he said. He tapped under my chin with the flat of the blade. I looked at him. He smiled.

"Want you to know," he said. "Want you to know she looked at me. Didn't know what was goin' on. Looked in my eyes and said *help*. Then I snapped her neck. Like a stick."

115

I DON'T KNOW if my body led, or my mind. Somehow it just happened this way—

I bowed my head. Like his words took the last drop of will from me.

"You gonna cry now?" he said.

Cry and fold and die and dry up—that could wait. It would wait, because now everything was without a thought as I took a short step forward and shot my head up, under his chin, hard as I could.

The impact told me I'd scored, hit his jaw flush. I pivoted, like I was in the low post, my back to him now, raised both hands up and elbowed him in the face.

In one motion I went around him and threw my hands over his head. Looking back on it now, this was another roundball move, a hot dog play. I used to hold the ball and the defender would come to my face, and I'd actually put the ball behind his head, then bring it back.

That instinct had served me enough to get Vargas around the neck. I pulled hard.

He flailed. He grabbed my wrist with his left hand. With his right he slashed back with the knife. It grazed my hip.

Before he could do it again I wrapped my right leg around him and forced us both down. He dropped beneath me.

I kept pulling. Kept it up until he weakened, wheezed, and went limp.

Why didn't I finish the job? I don't know. I only know two people shot through my mind—my dad and Jacqueline—and that somehow restrained me.

I used the strange knife, which was amazingly sharp, to cut my wrists free. With every bit of strength I had left, I managed to get Vargas up so I could push him into the trunk of the car. A Lexus. Blue.

Blue Lexus.

A blue Lexus followed me on Sepulveda one evening. Was it this one?

I wasn't going to ask. I slammed the trunk closed.

It was a good ride. In the fading light, I took a road leading away from the setting sun. Eventually shacks and single homes started to appear, then a paved street and a housing development. When I reached the first strip mall, I started to breathe a little easier.

It was evening when I reached the grounds of St. Monica's. I drove the Lexus all the way to the back of the property, behind the trailers. Father Bob must have heard me because he was out in two seconds as I emerged from the car.

He looked at me up close. "Mother of mercy," he said just before I fell into his arms.

116

I WOKE UP calling Jacqueline's name.

A cool hand touched my head.

"It's all right," Father Bob said. I was in the bed in my trailer. Father Bob sitting there like a nurse.

"How long have I been out?" I said.

"Half hour or so."

It started coming back to me. I started trembling, like I'd just been fished from the ice. Father Bob pulled the blanket up to my chin.

"I need a phone," I said.

"That can wait."

"No, now." My head was a bowling alley.

"You've been—"

"Please."

"Sister Mary has a cell phone."

"Would you mind getting her for me? There's also a card on the table, says Secret Service on it."

Father Bob found it. "What is going on, Ty?"

"There's a man in the trunk of the car outside. I want to get him out of here before he asks for hospitality. Can you get Sister Mary now?"

117

I USED SISTER Mary's phone to call Cisneros. Left a voice message. As we waited, Father Bob asked me if I'd like to explain.

"Not really," I said. Then, for some reason, I jumped in. "I almost killed a man," I said.

"The man in the trunk?"

I nodded. "The man who murdered Jacqueline. He was going to kill me and leave me in a hole in the desert."

"But you didn't kill him."

"Maybe I should have. I feel like I've crossed over. That I could have killed him."

"But you didn't."

I grabbed his wrist. "But I could have. I was never like that before. I don't even know who I am now."

"You want me to tell you?"

I waited.

"You are loved by God," Father Bob said. "You are not the exception."

"I wish I could buy that."

"Someday you will."

Cisneros called back.

"I've got somebody for you," I said.

"A name?"

"A body."

"What did you do?"

"It's Vargas."

"You have Vargas?"

"I got him."

"Dead?"

"Only close. He's in the trunk of a very nice Lexus."

I drove the Lexus to the corner of the Abbey lot. Vargas was yelling and pounding on the interior. I parked and looked down at the Valley, an innocuous blanket of colored lights.

Killer view. I listened to the breeze and the occasional sound of caged Vargas.

When Cisneros pulled up in a black Ford, he had someone with him. Another agent. Introduced him as *Smith-his-real-name.*

Smith nodded, all business.

Cisneros looked at my face in the single light of the parking lot. "Vargas do that to you?"

"They took me out to their ranch and worked me," I said. "They knew

I was talking to somebody like you. They were going to bury me out there. Vargas killed Jacqueline. But I don't know how to prove it."

Cisneros pulled a sidearm from under his coat, as did Agent Smith. "Why don't we start by popping the trunk?"

I did.

Vargas had his hands in front of his face. "Get me outta here," he said.

"Slowly," Cisneros said. "No sudden moves."

He struggled out of the trunk, his legs rubbery under him. Smith whipped him around and had cuffs on him in two seconds. Vargas turned back and looked at me. That heart of darkness stuff? I was looking at it then.

Smith shoved Vargas in the back of the Ford.

I'd brought the Bonilla journal from the trailer. I got it from the back of the Lexus and handed it to Cisneros. "This is probably going to interest you. It's something that came from Ernesto Bonilla's house. I think it was kept by his wife. I think that's maybe why he killed her, then himself. It's mostly in Spanish, but there's a very interesting spreadsheet. I had a sister here do a printout."

"You've done some pretty amazing things," he said. "Thanks for not giving me up."

"What are you going to do with Vargas?"

"Leave that to me."

"He'll know I got him. Barocas. He'll come after me."

"Let me give it some thought."

"I'd appreciate it," I said, "if you could think real fast."

118

NEXT DAY I ran up Sister Mary's phone bill by calling my lawyer. He was in court, but I got through to Gabrielle.

"Do you know how much trouble you're in?" she said.

"I think I do."

"Have you been watching the news?"

"I've been a little sidetracked."

"Sidetracked?"

"Will you have Marty call me at this number, please? And one more thing."

"Yes?"

"Would you mind going down to the parking garage, level two?"

"Why?"

"See if there's a red Taurus, circa 1995, down there? And maybe a cell phone?"

"What are you talking about?"

"It's a little complicated."

"I don't know if I want to hear it."

"You don't."

119

MY BODY FELT like David Hasselhoff's career. New places would start to hurt spontaneously. Instead of sitting around groaning, I called Fran, told her a sweet little lie about my being just fine. She didn't sound convinced.

What else could I say? I was a man on the run. How does that happen to a guy like me?

Something Jacqueline said to me kept rattling around in my mind.

We were going to go out to dinner, and I showed up at her apartment and found her in tears. What I finally got out of her was she'd been watching the news. They had the mother of an American soldier on. Her son had been captured by terrorists in Iraq. Tortured, killed.

"Evil is so real," she said.

I didn't pause for a philosophical discussion. She was distraught.

But now I knew she was right. Eggheads and Dr. Phil could pussyfoot all they wanted. Evil was real, and it did things to people. And sometimes it went after you.

The phone call was not from Marty Latourette. It was from one of the last people I expected to hear from.

"Where are you, boy?" Jonathan Blake Blumberg said.

"How did you get this number?" I said.

"That assistant of Latourette's, she—"

"Wait. Why is she giving that information to you?"

"Come off it, will you? Who do you think's paying Latourette?"

Stunned, I hardly knew what to say.

So I didn't say anything.

"Listen, it's getting hot," Blumberg said. "Marty told me you gave him the name Lattimore. He's a P.I., does a lot for big-name clientele. How'd you get that name?"

My brain jumbled around like Yahtzee dice.

"You there?" Blumberg said.

"I got the name from David Townsend."

"Good for you. This Lattimore has a rep. I know about him. He's a little too sold on himself."

"How so?"

"Dresses up in silk shirts. Parades around with all that curly hair and attitude. Guy like that starts to rest on his—"

"Whoa whoa whoa. Did you say curly hair?"

"It's sort of like steel wool."

The dice banged around even louder.

"What's going on?" Blumberg said.

"Where are you?"

"My office. Why?"

"I think I'm going to need your help."

"For what?"

"To hunt some meat."

"Now you're talking."

120

IT WAS B-2 who came up with Warren Lattimore's phone number and office location. We drove down in one of B-2's vintage Corvettes, something of a hobby with him, after he called Lattimore to set up a "discreet" appointment.

The office was in the back of a converted Beverly Hills duplex, the kind they turned into offices in the sixties. The front structure was Spanish-style and housed a hair salon. A black security gate on the side was the only indication there was a back office. No name on the gate either, or anywhere else that I could see.

Blumberg pressed a button on the call box and announced himself.

The gate buzzed open.

We followed a sandstone path under a trellis covered with clinging vines until we got to another Spanish building, a smaller version of the first. The oak door opened before we knocked.

Warren Lattimore was fifty-ish, about five-eight, and wore a black silk shirt open to midchest. Tufts of gray chest hair sprang out like ocean spray. The full head of sleet-gray hair was curly all right. I wondered if he had it permed by the folks in front.

"I'm Warren Lattimore," he said, extending his hand. He had a Brooklyn edge to his voice. "It's nice to meet you, Mr. Blumberg. I know a lot about you."

"And I you, Warren."

"Really?"

"Oh sure. You're one of the best."

"*The* best." Lattimore looked at me. "Hi."

I took off my shades. It took Lattimore about a second to recognize me. He looked at Blumberg. "What's this?"

"You know Mr. Buchanan, do you?"

"Sure, he's all over the news."

"Photographs well, doesn't he?"

Lattimore's face did a little tightening, like a poker player drawing to the inside straight. The bluffs were about to begin. "It would be a kick to help out Mr. Buchanan in his defense."

"I just bet it would," I said.

"I don't come cheap, but I could work out something. High-profile cases are my specialty. Come on inside."

Lattimore's office was done up in black and silver, leather and chrome. His large black desk held a computer monitor on one side and a console the size of a toaster on the other.

Which caught Blumberg's eyes. "That's a Z-11," he said.

"Yeah," Lattimore said.

"I make those."

"Right. I forgot. Great piece of equipment. I can call anywhere in the world and record anything, and it comes out clear as crystal. Well made."

"That's what I do," Blumberg said, "when I'm not killing people."

Lattimore, who was on his way behind the desk, froze. "I'm sorry, what?"

"Killing people. I used to kill for the CIA."

I almost burst out laughing. But Jonathan Blake Blumberg did not grin. He stared at Lattimore, who made it to his chair and slid into it. "That's news to me," he said. "Now how can I help you out?"

"You want to start?" Blumberg asked me.

"Sure," I said. "I appreciate your offer to help me, Warren, but we're here to listen."

"To what?"

"To you unloading your soul."

He looked chagrined and shook his head.

"You killed Channing Westerbrook," I said.

It took a second, but when his cheeks flushed it produced a nice glow. He looked at Blumberg. "What is this?"

"I think you better listen," B-2 said.

Lattimore shot to his feet. "Don't waste my time."

"Sit down, Warren," said B-2.

"Hey, you don't come into my office and tell me what to do."

"Sit down, Warren."

"Why don't you just turn around and—"

Jonathan reached under his coat and withdrew a gun. Just like in the movies. I think I was more surprised than Lattimore. I had no idea Blumberg was packing.

He pointed the gun at Lattimore. Lattimore put his hands in front of him and fell back onto the chair.

"Did I mention," Blumberg said, "that I used to kill for the CIA?"

I sidled up to Blumberg. "Jonathan, maybe it would be a good idea to put that thing away for now."

He shook his head, keeping his eyes on Lattimore. "Not until he hears what you have to say. I won't shoot him until you're finished."

Lattimore now looked to me for relief. "He's crazy. Make him put it away."

"I better get right to it, Warren," I said. "I'm going to tell you a little story, and then I'll let you decide what to do about it. I think I can even get Mr. Blumberg not to shoot you. Fair enough?"

Lattimore was openmouthed and silent.

"Maybe you could hold the gun at your side," I said to B-2.

He lowered the gun. I started my spiel. Lattimore listened. Blumberg didn't shoot him. Lattimore became quite amenable when all was said and done.

Now there was only one more person I had to see.

121

DR. LEA EDWARDS commanded the stage as usual. Speaking without notes, pacing back and forth, she looked more impressive than ever. Even from the back of the ballroom of the Renaissance Hollywood Hotel I could sense the vibe. This was a professional woman at the zenith of her career.

"Just remember," she said, "when it comes to human interactions and re-call, things are never as they seem. Divide up that perspective among twelve jurors, and your task becomes monumental. In a sense, because of the lim-ited reliability of memory, you must create the reality for the jury. You do not just reveal, you shape the facts. We would all like to believe there is ob-jectivity when it comes to truth, justice, and the American way. But that's for the comic books. You are for the courtroom."

This time there was no stunt. No shill yelling from the gallery. Just a standing O for Dr. Lea Edwards, holder of the golden key, who had just cre-ated about half a million dollars in more business for herself.

I hung back while a few stragglers made obeisance and got her to auto-graph her book for them. As the last one was fawning, I stepped closer and took off my shades. When she saw me, her head did a Richter—shaking before settling into uneasy disbelief.

She finished with the straggler, came over, and embraced me. "I don't believe it," she cooed. "What are you doing here?"

"Never too late to learn something."

She stepped back. "What's happened to you?"

"Somebody did a little work on my face."

"Aren't they looking for you?"

"I'm on the lam, as they used to say. Shall we go to the bar and live dangerously?"

We went to Twist, on the second floor, and took a little round table by a polychromatic window. It was almost as if Lea had planned the design herself. It set off her champagne colored suit perfectly. The jacket's embroidery almost bubbled in the dim light.

"I can't tell you what a pleasure this is, Ty," she said. "I've been so worried about you. Miss working with you."

"Al doing a good job for you?"

"Oh yes, workmanlike. But nothing like you."

A waitress stopped by the table and put a couple of square napkins down. Lea ordered a manhattan. I asked for Pellegrino.

"You ordered a manhattan last time we were together," I said.

"Always."

"See? Sometimes memory does serve."

She bit her lower lip slightly, like Bill Clinton being sincere. "Ty, I am so glad to see you, but what's going to happen? Is there anything I can do?"

"Actually, I'm here to help you with something."

"Me?"

"I want to help you stay out of prison."

Her expression went south. "What is that supposed to mean?"

"I remember us talking about a guy named David Townsend. I asked you about him, and you played like you didn't know who he was."

"Well, who is he?"

"We found Lattimore."

No change in her eyes. In a stone-cold voice she said, "Who, or what, is that?"

"He's the guy you hired to keep David Townsend from flapping his yap. What I figure happened is you were looking into Kendra Mackee's clients and used Lattimore. He got to Townsend and Townsend was going to talk about it. That would have supported the harassment story Claudia Blumberg is telling. So maybe you offered him money and he wanted more, or maybe you had Lattimore just pile on from the start."

"This is absolutely fantastic. Why are you saying this to me? I don't know anyone by that name."

"He certainly knows you."

She froze.

In court, a lawyer is ethically challenged. I mean, bound. Bound not to ask a question that doesn't have a solid basis in fact. But I wasn't in court now. I knew no bounds.

"What if I told you," I said, "that the curly-headed Mr. Lattimore is with the D.A. right now, pointing his finger at you?"

"Pointing?"

"For the murder of Channing Westerbrook."

Before Lea could react, the waitress returned with our drinks. She seemed to sense the mood and quickly placed the drinks and the check on the table.

I took the check. "I insist."

Lea said nothing. She studied me, not bothering to sip her manhattan.

"Did Channing start getting close to the story?" I asked. "And whose idea was it to include me in the mix? Did you just figure I'd be the perfect suspect?"

That was the point at which she imbibed. It was a long, contemplative drink. "Ty," she said, "can you help me?"

"Help you how, Lea?"

"With Lattimore."

"Whom you don't know."

She waved her hand. "You know what you know. But he's a liar. He did it all himself. And he'll try to implicate me. I need help. I thought I could handle him. But he went off on his own. I can prove it. We can get him, you and I."

"Why didn't you turn him over to the cops?"

"That would have brought it all crashing down, wouldn't it? My reputation. Gone. Everything. Now we have no choice. We have to move."

She reached her hand across the table. A plea. I took her hand. It was cold.

"I can arrange for you to talk to the D.A.," I said. "In fact, it may be sooner than you think."

She shook her head.

"You see this watch?" I said. I held up my wrist and removed Jonathan Blake Blumberg's prototype. "It's an amazing thing. I mean, there's a room on the third floor here where a Dragon Lady and a Silver Bullet are sitting with J. B. Blumberg himself and one Warren Lattimore. They've been listening to our conversation."

Now her face twitched. The cool exterior was cracking. "I don't believe you."

"Why would I make this up?"

"You can't use that against me. There are privacy rules."

"I'm not going to use anything against you. We just wanted Mr. Lattimore to hear you put the needle on him."

At which point Dr. Lea Edwards, Harvard PhD and Danforth Award winner, stood up, uttered some very unprofessional words, threw the rest of her drink in my face, and walked out of Twist.

Into the watch Blumberg had given me I said, "I think she's a little upset."

122

WARREN LATTIMORE SANG like a ten-year-old Michael Jackson. Real enthusiastic. In the hotel room with the Dragon Lady, the Silver Bullet, B-2, me, and a stenographer. He didn't even want a lawyer. What he wanted was to make a deal to get out of being charged with special circumstances and getting a lethal injection. Giving up Lea Edwards was the price.

"From the start she was out to get Mackee," he said. "That's why she brought me in."

"Why?" Marie Antoinette Rocha, the Dragon Lady, asked. "What did she have against Mackee?"

"Lea caught her husband and Mackee in the old compromising position. She came home early from a lecture trip one day, walked into the dining room, and found more than a bowl of fruit on the table. I got involved during the divorce, which was kept low-key. Nobody wanted any bad publicity. Everybody said, Hey, let's forget about it. Only Lea Edwards don't forget. She was gonna take down Mackee no matter what. And she would've done it, too, but that reporter came around. She said she was doing some background on the case Peter Pan here was handling"—Lattimore nodded my way—"but she started to ask about David Townsend and in a real pushy way, if you know what I mean. She made it clear she was going to keep looking into this thing and that's when Lea asked me to get rid of the problem."

"Why'd you agree?" Rocha asked.

"Lea Edwards gets what she wants," he said.

"Were you sleeping with her?"

Lattimore nodded slowly, with a faraway look. "She will eat you alive."

"I've got some teeth, too," Rocha said. "Do you have any tangible proof to corroborate any of this?"

"You can thank Mr. Blumberg for the Z-11. I got recordings for you."

B-2 smiled. "It's what I do."

I said, "You have a recording of you calling me with a Mexican accent?"

Lattimore smiled. "You'll just have to trust me on that one."

Two days later, the D.A. formally dropped the charges against me.

Two days after that, Lea Edwards hired a top-gun lawyer—ironically, a former partner of Latourette's—to defend herself against the murder charge the D.A. dropped on her. The press loved it. Another celebrity trial had come to L.A. It would be fat city for a year.

Two weeks later, another fugitive replaced me in the news.

Rudy Barocas, American success story, was reportedly in France. When I saw that little item in the paper, I tried to get through to Cisneros. I'd tried several times before that, never getting a callback. So I left yet another message.

This time, he did return the call. To Sister Mary's phone. Gave her a location to give to me.

I met him on a fire road off Mulholland Highway looking down at the Encino Reservoir, a patch of water in the middle of brown scrub and dirt.

Cisneros was leaning on his car when I got there.

"Anybody in the trunk?" I asked.

He smiled. "Not today. How you feeling?"

"My body's just getting around to talking to me again."

"What's it saying?"

"Don't get hit anymore."

"Good advice."

"I'd love to chat," I said, "but I saw that Rudy is sipping French wine. What is up with that?"

"Wanted to tell you about that when the time was right. Now it's right."

"Hit me. I mean, tell me."

"Vargas is dead."

"What?"

Cisneros nodded. "Barocas got him. Vargas was going to talk to us about what was in that journal and disk you gave us. It's a pretty complete record of the Barocas counterfeit trail with all sorts of contacts. Good enough to go to the federal grand jury. Unfortunately, Vargas got bonded out and then didn't want anybody to know where he was. Barocas found him before we did, at a house in Silver Lake. Took out two other people who were there, too."

"You know who they are?"

"Not yet."

"One of them's a guy named Gustavo, I'd be willing to bet. The brother of Alejandra Bonilla, who kept the records." I felt numb. Even with Vargas dead I wasn't relieved. Business still seemed unfinished.

"We're not going to give up on Barocas," Cisneros said. "But it might be a good idea for you to lay low for a while. You need any help finding a place?"

I shook my head. "I have somewhere in mind."

"You sure?"

"I'm sure. God himself watches over this place."

"Sounds better than witness protection." He stuck out his hand. "Take good care, Mr. Buchanan."

"Same to you, Agent Cisneros."

123

A FEW HOURS later I was waiting across from the NoHo Theatre for David Townsend to show up for the evening's performance. When he entered the front doors, I crossed the street and pushed my way past a guy who said, "Can I help y—"and caught up with Townsend going down the aisle toward the stage.

When he saw me, he looked like he was going to scream.

"Easy," I said. "It's over."

"What is?"

I told him about Lattimore. He didn't believe me at first. We went into the theater office, and I pulled up the story on the *Times* website.

Townsend almost started crying.

"You can rest now," I said.

"I guess I should say thanks."

"You can say it by doing one thing for me. And for yourself."

He waited.

"I know a camera guy from KTLA. I want him to tape your statement."

"What statement?"

"You're going to come clean, David. Kendra Mackee manipulated you to come up with a repressed memory you didn't have. That was used to bring down a good priest. You need to make that right."

He didn't respond for a long moment. Then he started laughing.

"What's funny?" I said.

"You got it wrong."

"What?"

"Mackee didn't do anything to me. I was the one in control. See how long it lasted?"

"You saying you think you *did* repress those memories?"

"No."

"Then what?"

"It was the other chick who hired me."

"Hired you? Who—"

"Dr. Edwards, idiot. You better sit down."

I did, on a folding chair.

276 JAMES SCOTT BELL

"It was her deal all the way," he said. "Found me and coached me so it would look real. Paid me a good chunk. Then she was gonna use me to expose Mackee. Only when this Blumberg thing happened, I told her my price had gone up. That's when she let Lattimore start convincing me otherwise."

"You are lucky to be walking around."

He laughed again. "I did one of those old movie things, told 'em if anything happened to me I had a statement on tape that'd go to the cops. They bought it."

"No tape?"

Townsend shook his head.

"Now you can make one for real," I said.

"If I do, what happens to me? Do I go to jail or anything?"

"Nah. The only one who'd come after you is Father Robert. And he wouldn't do that."

"I know," he said. "He'd forgive me."

"He already has," I said. "But I haven't. You know what you did to an innocent man?"

"Yeah, I know all about it."

"So come clean."

"Why should I?"

"To make things right for Father Bob. You can help him and do a little good for your own soul."

"If I believed in a soul."

"I think you should," I said.

"Maybe I'll think about it."

"Think fast."

124

NEXT DAY I was in McDonough's office. It was like a strange, parallel dimension. All the wood and leather and teak. All the glass-enclosed bookcases and corner windows looking down at the earth.

A year ago I was picturing myself in an office like this someday. Now I couldn't force myself into the picture at all.

McDonough was all warmth. "Ty, we'd love to have you back with us. Despite what's happened, all that's water under the bridge. I know you were under a lot of strain. But you're one of the best lawyers we've ever had here, and I'd hate to lose you."

"Aren't you afraid I may dance on somebody's conference table?"

He snorted a laugh. "Not at all. Over and done with."

"But that's the thing," I said. "*I'm* afraid I might."

He looked at me.

"I'm afraid I won't be able to go back to doing things the way I did," I said.

"I think you can."

I shook my head.

"But you have to do what you're trained for," he said.

"I've been thinking about that. I might go out on my own."

"Do you know how hard that is?"

"I figured out the secret, though. It's real simple. Low overhead. No office. No home. A phone. And this." I tapped my head.

Pierce McDonough said nothing. A man who makes $750 an hour is not likely to process the term *low overhead.*

"Pierce, I enjoyed working here. I really did. But I'm just not the same guy. I wouldn't do the job you expect. Thing is, I don't even know what to expect of myself. But I want a chance to find out."

"What do you think's out there that isn't here?"

I shrugged. "More, I guess."

"More what?"

"Just . . . more."

125

ON THE WAY out I stopped by Al's office. He was sitting at his desk when I poked my head in.

"How goes it?" I said.

He looked surprised, then sheepish. "Hey. A lot more work since Edwards got arrested. Thanks for complicating my life."

"It was already messed up."

He ran his fingers along a sleek, silver pen. "Ty, man, look—"

"No need to explain. I just wanted to say good-bye."

He stood. "Why don't we go to lunch?"

"Another time maybe."

"Drinks after work?"

"Go home to your wife and kids, Al."

"Ty—"

"I mean it."

"What about you, man? What are you going home to?"

I thought a moment. "I'll let you know when I get there."

126

ON A PRISTINE Friday night a week later, I went to a Brazilian place near the Northridge Fashion Center. Jacqueline had liked it. It was small but rated A and had a funky feel and all sorts of meat.

I ate alone but didn't feel alone. It was like somebody was with me the whole time, telling me it was all right now, that I could rest. Move on.

Or maybe it was just my body and brain trying to convince me hope was more than just a four-letter word.

My prospects were hardly the stuff of law school dreams. But I didn't care, and it was nice that I didn't. It wasn't like I was completely tapped out. Jonathan Blake Blumberg had paid my defense fees because he said I was getting to be a good "hunter," and he wanted to keep me on to help him clear his name. Said he'd submit to polygraph tests and do whatever it took. I said okay, because clearing names now seemed like a good specialty to be in. And David Townsend had agreed to talk, for Blumberg and Father Bob, too.

After that, who knew? I had options. Living below my means for a while seemed like a good one. Not having to wear a suit every day would be sweet. The little things in life.

I paid the check and went outside to a balmy Valley evening, wind coming out of the north and a near full moon rising.

And a cool sound from the corner. Street music. A kid, maybe fifteen, was drumming on a plastic water bottle. Had a hat out for change.

I fished out a buck and dropped it in the hat. Let him finish his solo.

"Very cool, my friend," I said. He had a tat sleeve and gap-toothed smile.

Then I heard myself say, "Mind if I?"

The kid was sitting on an upside-down paint bucket. He stood and said, "Go for it," and handed me the sticks.

They felt good in my hands.

I sat and started in. Started slow and built, and in about a minute I was going like I'd never been away. Going and going under the moon and stars.

I was all of them at once, the greatest drummers, the sultans of the skins, and I played on and on, lost in the music and the night.

127

"YOU WERE RIGHT, by the way," I told Sister Mary the next day. It was morning at St. Monica's and she was on the basketball court in her sweats, shooting around.

"I was?" she said.

"Wrath was the sin. Lea Edwards wanted good old-fashioned revenge. Isn't there something about hell hath no fury like a wo—"

"Watch it, bub, there are nuns present."

"Got it."

"So," she said, "when will you be leaving?"

"Is that any way for a Benedictine to talk?"

"Let me rephrase. Will you be staying?"

"Yeah. I think I will."

"Sister Hildegarde will be thrilled."

"I won't be a slack."

"I know. The new ovens arrived yesterday."

"New ovens?"

"As if you didn't know. Thank you."

I cleared my throat. "I figure you all could use some legal work around here. Maybe some of the people in your parish, the poor ones."

"A lawyer who doesn't want to make money?"

"I'll be the Bizarro World Johnny Cochrane for a while."

"We'll keep you in fruitcake, if that'll help."

"Sounds more like purgatory."

"No. Your purgatory will be on the basketball court."

"Why Sister Mary Veritas, it almost sounds like you're calling me out."

"Just be warned. If you think hell hath no fury and all that, you don't want to challenge me to one-on-one. I take no prisoners."

"What? A sweet, unassuming woman of God? I don't believe it."

She bounced the ball once. "Try me," she said.